# 'IT'S A DOG'S LIFE'

Tales

from

An enchanted island

**By**

# Noel  C Stuart

Published by Two Oaks Press
Tenderah Road
Helston
Cornwall

First Edition

All characters in this book, with the exception of Val and Roy Callin, are fictitious
and any resemblance to actual persons, living or dead, is purely coincidental

A catalogue record for this book is available from the British Library,
ISBN 0-9553663-0-5
ISBN 978-0-95533663-0-5

Printed in Cornwall by
R Booth
Antron Hill
Penryn

## DEDICATION

My grateful thanks to my parents whose faith and trust helped me through college
to achieve my dream and to Margaret, my wife, who has constantly supported me
throughout my forty years in practice and has laughed at my funny stories and shared
in the joy of my vocation.
Colleagues in the Helston Writers Group, particularly Barbara Allen and Sheila Jefferies
have encouraged me constantly as has my tutor Anne Morgellyn and Anne Bailey who
checked the copy and kept me on the straight and narrow.
My friend Mike Carter who skilfully arranged the outside cover deserves special mention.
Above all I must thank my clients and patients who over the years have been the
inspiration for this book,

# A Knight in Shining Armour

A sharp click announced the arrival of the mail as the letter box snapped shut. Bert, my flat mate wandered into the kitchen, still yawning the night out of his system.

"It's a letter for you, Ned," he muttered and disappeared into the bathroom. It was a plain envelope with the address written in a bold and generous hand. I recognised the unmistakable script of Maeve Plunket, an alluring little will o' the wisp who had bewitched me for the past six months.

*The letter started off, "Dearest White Knight. We have been drifting apart recently through no fault of our own - different interests and you trying to study so hard. I'm afraid that I didn't help much! We have had lovely times together, which I shall always cherish but I have been going out with another man recently.*
*We have become very involved with one another and he's asked me to marry him. It is that big handsome man Tom Gleeson who nearly killed me last year! We are very happy and I only hope that you find a girl to match your charm.*
*Love from Maeve."*

I crunched the missive up and threw it into the fire. 'Thanks be to God for small mercies! At last I'm free from that young lady and her family. We've had some lovely times together. I wonder how much she knows about the murky world in which her father is involved.

After a hearty breakfast I wandered up Anglesey Road and into the side door of the Dublin horse show grounds. Apart from a couple of groundsmen trimming the verges, the grounds were empty. I sat in the stand looking out across the arena recalling the times I had watched Maeve competing in the show-jumping events. I felt that I just wanted to mull over the events of the last twelve months.

The heat, the intense silences and the tension, willing Maeve and Dancer to finish a clear round came to me clearly. Afterwards the horses would be rubbed down, fed and watered before we went off to the city for a celebratory meal provided by her father, Dan-Joe. He was overgenerous and possessive of those surrounding his family. Sometimes I felt like a young stud retained for his daughter's pleasure. It had been an incredible summer, full of happiness and romance, with an incredibly attractive young lady. In a paradoxical way, a load had just been lifted from my shoulders. No longer was I a kept man. I stood up to go back to the digs realising that I had broken one of life's basic tenets. It's a foolish man who lets a pretty face distract him from a day's trout fishing!

Looking back objectively at the events of the summer term I could hardly believe that it had happened. I had never really considered myself as a knight in shining armour. It had been yet another adventure.

Mine were the simple pleasures of drinking Guinness, rugby and fishing. I was finding that the necessity of passing examinations was beginning to dominate my thoughts, leaving precious little time for minor distractions such as rescuing fair maidens and for cultural activities like the Abbey Theatre.

My problems had started when Mike, Bert and I had spent a weekend in County Meath in order to escape from our studies. We camped in a field beside one of those little white Irish cottages. It lay just below the road in a rather rough meadow dotted with thistles and patches of sedge grass. A fine plume of blue turf smoke crept lazily out of the chimney pot to dissipate in the air. Mike knocked on the door and a tall dark woman in her thirties greeted us. We noticed that she gave a welcoming smile on seeing Mike's Nordic good looks and clear blue eyes.

"Of course you can use the field for your tents. You're as welcome as the flowers in springtime," she said smiling radiantly as if we were doing her a favour.

"I'm Grainne O'Farrell. I'll call my husband." Glancing over her shoulder she shouted "Padraig. These young gentlemen would like to camp in the meadow for the weekend. Take the scythe and make a space in the thistles."

Padraig appeared from the inglenook where he had been stacking turf beside the fire. His weathered features peered out from beneath a battered trilby. His bent old body seemed to scuttle sideways in a crab-like fashion due to a disabled leg. He must have been at least twenty years older than his wife - little wonder that the sight of Mike had entranced her. "You're welcome," said Padraig.

"Just give me a minute while I run the stone over the blade of my scythe. The edge leaves it very quickly." Despite his disability, it was a pleasure to watch the rhythmical sweeping action of the scythe and the gentle hiss as the thistles prostrated before him. Grainne insisted on bringing us out milk and a rice pudding each day in case we starved.

The days were spent wading in the river, clad in trousers and gym shoes, casting a line in our hunt for the elusive trout. Nature was at her best. The lush meadows, rippled by light airs, were dotted with flowers of every hue. Contented cattle grazed in the knee height grass. Their hind legs were muscled all the way down to the hocks, bringing alive the old saying, "Beef to the heels like a Mullingar heifer".

# **Chapter 2**

A peerless blue sky looked down with white clouds gently drifting by. It was fish for every meal, with the evenings spent sampling pints of Porter that tasted like nectar after the days efforts. Who could ask for more!

A scream of pain broke the silence as a car roared along the country lane. Dropping my rod on the side I scrambled up the opposite bank. A set of horse's legs was flailing the air and as I rushed across the paddock I saw a slight figure lying in the ditch. I could hear moaning and the figure of a girl with arms spread-eagled like a rag doll. "Are you all right, Miss?" I said concernedly, kneeling down beside her.
Deep green eyes, haloed in a circlet of auburn hair, looked up at me from a bloodied and tear- stained face.
"Thank God you've come. I could have been killed. Dancer fell on top of me."
Gently lifting her up into a more comfortable position I found that she was only the weight of a doll! She screamed out as she tried to move her arm.

"Just lie there," I said. "There's a man coming down the road on a bike who can fetch some help. You're fortunate the mud was soft or Dancer's weight would have crushed you."
Waving down the cyclist I explained the situation. His face darkened as he surveyed horse and rider.

"Ah! That'll be Maeve Plunket from the village. A pretty little slip of a thing she is. I'll bet that the sports car driven by young Tom Gleeson spooked the poor horse. Sure, didn't he nearly drive me into the ditch. Too much money and too little sense. I'll ask at the big house for the use of their 'phone."

I rushed back to the bank where Maeve was lying and found her trying to stem back tears of frustration. "I can't move my right shoulder and my ankle is agony to move," she muttered.

Attempting to distract her I talked about Dancer, her young chestnut mare, who was standing disconsolately, shaking in every limb

"I'll just have a look at the mare as she appears to be pretty shaken up. Back in a second"

I walked over to console Dancer and led her quietly over to Maeve on the bank, talking all the while and smoothing her down. They both relaxed although Maeve was having a lot of trouble with the smallest movements. It occurred to me that I was using the same therapy on horse and owner. They both seemed to listen to my light chatter as I talked about sport, fishing and the student life in Dublin that might now have been a thousand miles away.
I held her hand, as comfort, whilst we awaited assistance. The warmth of the sun as we lay in the meadow grass, the gentle song of the bees and soothing summer heat made my job quite pleasant. I asked her how the accident happened and a pink glow suffused her face as her eyes flashed in frustration.
"It was that stupid yahoo, Tommy Gleeson in his brand new sports car, came flying round the bend and just missed Dancer. Of course, she cat-jumped sideways and fell over the hedge. To think that I ever considered going out with him. He's fancied me ever since the ceilidh at the village hall."

She screamed in pain as she attempted to change her position.

"Hold on." I said. "Keep it until later. Now I've got to tell you a lot more stories to calm you down again."

After half an hour we had discussed our lives at length and I learnt that much of her life was involved with horses and show jumping. The arrival of a car at the roadside intruded into our tête-à-tête. Out of it scrambled a tweed clad figure wearing plus fours and a fore and aft hat. Dr Sean Brennan was a Falstaffian character with a red face and mutton chop side-whiskers. With bag in hand he scrambled over the hedge and accepted my help to avoid a muddy landing in the ditch.

"My dear Maeve! What happened to upset Dancer? I thought she was a steady young filly. Just lie still and tell me whilst I examine you."

"Uncle Sean. I'm glad you've come. It was that Tom Gleeson driving like an 'eejit! I'll kill him, so I will!"

"You'll do nothing of the sort young lady," he replied, chortling with glee as he visualised the confrontation. "Five foot nothing of you could hardly stand on the boot of Tom at six foot three."

I couldn't resist a chuckle at the thought whereupon she turned to me with a wild look in her eyes.

"As for you. A fine white knight you are! Rescuing a lady in distress, dressed in a polo neck and wet up to the waist as if you'd just came out of the bogs. Do you realise how wet you've made me. I'm drenched. We'll be the talk of the district so we will!"

"Maeve," continued Sean. "You've got a dislocated shoulder. Hold on and I'll put it back for you."

"It won't hurt will it, Uncle Sean?"

"Hardly a thing" - at which point he put his knee on her ribcage, pulled the arm across her chest with a twisting motion. Maeve gave a high pitched scream as the joint clicked back into position.

"Hush child. It's back now. You scream just like your mother used to when we were children and she couldn't get her own way."

At that moment the ambulance arrived and Maeve was lifted onto a stretcher and headed off towards Mullingar. Sean stayed behind for a moment whilst we gazed down over the bridge and considered the possibility of catching the resident trout below.

"I wouldn't be too bothered," he said prophetically. "It's like wasting your energies chasing a pretty girl when there's thousands more you could be having sport with!
Many a true word is spoken in jest!

"We'll leave Dancer where she is until the stableman collects her. She'll be happy enough in the field. By the way, that young man, Tom Gleeson is a decent enough lad. He's studying medicine in Dublin and was probably only showing off his new car."

4

# Chapter 3

I arrived back at the camp site to find Bert and Mike organising the meal over an open fire. "Where did you get to! We thought that you'd been carried away by a water nymph" commented Bert. "Here we are slaving away and you arrive back late with a couple of scrawny little fish - guess who's doing the washing up and buying the first round."

"I've already collected our rice pudding from the lovely Grainne, so that's my duty done" added Mike, chuckling at my apparent discomfort.

"Well," I replied vaguely, "I got carried away in pursuit of my professional duties as a carer."

After our meal we headed into the village to sample Mick Carolan's Porter. Carolan's Bar was not so much a bar as an emporium. As we walked through the door we passed the ironmongery department, smelling of age old dust and paraffin, with rows of shining galvanised pails, brooms, coconut mats and cooking utensils. The next room was the haberdashery area, and had a much cleaner smell and sold boots, men's trousers and shirts, and dresses and vast quantities of ladies wrap around floral overalls. The back room consisted of the café and public bar that also served as the social centre of the village.

The bar was fairly empty when we entered, in contrast to market day, when the whole shop and bar was a heaving mass of country folk shopping, swapping tales and drinking.

Bert leaned across the table to Mike as Mick brought along our drinks. "I'm a bit worried about Ned. He's developed that far away haunted look that appears when there's a woman in the offing. Maybe he's missing one that he's left behind in Dublin or a mermaid called him from the river."

"I recognise the symptoms Bert. Quite a serious attack of hormonal stimulation I should say. It could be your little sister plucking away at his heartstrings."

"Not at all. She's too sensible for him. Anyway, I'd kill him if I caught him kissing my wee sister!"

I let them gossip on for a few minutes and offered to tell the true story if somebody bought the second pint. Without disclosing my more personal feelings I gave them a blow by blow description of my adventure, that ended with the ambulance disappearing down the road in a cloud of dust. All the time, I was aware of those deep green eyes, flecked with brown staring into my innermost thoughts.

"I wonder how she is?" I said suddenly, drawing worried glances from my companions.

I glanced over to the bar where Mick was talking to a well-built man, with wavy black hair, and pointing in our direction. The man strode across and sat down beside us. "Hello lads! Which of you is Ned Carson? My daughter refers to you as the Knight in Shining Armour", he said. I admitted to being Ned, amidst ribald remarks from my friends about the age of chivalry.

"I'm Dan-Joe Plunket. I've come to thank you for coming to her assistance so quickly. Things might have been much worse but for you. I've asked Mick to bring you another round of drinks, so if you don't mind I'll join you."

We nodded our approval on seeing Mick approaching with glasses full of Porter

"I'm very grateful to you," continued Dan-Joe. "As you are young vetinries I would like to take you down to see Maeve's eventing horses tomorrow and you could then have dinner with us in the evening. God willing, she should be home by then. Only a shoulder dislocation and sprained ankle to show for her tumble. She's even forgiven Uncle Sean for putting the shoulder back in place."

We arrived back in our tents feeling rather pixie-led from drink. As we dozed off to sleep Bert muttered something to the effect that he had met Maeve somewhere before, as I slipped into a night dominated by deep green eyes flecked with brown.

The following day we called round to see Maeve at Ballinagar House, an imposing country residence set in some thirty acres. A tennis court stood invitingly at the side, whilst our eyes were at once drawn to the lawn running down to the private lake just waiting to be fished.

We entered the sitting room to meet Maureen Plunket and Maeve. Maureen was petite and very much a mature version of her daughter. My gaze at once went to Maeve, resting on the settee and clad in polo neck and slacks.

"Mummy. This is my white knight, Ned Carson, who tended me so well yesterday. He didn't tell me that he had two other gorgeous men with him. Maybe fate meant me to have an accident. I shall enjoy their company until I can go and throttle Tom Gleeson or maybe they will do it for me. He fancies himself as a horseman but he really couldn't ride a three-legged donkey. Did you show them round the yard Daddy? How is Dancer, Mr Vet?"

"Looking pretty good despite her fall. One or two abrasions, a bit stiff."

Sitting near the window was young man in his mid twenties. He had dark wavy hair and the good looks that must have made many a young girl turn and look. He was a younger slimmer edition of Dan-Joe.

Maeve introduced him proudly "This is my brother Liam. He helps Daddy train the horses and is as keen on steeple-chasing as I am on show-jumping". "If he was not my brother," she continued, smiling fondly at her sibling, "I'd say he's got a good future". Their eyes met in mutual understanding.

He turned to us, with a hint of a smile. "Thanks to you, I still have a baby sister to tease me incessantly. I shall be having words with Tom Gleeson before this day is out. He is the kind of man, who gives the country a bad name and unless he comes to his senses he will come to a sticky end".

"Liam" interrupted Maureen sharply. 'I don't think that we need discuss young Tom like that. Yes! He is a bit of a spoiled brat but he'll grow out of it.'

6

Liam walked across, kissed his mother fondly and apologised to us before departing for the stables.

"Ah!" continued Maureen. "Tom behaved very badly to Maeve at the ceilidh last year, when he was full of drink and Liam knocked him down, despite being four inches shorter. Nobody insults his little sister and gets away with it. He has quite a volatile temperament like his father. Little wonder that I call him my 'Stormy Petrel!' I'm surprised that he made no comment about your Ulster accents. Let us sit down now and enjoy a meal, thankful in the knowledge that you were so near at hand , Ned!"

The evening slipped past rapidly as I was captivated by Maeve's happy laughter. The hospitality was excessive and next morning we recalled little of our journey home and were glad of a quiet day.

This was the first of many visits to Ballinagar during the next few months. I used to follow Maeve around the show jumping circuit and stay at the house for the weekend before heading back to Dublin. There were lots of parties and dances with her friends. My work suffered and when I had abysmal marks in a pathology exam the warning bells began to ring. I was neglecting my studies to enjoy a style of life that was really not my scene.

I was finding that Dan-Joe was very flattering and a bit demanding, when he kept dragging me down to the stables to see any problems that had arisen with the horses. "Ah! Ned, you certainly have a nice touch when it comes to horse medicine. I sure hope that you settle nearby when you qualify!"

I might have succumbed to some of his patter if it hadn't been for some comments from Sean Long, his old stableman and retainer. We were sitting down together cleaning tack and talking when Sean told me that Dan-Joe started off with his father as a horse dealer, 'fixing' some of the flapping races to try and make a few shillings. I knew enough about this type of racing to know that lame horses could be 'nobbled' to run sound and by the use of various potions it could be arranged to win or lose races. This was all a bit shady and led him into the second-hand car market, where the same rules applied. "The man had a hard life to start with, particularly when his mother was shot in the back by the bloody Black and Tans as she was walking into chapel. The bastards were just assassins hired by Westminster. Dan-Joe was the eldest son and swore to avenge his mother's death and joined the Nationalist cause."

"That was a long time ago, Sean. How does he feel now that the country is at peace?" I commented.

"He doesn't believe in the present government at all - too close to England he says. I know that he goes off to secret meetings often enough. It's a pity that he's still so full of anger but he knows that the association is good for his business. They have links across the country. I lost relatives to the Black and Tans and joined him for several years until I realised that hatred was destroying my life. When I backed out there were several threats aimed at me but I had some protection from my friendship with Dan-Joe. Indeed, he saved my life more than once. My great worry is that young Liam seems to be following in his ways. I've watched that boy grow up and he's like a son to me".

Sean noticed that I was showing some signs of alarm and continued, "Let none of this go any further Ned or we could both be in serious danger. You are young and genuine but we have a common interest in animals and the country. Dan-Joe would not be averse to using you for his political aims as I believe that he's involved in cross border smuggling and protection rackets in the North. Be careful in case you get sucked into something you don't understand. I don't think that young Maeve knows any of the facts - too interested in partying and spending her father's money."

'Sean', I said, 'I'm very grateful for your advice. The whole situation is a bit beyond what I want in life and it makes me truly sad that such dark problems are still lurking in this lovely country.'

The following weekend I stayed at Ballinagar and went down to the stables with Maeve as she exercised her horse. I was busy mucking out one of the stables when I noticed a shadow, cast by the sunlight, across the floor. It was Dan-Joe, looking a bit preoccupied. "Tell me Ned. You're a smart sort of fella. How would you like to earn some good money?"

Rather taken aback I looked up, feeling somewhat uncomfortable. "What do you want me to do Dan-Joe? I don't really need anything at the moment."

'Oh!, he said casually.' With your knowledge you could help me solve a problem. I've put a lot of money on a filly at the Curragh this weekend and now it looks as if her stable mate might beat her to the post. I know that Phenacetin will slow her down but I'm unsure of how much to give her.'

I suddenly felt tense, almost entrapped. If I gave him the information that 200 grains of the powder would slow a horse's heart, possibly killing it, he could hold this as evidence against me and jeopardise my career. I looked thoughtful for a minute. Then, my mouth dry, with fear, I replied, "I'm not really sure offhand as we don't use it much now but I'll look it up when I get back to the city". Strangely enough I had been asked the identical question by a man who raced ponies in Donegal only two weeks before. The warning bells were ringing and I must get out of this relationship!

I could not relax during the rest of the weekend, despite Dan-Joe plying me generously with Power's whiskey. I felt that he was trying to set me up. Maeve was very aware of the atmosphere and did her best to please me. Eventually, I left after lunch on Sunday to arrive back home with a tale to tell.

I repeated Sean's tale to Mike and Bert, when I got back to the digs. They were very concerned and suggested that I distance myself from Maeve and Dan-Joe before the situation got worse. Rather feebly, I wrote to Maeve saying that our relationship was interfering with my studies and we should not see each other as much. After making my excuses several times Maeve became quite petulant when I was not at her beck and call and eventually her calls petered out. I was quite worried as I had informed Dan-Joe that I was unable to find the true dosage of Phenacetin to 'nobble' the horse and suggested a very low and safe level after consulting with my pharmacology lecturer. His comment was, "Dan-Joe Plunket has an unsurpassed reputation as a rogue in the horse world".

# Chapter 4

After this episode we pledged to be semi-celibate until our final exams to eliminate Ballinagar from my thoughts. The cure was to go down to the rugby club bar and get into serious training for the season. So commenced a serious spell of study, sport and partying to eliminate this affliction from my mind and only occasionally I spoke to Maeve. I still had daydreams about her but my jailers kept taking me out on diversions. Slowly the pain eased as I realised that most of my worries stemmed from a rebuff to my own conceit and the necessity to concentrate on my studies drove her out of my mind.

Several times I found myself playing rugger against Tom Gleeson and the word got about that he and his cronies were out to kill Ned Carson or maybe only break a leg! We were in great training and managed to repel all their advances and came away the victors at each encounter.

It was a king-size hangover with lights flashing, humming in my ears and the granddaddy of all headaches. Eyes closed, lest my eye balls fell out, I revelled in the lack of communication and responsibility of facing the world.

How did it all happen? Slowly, a recollection came to me of spending the evening dancing the night away in the Metropole Hotel. One or two pints of Guinness, but not enough to even get tiddly. The talent wasn't all that great but Bert and Mike went off home with their girlfriends leaving me to walk home along O'Connell Street. As I crossed the end of Moore Street a voice called out, 'Hey there'. Turning to look down the darkened street I saw three figures approaching and then a quick flash of light followed by oblivion.

A welcome hand, cool, female and reassuring rested on my forehead. "Ned, Ned are you feeling a bit better," came the angel tones. This had to be heaven! My eyelids flickered to see the blurred figure of a young and pretty nurse leaning over the bed.

"Tell me, where am I" I responded recognising that I must be in hospital.

"You're in St James's emergency ward', came the reply. 'You were found lying unconscious and covered in blood at the entrance to Moore Street by a young medical student. Don't be moving now as you've had a fair beating and you'll ache all over for a few days. You've got a great black eye but fortunately no broken bones. The girl friend won't look at you for at least two weeks", she added, smiling. "The doctor will be here to see you in a wee while but in the meantime there's a couple of visitors for you."

In walked Mike and Bert trying not to look too concerned. "Well, where did you get off to last night? chuckled Bert. "Haven't we always told you that trying to rescue young maidens from the arms of their boyfriends is bad news. Seriously though, what on earth happened after we left you?"

"I've no idea", I managed to mumble despite my aching face. "I can't remember a thing. I wasn't robbed because I only had a few shillings. Who could have a grudge against me?"

At that moment a doctor appeared surrounded by a covey of nurses and a few white coated students. We at once recognised the tall figure of Tom Gleeson amongst the students. "Good

9

morning gentlemen, I'm Dr Kelleher and have just called in to check up on you. It looks as if you can go home today as long as you rest for a couple of days - post traumatic shock can still catch up on you. It was fortunate that Tom Gleeson and his friends appeared on the scene in time or you might have been more seriously injured."

Tom came to the bedside and leered down at my prostrate figure. "Well Ned, you certainly got the better of us on the rugby field but it was lucky that we were nearby last night to rescue you. I've no idea who they were but they ran off in a hurry. It might even be Liam - jealous because you're chasing his sister!"

"Thanks Tom," I muttered, "I owe you a pint next time", I responded, too confused to believe my eyes. Here was a man, who had sworn to get me, had arrived in the nick of time to save the situation. Was this all bluff or was there another agenda and where did Liam come into the picture. Mike and Bert exchanged knowing glances and said nothing!

Later that evening, we sat at home pondering the situation, unsure of which way to turn as we all suspected that the evidence pointed to Tom being involved in the incident and yet it was too open a case for it to be true. Mike commented that a few of his friends were in the same year as Tom Gleeson at medical college and he would get them to look into the matter. It was a bit scary to think that I could be attacked at night for no reason.

It didn't take long for the medical college grapevine to report back to Mike about Tom Gleeson. "It appears that he has been mouthing off to Dan McIlvaney that Ned Carson, who has come from Northern Ireland, is trying to take his girl friend and must be sorted out. A more worrying aspect that has come up is that he is a member of the Republican Brotherhood, a group of young hotheads, who feel that the Nationalist party are not aggressive enough and they want to take direct action against any one associated with Ulster. It appears that Ned could be on the list so we must keep our heads down until graduation".

It did not give us any more information as to my assailants but I felt that if Tom was left to pass on his opinions to his future father-in-law it would keep them away from me and they could sort out their own differences.

It was a long hard slog for the next six months as our final exams drew nearer. We had the odd break to go fishing but otherwise led a moderately celibate existence. Even when we went out to the pub to ease the stress we carried little aide-memoire notes in our pockets. The days of our final exams were tense and tempers became frayed easily. The best treatment was a Porter before bedtime! We all had nightmares about failing the exams and letting down our long suffering parents. I had memories of being dragged through my dietetics exam the previous year.

We had awoken with throbbing heads, and a cup of milk was all we could manage for breakfast. Staggering around the flat at seven thirty am, we tried to prepare ourselves for the final's results being posted at ten o'clock. Better not to think of my nightmares of being attacked or shot some dark night, that lurked in the recesses of my brain.

I stared out of the window at the steady Dublin drizzle. It was a morning only fit to grow grass!

I recalled the events of the previous night. The three of us at Crowe's Bar, in Ballsbridge, drinking ourselves all but under the table. I was in company with the incredibly handsome Bert with his dry Ulster humour and blonde Mike with his silver tongue. They had always seemed to be surrounded by the prettiest girls.

A quick splash under the tap, and then we were cycling off to college like men possessed and cursing the demon drink, which was the ruination of all students. The murmuring crowd in front of the notice board parted to let us in. The doubts that had been nibbling away at our brains evaporated like mist before the morning sun, accompanied by cries of exultation at seeing our names on the pass list.

After the initial euphoria the emptiness of anticlimax gripped my stomach as the first realisation overtook me that this was the parting of the ways after five years of sharing our triumphs and disasters. We had been inseparable over the years. Playing rugby three times a week, drinking and partying seemed to keep us in good fettle. When we tired of the city life we would retreat to the country for a few days fishing. The thought of facing reality became quite daunting after our irresponsible and cosseted life style. We headed once more for Crowe's Bar to discuss the new aspect of our lives, making sure to take our less fortunate colleagues along for a final celebration. After all we couldn't have stood out in that rain all day although there is a very haunting quality about Ballsbridge when the pavements are wet.

# Chapter 5

Tomorrow was graduation day. Here I was, a fully qualified vet at last with the world just waiting for me. T. G. Brown, our principal had said to us only yesterday, "Ladies and gentlemen, you are fully qualified veterinary surgeons, high in knowledge but low in experience, about to be let loose upon the unsuspecting public. Be humble in your dealings with others and always be aware of your obligations to those animals under your care," before dismissing us to our fate.

I had been up early to finish my packing in the flat and to give my thanks to our landlady, Mrs Gallagher, for tolerating us for the past two years. She had mothered us during our stay. She never intruded into our lives, but was always available for advice. She was a slim fifty-year old with a shining head of grey curls. Both her daughters had left the nest some years before and she would occasionally disappear off to Cork to be with her grandchildren. When we returned from receiving our final's results she had left three bottles of Guinness on the stairs with a little note, "You gentlemen must be just full of knowledge!"

As flatmates we had stuck together throughout our college days and after last night's celebrations we made the rather ambitious promise to keep in contact during the years to come. We did feel sad for those who had to resit various papers and three of our colleagues who could not go into practice for a few months until they reached the mature age of twenty one years!

The sun had its best suit on, the air was clear and a dazzling blue sky lifted one's spirits. A quick breakfast and off to Dublin Airport to meet my mother and father who were flying in from the Isle of Man with Moira, the girlfriend I had not seen for over two years since she went to work in Africa. The north road was almost devoid of traffic and the airport half empty. One of my friends referred to it as a white elephant- "Sure, how can you make a place like that pay in a country with such a small population?"

We were intending to head up country to enjoy a family fishing holiday before I faced the serious problem of earning a living. I arrived early, had a cup of tea and headed for the reception lounge as the plane taxied up the runway.

My father and mother appeared through the passengers entrance as I went into the reception lounge. Dad, prepared for the holiday, carried his most precious Hardy split cane fly rod. He wore his fishing garb, a grey tweed suit, and my mother, clad in a grey skirt and powder blue twin set was looking about anxiously for me. We smiled and waved as I hurried across the room to greet them.

Then Moira appeared, framed in the entrance and I was suddenly stopped in my tracks, all thoughts of Maeve were banished for ever. She wore a mustard coloured suit, cunningly tailored to fit her slender figure. A cheeky red cone of a hat, perched on a halo of sun-blonde hair set off her beautiful face with its full cherry lips and eyes the colour of cornflowers. I stood spellbound as this vision came across the floor to greet me. I had always known as a rather earthy young student, that it could never happen to me-but now my mind was transported into the realms of fantasy. I had always tried to persuade myself that love and infatuation were temporary mental aberrations caused by the endocrine glands going into spasm.

My feelings must have been very evident as an arm linked into mine and my mother said, "Don't I get a kiss too dear?"

I could also see that she was thinking what a beautiful daughter-in-law Moira would make. Dad, the original quiet man, just smiled over towards the young woman and said, "Well, I hope Moira enjoys fishing."

The next few days went by in a whirl although I recall little of the graduation ceremony and celebrations. I took Moira to the Veterinary College (now strangely empty) and to Trinity College where I had also studied, as well as to many of the more acceptable venues that we visited as students. It was like a stroll through a summer's meadow, my mind full of her smile and happy laughter and my pleasure to suit her every whim. I showed her the sights around Ballsbridge that had given me such pleasure. The broad tree-lined avenues flanked by the gracious Georgian residences, St Stephens Green, a favourite place for walking and gazing at the delightful variety of house doorways. The many barefooted boys selling newspapers and the old crones, "shawlies", begging in the streets, which depicted the poverty still present in the country.

It was hard saying farewell to Dublin. It had come to mean so much to me during the past years. I had always looked upon it as a city of light and happiness, where I had worked and played hard with one goal in mid, to repay my parents trust and financial backing throughout my course.

"I have been offered a job in Leicestershire," I commented to Moira. "I have to go off for interview at the end of the holiday. Would you like to come with me for company as we have so much to talk about? No doubt you will be looking out for a teaching post now that you've returned."

"It all depends on what positions are on offer. I have several problems on my mind at the moment. I might even return to South Africa!" she responded mysteriously.

Alarm bells started to ring and feeling a growing sense of panic starting in the pit of my stomach, I continued urgently, "What on earth for? Do you feel that your future is in the sun?"

"I don't honestly know. I came back to see you and sort out my feelings. I have been going out with a friend in South Africa. I am very fond of him and now you have come back into my life. I must have space and time to work my way through the problem!"

My heart sank, as I realised that Moira had problems and I had competition. I had always been the guy who could love 'em and leave 'em without a backward glance and now the roles were reversed. Consumed with jealousy, I could only say lamely, "I shall try to leave you to make up your own mind but I can't help letting you know my own feelings."

At that moment I hated this intruder into my dreams. He was probably handsome and wealthy with a house of his own. What chance would an impoverished young graduate have against such opposition?

I felt angry that Moira had intruded into my own happy life and then dropped this unwelcome news. I had three weeks to prove myself so decided to start it off with a bunch of red roses. We spent the next three weeks in the County Donegal and Mayo on a fishing

13

holiday, although the rivers were so low that we came away with very small catches. Not that it mattered one farthing as my mind and thoughts were fully occupied with this lovely nymph who had cast a spell upon me. Every morning we would call upon Markie, the ghillie, to row us around the neighbouring lake, trolling for pike. Markie would take us to little caves at the lough side, to shelter from the rain, where he would regale us with stories of hiding in them from the "Black and Tans" during their fight for freedom. On one of these outings I even helped Moira to land a seventeen-pound pike without a twinge of envy-the ultimate self-sacrifice by a lovelorn angler! I tried to push thoughts of my rival into the background and carefully avoided mentioning the situation as Moira had to work through her own problem.

# Chapter 6

I had been offered the opportunity of several jobs in England and Wales. During the next few weeks I had to attend the interviews. The thought of my first job amongst new friends filled me with excitement and some apprehension. If I could spend a couple of years gaining experience "across the water" I could look forward to returning to my Celtic roots either in Ireland or the Isle of Man.

I was sad to leave Ireland after ten years of happy memories. Despite its damp reputation, it has riches beyond compare, a green and pleasant land full of silver lakes and pleasant people. The Irish are born with an innate courtesy and charm. The towns with their broad streets that were liberally scattered with small bars boldly stating that mine host was Rafferty or Flanagan. Inside, past the ironmongery and groceries the landlord was prepared to give you all the time in the world to have a bit of 'craic'. At college I had been gently teased for having Ulster Presbyterian roots but the majority of the population has a tolerance of all people and a willingness to accept you for what you are.

Moira decided to keep me company on the journey whilst at the same time she could be reading through the Educational Supplement for job vacancies. After scanning the papers she said, "There are quite a few jobs available that would suit me but would I enjoy them? Can you see me as Physical Education organiser for Lancashire, based in Preston or instructing in a college in Birmingham? I shall phone some of my college friends and find out if they know of any vacancies coming up!"

After looking at several job situations I decided that none was as good as home and resolved to phone my friend, Brian Scanlon to see if there was still a vacancy in his practice back at home in the Isle of Man. Brian had bought the practice in the Isle of Man several years earlier, after leaving his native Ulster. I felt that he was lonely and overworked in the growing practice and that my presence would ease both situations. He had been a widower for several years and because of his undoubted charm, was regarded by the local ladies as a very eligible bachelor.

I had seen practice in England and although the farms were much bigger and more efficient than those that I had been used to in Ireland and the Isle of Man, they lacked the personal touch of family farms. Oftimes, I had called at cottages in Ireland on a hot summer's day, merely to ask for a drink of water but according to local custom, had been presented with a table groaning with food. A similar hospitality was evident in the Manx people. It was a love of my culture that was drawing me back home.

I telephoned Brian from our hotel in Cheshire. His soft brogue sounded on the line. "Och! Hello Ned. Is that you? Where are you calling from at all? Have you got yourself a job yet?

"It is Brian. We are staying in a nice wee hotel near Wilmslow. So far we've had an enjoyable trip. The drawback is that I don't speak Welsh, which is necessary in parts of Wales and the other jobs are too far away from the sea for my comfort. Are you still wanting help because I should like to apply if you have the patience to teach a new graduate the ropes?"

"I should be delighted" replied Brian, "I've already given Calum Gray his notice as he is becoming a hopeless alcoholic and costing me a small fortune! It's a pity as he is a very

15

competent vet. When are you due back on the Island? Has Moira got herself fixed up with a job yet?"

"Not yet. She's standing beside me here. I shall drop her off home in Formby and be back by the weekend."

Moira had taught on the island before taking up a post in South Africa and had heard on the grapevine that there might be a job advertised for a P. E. teacher in Douglas to start in the spring term. We headed for Liverpool, where I spent a couple of days with Moira and her parents before boarding the boat for the Isle of Man. I planned to stay in Douglas with my parents temporarily and then move out to Peel on the West coast as soon as possible.

Moira shared my excitement as she was hoping that the job vacancy might be available on the island. During the journey she had kept a careful eye on me in case I became drowsy in the heat, and insisted on stopping for regular tea breaks. It gave me a comfortable feeling that we were sharing one another's pleasures and concerns. So much for that independent guy who had been so self sufficient and liked to play the field.

The journey to Liverpool was a nightmare. The new motorways were still in their infancy and as we turned onto the East Lancs. Road we found ourselves behind a convoy of heavy vehicles, covered with dirty tarpaulins and belching out diesel fumes. It was a day of early summer showers. The sky was leaden with continuous drizzle that made everything appear mucky and grey. The lorries were covered in mud and all the colours dimmed in the half-light. The windscreen wipers of my Morris Minor struggled bravely to clear the smeary coating of diesel and dirt from the glass. I became impatient with the stop start driving and traffic congestion as we edged our way towards Formby. The side windows were closed to keep the noxious spray out, whilst Moira was kept busy wiping the misty windows clear with a duster. To ease my irritability, I muttered an aside to her, "Thank the Lord that you dissuaded me from applying for the job in a Merseyside practice." She placed a hand on my arm, realising that I could not have lived in these conditions. Despite my frustration I could already sense the welcome tang of the salt air as we passed the docks. I had a sense that Moira and I were growing closer together and any mention of a return to South Africa was becoming less frequent.

Liverpudlians have always been a vibrant people with a resolve and wit that carried them through the dark days of the war years and the city hummed with activity as we drove towards the docks. Any city that could give birth to the Beatles, the Spinners and myriad comedians had a special place in my heart. The pavements were bustling with people hurrying to work, exchanging greetings and jostling at road crossings as they tried to thread their way through the taxis in Bold Street.

It was a resplendent morning in full summer as the pride of the Manx fleet, "Mona's Queen", lay alongside the Princes Dock landing stage. She was replete with holidaymakers bound for Douglas. They were all laughing and joking. "Kiss me quick" hats already adorning many a pretty head. There were grandparents, who had visited every year since they were courting, mums and dads, on holiday with their children and the young people already casting eyes at the opposite sex. Bright sunny days always highlighted the joy and anticipation of the occasion.

The Mersey ferries, abrim with workers from New Brighton and Wallasey shunted back and forth, like a stream of bees returning to the hive under the Liver Building. The river was seething with small boats, tugs and cargo vessels weaving ever changing intricate patterns across its vast expanse.

Despite the glorious day I felt torn in twain as we embraced and said our farewells. Moira was wearing a light blue summer dress and I found myself lost in a torment between the anticipation of love and realisation of duty. Understanding my predicament, she kissed me brusquely and stepped back into the crowd as the crew were drawing up the gangway.

## Chapter 7

Heading towards the open sea, I collected my hand luggage and staked a claim in the for'ard saloon. My excitement was intense at the thought of setting out on a new adventure in life. Unable to relax, much of my time was spent pacing the deck or leaning over the rail, watching England sink into the horizon. My mind was in turmoil and thoughts churned round in random fashion. Things were happening much too quickly. I felt a deep joy at returning home, concern at my growing feelings for Moira and a degree of trepidation about facing up to "real life". Was I ready for a steady relationship? She had not yet sorted out the South African dilemma! Would I make a success of practice or join the government service and become a puppet of political whim?

Millions of stars danced and sparkled on the wavelets as we set course for Douglas. The passengers were bustling around, claiming seats on the covered deck and pulling out deck chairs to enjoy the sun during the journey. Snatches of conversation drifted through the air- "Well it didn't take you long to settle down wi' tha paper George. Get up out of tha' seat yer great lummock and bring us a pot of tea and scones. While yer at it put out that stinkin' pipe or we'll all be throwin' up! You're making more smoke than the Queen Mary."

In a corner of the deck a worried looking woman, in a flowered dress was looking around, desperately shouting "Percy, will yer stop those bloomin' kids playin' tig around the ship. Next thing is they'll have fallen overboard and got drownded. Then what'll I say to mother?"

Further along the deck young lads in the pursuit of love were leaning over the rail chatting up a group of giggling girls. "Eh! What's yer name love? Do yer fancy me or me mate the most? He cuts a right figure on the dance floor"

At this the noses went up in the air. "Ee! You cheeky thing. 'Ave yer no manners? Don't they teach yer how to talk to ladies up in Burnley?"

I embarked on my usual tour of the ship just in case there had been any changes. There was always a companionway leading down into the engine room from which a smell of hot oily fumes drifted across the deck. This and the strong odour of cooking kippers from the galley made many would-be sailor turn a light shade of green.

The weather freshened on the beam after we crossed the Mersey bar and the ship started to roll. Once happy holidaymakers became much quieter and a few leant over the rail, looking rather white and shaken. A rather rotund gentleman, dressed for the occasion in Panama hat and British Legion blazer regarded his wife, in the adjacent deck chair "Ee! Mabel, You're looking a bit under the weather, lass! I rather fancy a plateful of fish and chips. Would thee like a few? It might settle your stomach." Mabel, looking quite pale, glowered at him. "Go away you silly bugger!" she growled. And promptly vomited over the deck. The more dignified travellers had already disappeared into the lower saloon where they could be seasick in private.
Leaning over the stern rail I watched the ever-attentive gulls swooping down for titbits in the foaming wake behind the ship or waiting for the crew to throw food out of the porthole. Many of these birds fell behind until only the stalwart few were left in attendance. The

Manx contingent of gulls would soon appear and take over escort duties and I could swear that they call with a different accent to the Liverpool birds. I saw several groups of razorbills and guillemots flying fast and low, almost skimming the wave tops, and graceful gannets, pristine white in the sunshine, effortlessly gliding through the troughs in the waves.

At the thought of arriving back in my beloved homeland butterflies of sheer joy and excitement were cavorting around my stomach banishing any thoughts of a full meal. After two hours, I opted for a cup of tea and one of the buffets renowned Eccles cakes, which lived up to their nickname of "Flies Graveyards." The outer covering was so thin that it brought a new meaning to "short pastry."

The weather was brisk in mid channel with intermittent sunshine and clouds scudding rapidly across the sky. The nearer we got to the Island the choppier became the sea. The bows of the ship would rear up and then plunge into the crest of the next wave as tons of foaming tide slewed across the fore deck. Spume, plucked from the wave crests, lashed across the deserted deck and on the leeward side there was one long row of not-so-happy holidaymakers leaning over the rail in the abject misery of seasickness. Only the hardened sailors were left to carouse in the bar. Even to walk along the deck was a steeplechase of stepping over the prostrate, moaning bodies.

Douglas promenade would be busy on my arrival at home as we were right in the middle of the "Wakes Weeks" holidays, when the factories throughout Lancashire closed down and the workforce headed for the seaside resorts. Thousands of Lancastrian lads and lasses headed for the island, intent on two weeks of fun and romance, and determined to go through their year's savings in the process. It was an everyday occurrence to see groups of happy lassies, still attired in evening dresses and curlers in their hair, walking arm-in-arm along Strand Street, just singing for joy.

Compared with their own unending grind in the mills and smog of the industrial towns Douglas was like heaven. It had always amazed me just how many adult holiday makers were very short in stature and it was only later that I learned that they had probably grown up in conditions of great deprivation, lack of food and industrial smog, which cut out the sunshine that we had all taken for granted.

Swimming and sunbathing on the beach were the order of the day whilst the evenings were assigned to shows and dancing to the rhythms of Joe Loss, Ivy Benson and Ronnie Aldrich. The Villa Marina and Palace Ballrooms were packed every night. The local lads were there, like bees around the honey pot, to look over the new talent.

Gradually, the island appeared as a cloudy smudge on the horizon, becoming more defined as Snaefell, guardian hill from which one can see seven kingdoms, arose through the haze. This sight had welcomed the invading Norsemen a thousand years before and set their hearts pounding with excitement. I was coming home! I stood at the bows, pulse racing and eagerly watching as I identified each landmark.

Sliding quietly in between the Battery Pier and Conister Rock, the "Mona's Queen" berthed alongside Victoria Pier after announcing her arrival with a sharp blast of her klaxon. I was home at last!

The long queue of passengers waited to disembark. Those happy holidaymakers of five hours ago were very subdued as they dragged heavy suitcases down the narrow gangway towards the hoard of busy porters who would lead them away to the nearest taxi. I stood at the rail taking in the sights and sounds that I knew so well and looking for any changes in the pattern of life. Change did not come quickly on the island and it was much the same as I had always known it.

# Chapter 8

It was good to be back on the Island. My mother fussed over me like a broody hen, delighted to have her youngest chick back in the nest. Before starting work I spent a few days getting my bearings and looking around Peel for a house. Peel was a town apart from the rest of the island. A cathedral city on the west coast that lived up to its name of the sunset city. The ruined cathedral was on St Patrick's Isle down by the harbour and is meant to have been founded by St Patrick when he brought Christianity to Mann.

The nearest town was Douglas, twelve miles distant. Peel had its own farming hinterland, a cattle market at St Johns and a thriving herring fishing and kipper industry. During the herring season the harbour was often packed with herring boats unloading their catch to supply the kipper factories. I regarded Peel as a place where I could happily settle and it was also strategically placed from a veterinary practice viewpoint. There were several houses that caught my eye but I resolved to wait until Moira arrived in the island in order that she could help me to make a decision.

I drove around the island, reliving old memories. Glen Mooar where I had recuperated from TB, then down the west coast to Port Erin, around which my childhood memories were based. The chasms and Port St Mary had all figured in my adolescent years. These villages were still unspoilt with little indication of the changes to come.

The Isle of Man railway, resembling a toy town express when compared with the British rail system, still ran to all towns in the island and was an important means of communication. I have travelled many miles in its rickety old coaches between Douglas and Peel or Port Erin. One of our favourite games as children was to bombard the railway crossing men with peashooters as the train chugged on to its destination. The damage inflicted cannot have been very severe, as we were never reported to my father. It was on these journeys that my brother would give me half a fag so that I would not tell tales about his smoking habits when I returned home. Being a very far seeing young man I gave up the habit at eight years old as I had heard that it would make my heart turn black - what a frightening prospect!

Returning to Douglas brought back a flood of memories. The excitement of the summer season when the beach was covered with wall-to-wall sunbathers, some equipped with umbrellas others with windbreaks, but all intent on sun worship. There were the pink and blistered ones who had just arrived and the bronzed goddesses who stirred up my first thoughts of masculinity. I used to walk with my two cocker spaniels along the beach each day and enjoy the ice cream and holiday atmosphere until one day a scream of indignation caused me to turn round. Nobody had told Sean, my dog, that he should not cock his leg on ladies, lying asleep on the sand. Pandemonium broke out as everyone but the victim enjoyed the situation. "Ee Love! It'll make a lovely story to tell, back in Wigan! Covered with embarassment, I pretended it was someone else's dog and walked on, hoping that he would follow without incriminating me!

The promenade was crowded with folk strolling along in the sunshine and older couples just sitting and watching. The men in braces, their heads protected from the sun by handkerchieves, knotted at the corners. Newspapers converted into inverted paper boats also added a certain sartorial elegance to the headwear.

A background to all this excitement was the steady clip clop of the horse-drawn trams running from Derby Castle to the bottom of Victoria Street. These fine draught horses with their " fluffy" plumed feet moved tirelessly back and forth along the promenade, much to the joy of thousands of holiday makers. The stables at Derby Castle were home for up to sixty horses during the summer months and each horse was rested after three trips along the promenade. When they reached retirement age they spent the rest of their days at the "Home of Rest for Old Horses", a very worthwhile charity developed to suit their needs.

From the Derby Castle end of the promenade, the electric railway ran all the way along the coast to Laxey, where a branch line veered off to climb to the summit of Snaefell and the main line continued onwards to Ramsey in the north of the island. With all these interesting means of transport provided, the holidaymakers had no need of their own transport. Perhaps as well, since in all probability, the great majority of them didn't own a car anyway.

I decided that, before moving to Peel, I must be fully independent and acquire lodgings of my own in Douglas. A very motherly widow, Mary Careen, who looked after all the young men who had worked for Brian, ran my "digs". She told me about my predecessor who had been an alcoholic and who, in order to feed his habit, eventually resorted to selling antibiotics in the pub to farmers. As far as I was concerned, Mary was extremely kind and always felt that I deserved a large breakfast and evening meal to make up for my hard life!

I hobbled in one evening; rather lame after a Shire horse had stood on my foot. She sat me down on the stairs, despite my protestations, saying, "Just you take your socks off my dear and let me see the bruise."

"Really Mrs C. I can get my father to look at it tomorrow"

"Now let's have a look at it. Doctors are much too busy to be looking at minor little things. I shall pour some of this tincture of Arnica and Witch Hazel over it and it should be much better before you see your father. My mother was very good with herbal remedies and homeopathy and cured most of our ailments as children."

I had never encountered this "herbal" treatment before but the effect was dramatic. Almost immediately the pain was relieved and I was left to meditate over the use of alternative forms of medicine. All through my college life I had wondered why my lecturers denigrated the use of country cures like garlic and herbal medicines, when one of our most powerful drugs-Penicillin-was obtained from a mould grown on bread. For centuries the gypsies had used poultices of mouldy bread to dress wounds.

Many years later it was announced in a medical journal that extract of garlic would control the development of Salmonella bacteria that cause Typhoid and many other unpleasant conditions. People living in hot countries have for centuries used garlic in their cooking. Meat goes off very rapidly in these countries so we can surmise that the taste of garlic cloaked the flavour of over ripe meat and would also suppress the development of infection after eating tainted food. A most agreeable hypothesis had been put forward that not only is wine drunk for its medicinal properties but that our ancestors discovered that the alcohol in fermented grape juice killed bacteria, when many of the wells and streams were contaminated with sewage. To me this seemed a strong case for imbibing for my health's sake.

I was engrossed in a game of poker with Mum and Dad on my evening off when the phone rang. Half expecting a call if Brian was very busy I was surprised to hear Moira's voice. She was bubbling with delight. "Ned, are you avoiding me, I've been phoning all over the place to contact you!"

"Not really!" I retorted, "I called in at The Jolly Farmer after work for a convivial pint. That's the pub with the voluptuous barmaid, who gets on so well with all her customers. She wanted to have a drink with me afterwards but I managed to resist her charms and came home for a game of cards instead."

"Guess what! I've got the job at Douglas High School so you can kiss goodbye to your gorgeous barmaid and take your lovely girlfriend out for a drink instead."

"That's great!" I exclaimed in delight, barmaid forgotten. "That's really made my day. When are you coming over? Mum was saying tonight that you could stay with them whilst you are hunting for digs. What a relief as I didn't fancy a boat journey to Liverpool every second week during the autumn."

Moira eventually found a flat quite near to my lodgings so that on my nights off duty we could enjoy each other's company, whilst she could practise her developing culinary skills on me. It had to be so, as we could not afford the great expense of eating out in a restaurant and besides which, she did cook an excellent casserole.

Being in love and working hard were a very stressful combination. The thought of parting once more was too much and by November I had proposed and was very surprised to be accepted. We decided to keep our engagement secret until I could formally ask her father for his daughter's hand in marriage. I tried to be very nonchalant about it but beneath the surface I was in turmoil at the thought of him saying, not without reason, "No! All vets are drunken layabouts," and then we should have to elope, as had my father and mother in years gone by! I needn't have worried, for it came about that he was delighted to have me in the family. Unbeknownst to me, my own family had been taking odds on when we would become engaged and breathed a corporate sigh of relief that I was at last showing signs of responsibility. They had already earmarked Moira as my future wife to the extent that my sister presented us with "his and hers" casserole dishes, before any official engagement was announced. Perhaps they had seen the stars in my eyes!

# Chapter 9

Brian Scanlon, also a Dublin graduate, was very kind and welcoming. Coming from a strict Nonconformist background, Brian had been raised with a work ethic and made me feel very humble when he said that he had not missed a single lecture at college, whereas my friends and I had maintained a much more relaxed attitude to academic life. His integrity was remarkable and I have several times seen him enter one dozen eggs in his daybook, payment for work done and duly recorded for tax purposes.

He lived in an old Georgian town house, set in a two acre walled garden. The stable yard had been converted into a consulting room with a kennel area alongside a garage and stabling for his grey hunter, Baska.

When he bought the practice he also acquired Ruth, the housekeeper, who had looked after his predecessor. Ruth had dedicated herself to caring for her employer, but was very much a part of the household and the practice. She had come to the job as a temporary housekeeper some fifteen years before and blossomed into her present position of practice organiser, bookkeeper, cook and general mother hen in the business. Woe betide anybody who offended her sense of right and wrong. As a farmer's daughter she knew all the clients, their relationships and credit worthiness. She was also a competent horsewoman and could often be seen exercising Baska on the sea shore in the early morning.

Although he was brought up in the farm animal tradition Brian was also a skilled small animal practitioner. I had 'seen practice' with him as a student since he arrived on the Island, when he was building up the small animal side of practice so, I felt that I could contribute greatly to that side of the business.

After buying the practice he was living very much hand to mouth, but by dint of sheer hard work and introducing modern techniques into the business it slowly grew. At that stage he had very little equipment, relying on his skill and knowledge, but gradually saved enough to develop the premises. Disposable hypodermic and suture needles had not been developed at that period so every Friday evening was sharpening time. The needles were pushed through a cork so that the tip appeared at an angle through the base and we would sharpen them on a carborundum stone until they developed a keen edge. They were then cleaned and sterilised ready for the following week.

Despite my years as a student I very quickly found out that the responsibility of being a diagnostician was a very different situation. His whole approach to his assistants showed great understanding of the problems facing new graduates. First thing in the morning we would divide the calls between us and then he would look carefully through my list saying, "You've done quite a bit of dehorning of cattle, so your first call should be no problem. I see John Fayle has half a dozen ruptured pigs. Do you feel quite happy about the technique? If not, shall we go through the procedure so that you don't make a fool of yourself?"

I have never ceased to be grateful to him since he told me not to be too proud to call upon him, as a second opinion, at any time. I requested his help many times during those first few months, as the surgery premises were part of the house and he was readily available.

Increasingly, we were carrying out routine surgery such as cat and bitch spays, which thankfully reduced the necessity of putting down unwanted litters. Our anaesthetics were fairly simple and entailed prolonged recovery times in dogs. Cats were still anaesthetised using anaesthetic apparatus that involved blowing air through ether by manually squeezing a rubber pump that was connected to a mask held over the unfortunate patient's face.

Every time that I used this mask technique it reminded me of my first tooth extraction when I was a child. I was laid on the settee, my arms were restrained and a chloroform - soaked mask placed over my face. All I could do was struggle as I breathed in the sickly sweet fumes until I slid into welcome oblivion. I recall being very frightened after recovering from the operation as I vomited up congealed blood.

In a similar manner my patients would fight against the anaesthetic and were allowed to recover in peace and quiet. Any disturbance at this "excitability" stage of recovery could start convulsions when they might unwittingly damage themselves.

The postoperative nursing facilities were very unsophisticated. Heated kennels, saline drips and blood transfusions were yet to come. Nursing was based on the TLC factor; the vet or his wife maintained a watch over the anaesthetised patient. Ruth, the housekeeper was a tower of strength at nursing the postoperative patient. She would sit beside the fire in the kitchen making sure that the patients were comfortable and talking to them quietly. "Come along my little treasure, we'll soon have up on your feet and ready to go home looking all smart." Every animal was examined carefully to make sure that all blood and stains were removed. "Mr Scanlon. You have not cleaned up this dear dog properly. Whatever will her owners say? Don't expect me to look after her until she's all tidy."
Brian, with a wry smile, would then set to and carry out the necessary ablutions. "Och! Ruth. Do you not think that you are being a mite fussy?"

As we had few antibiotics, sterilisation of hands and instruments had to be extremely thorough. For years many vets regarded the use of antibiotics after a surgery as an excuse for poor sterility. The operation site was washed, painted with tincture of iodine and then re-washed again with surgical spirit.

Prior to carrying out these procedures, I would scrub my hands for five minutes in carbolic soap and then drench them in surgical spirit. Although surgical gloves were unheard of in that era, it is a credit to the standards of hygiene that we had minimal postoperative infection. The instruments were boiled for ten minutes and then placed on an enamel tray that had been washed with iodine.

My initiation into practice was made easy by Alan Ramsden, who assisted us in those early days and was indeed a Jack-of-all-Trades. Herdsman, motorcycle racer, rifle shot, mechanic and engineer were all within his remit. He could turn his hand to anything. He was a most charming Yorkshire man, who had attained his Higher School Certificate and made a positive decision that further education and an office job were not for him. He escaped to the Isle of Man, together with his wife Betty, as he had a great love of motorcycling and was determined to fit the job to his pleasures.

Eventually, he joined Brian as lay assistant, trouble-shooter and debt collector. Many an outstanding debtor found this happy, smiling man irresistible when he came "bill chasing". 'Eh now, Mr Jones. My old boss cain't afford a new shirt at t'moment, so he asked me to call and collect the bill. We were that pleased to see those lovely bullocks of yours in the mart last week'

He loved handling animals and as a great wildlife enthusiast he helped to develop my love of wild birds. We would go out flighting duck together and whilst we were awaiting their arrival he would teach me about the natural history of the other birds flying past. "If you watch 'em carefully Ned you can tell nearly all t'birds by way of their flight pattern."

Alan had assisted with so many operations over the years that he talked me through my first few bitch spays, as a confidence booster. These operations were just gaining popularity but at that time were still quite uncommon. "Yer know Ned! I've 'elped Brian wi' so many operations that I could almost do 'em blindfold" and his face would wrinkle up in a smile like a naughty pixie at confession. "I reckon that you and I should get through this in double quick. Soon we'll be doing them quicker than Brian," he added conspiratorially.

Alan never wished to graduate from the strictly amateur Manx Grand Prix racing to the more professional atmosphere of the T.T. Races. He was quite content to get around the course and get a finisher's medal. After early morning practising, his aim was to get home to one of Betty's enormous fried breakfasts. This was finished off with "A bit of toast and some reet sharp marmalade to cut the fat!"

No matter how skilled and knowledgeable one may be in veterinary science, one will get nowhere without the veterinary art. It is essentially a people business where bedside manner is of the greatest importance. Communicating with people from all walks of life and gaining their respect is paramount and this is only acquired by experience. The ability to deal with adverse conditions in work and weather with equanimity is also an essential for success. Many of my very bright colleagues at college ended up in teaching or research because of their academic bent and inability to communicate on a layman's level. The post-war graduates, to a large extent came from a different background to their predecessors, were often town reared and unfamiliar with handling stock. This knowledge had to be acquired during the college years along with the scientific advances in medicine.

When I look back at the training of those veterinary surgeons who qualified in the first quarter of the century I am filled with admiration for their skill and knowledge. They were much closer to the stockmen and the animals they handled as many of them were brought up in agricultural areas and did their visits either on horse back or pony and trap. Consequently, they had a much better rapport with the animals under their care and nursing the individual beast on a farm was of much greater importance, as the loss of one animal could be twenty per cent of the herd. In my student days I have seen many farmers sit in the shed all night, rolling Primrose (every cow had a name) over every hour in her thick bed of straw. She would be constantly offered water, fresh greens or a bit of ivy - for the appetite. Unfortunately, under intensive farming conditions this individual care is impossible. The compassion shown by the stockman today is still there, but life is too busy to provide the same individual attention.

Diagnosis for the early practitioner was carried out by using a strict routine of examination with eye, ear, hands and knowledge of stock. Skills largely forgotten. There were none of the modern diagnostic tools such as blood tests and laboratory facilities available. Almost all medicines were made up in the surgery as drenches, to be given by mouth. Injectable sulphonamides, the tip of the technological iceberg, only became available in the nineteen thirties.

# Chapter 10

My first problem occurred after I had been in practice a few weeks. On first qualifying, I believed that I had all the veterinary knowledge in the world at my fingertips and that everyone would be rushing to hear my pearls of wisdom. Six weeks later I had reached the bottom of my self-esteem as so many of the cases did not follow the textbook. I was beginning to realise that I knew very little and that my most important task was to gain the respect of my clients. As a young graduate I came up against the problem met by all beginners. As far as farmers are concerned they requested assistance from a competent vet who looks as if he knows what he is talking about. They have hard lives and don't want to risk the care of valuable stock to apparent schoolboys, who rush off to study a textbook in the car if the case is confusing. Several times I arrived on the farm to be met with retorts such as "Who are you? I called for a vet, not a student," or "I was expecting Mr Scanlon but I suppose you'll have to do. I hope you know what you're at." None of these situations help a young graduate's ego and it only makes things worse to answer back. Early on I determined that, when I received the aggressive treatment, the only answer was to agree with anything that was said and be so nice to them that within a few weeks they ate out of my hand.

It had been a rain sodden week in a grey November and everybody was feeling somewhat down in the dumps. On a particularly overcast, mizzly autumn day, I arrived to calve a cow at John Broughton's farm at Ballyronan. Fortunately, I had been there a couple of times before and had formed a relationship with him. We had had a difference of opinion, when I first visited one of his cows with mastitis. As John had expected Brian, and felt that he had been rather fobbed off with a junior member of the practice, he made the visit rather hard for me by breathing down my neck and impatiently asking awkward questions such as how many times had I treated cases like that and what were the chances of cure? I managed to keep cool and answer all his queries, adding that it was severe enough to require another visit next day. Brian had warned me that he might be awkward and that we should drop in whilst passing for a couple of days to overwhelm him with kindness and concern for his cow. The ploy worked remarkably well and after a day or two I found that I was a welcome visitor.

John was a self made man as he always insisted on telling me. A hard businessman, who was reputed to be sharp in his dealings and stood no nonsense from anyone who opposed him. After leaving school at fourteen he had taken up various odd jobs including a bit of totting around the council dump. Gradually he increased the scrap side as the price of metal improved and eventually set up his own yard as a scrap merchant. Builders and plumbers waste, wrecked vehicles and old rags were all his stock in trade. By shrewd business deals and working very long hours he built up his little empire, alongside pig swill collection and a few scrawny cows behind his scrap yard. Needless to say the piggery stank out the neighbourhood, but pigs were profitable and the farming side kept on growing.

When John's two sons left school he put them into the scrap side of the business, under his supervision. He then bought Ballaronan Farm, which had a hundred and twenty acres of land suitable for dairying. Ballaronan House had been built for a wealthy merchant who had retired to the island during the industrial revolution. It was an attractive Georgian house. Set back off the road and approached by a tree-lined driveway, it had an air of quiet repose, sitting at the edge of extensive parkland. There was an open view across the

27

lawn, which was bordered on each side by well-tended shrubberies and herbaceous borders drawing the eye across the park to the distant woodland. The lawn terminated sharply in a haha, overhung by delicate leaved maples.

Beside the driveway was the entrance to the farm buildings that lay across the meadow, some two hundred yards distant, beside the more modest farm manager's house. The red brick farm buildings were built in a square, and the main entrance was through an archway into the large yard, with a central manure pit to ease the chore of cleaning out the cows' houses and calf pens. Separated from the calf pens by a feed store and barn were the piggeries where he kept a dozen Large White sows.

On entering the yard I was met by George Andrews, the farm manager, who had grown up with John, helped him build up his scrap business and as a farmer's son, was the motivating force in encouraging his friend to go into farming. George was a sturdily built character of medium height, with a generous girth acquired from supping ale in the 'Jolly Farmer.' He always looked the same with a worn cap sitting askew on his head, shirt with no collar, waistcoat, brown corduroys and brown leather boots and gaiters. Those boots and gaiters were lovingly cleaned and polished every day by his wife of many years and mother of three young boys, each one the image of George. I appreciated such organised help, and it was a pleasure to have a table provided to put my gear on.

"I've got Buttercup in the loose box, Mr Carson," said George, "'Ah thought she were due this mornin'. The water bag burst about breakfast time but she's not gettin' on wi' it. I'm sure I don't know what's to do but she has three feet showing. Perhaps it's twins. The lad has just gone to fetch thee some warm water and soap."

George had tied up the young Shorthorn cow by the neck in one of the stalls of the disused stable, rather grandly referred to as a loose box. She was standing patiently with occasional forcing that caused three little feet to pop out of her vulva, and as if changing their mind disappear again. Of course, every time she strained, a couple of dollops of soft dung would drop from beneath her tail onto the exposed feet. As the feet vanished once more inside the vulva yet another lot of manure would arrive inside as contamination. In these days of efficiency and design awards the parturient mammal would not really win any major prizes. Despite all these drawbacks there is very little postnatal infection in cattle!

I put on my wellington boots, stripped to the waist and donned my new red rubber apron that gave me some protection from wet and dung. Adding disinfectant to the pail of steaming water, I got up a good lather with the soap and washed up Buttercup's rear end - then she strained once more and I had to repeat the process. Gently, I slid my arm into her pelvis amongst a mêlée of legs. First of all a head, then a tail and deep inside I thought that I could almost touch something else. All my lectures on parturition flashed through my mind and nothing came to me that answered the situation. First, I pulled on one leg with its mate - or was it? Nothing happened! Then I moved over to the tail and slid my hand over the rump to familiarise myself with the local anatomy. Sliding my hand along the hip and down the calf's leg I found the stifle joint and then moved onwards to the hock or heel joint. At this stage I was at full stretch and rapidly running out of arm. Buttercup came to the rescue and forced quite hard. In the process she very nearly broke my arm, that was jammed between the calf and pelvis. Simultaneously, a gallon of uterine fluid shot over the top of my apron, down my chest, trickling quietly down the trousers and into the boots where it oozed through my socks, very efficiently lubricating my toes. Fortunately, the hind leg then moved towards me and I managed to grasp the fetlock before it disappeared. Cupping my hand around the foot I could then flex the leg and ever so gently pull it outside. I then was faced with four legs and there was another one that I could not reach and that made five! Problem-of course it must be triplets at least. No matter how I worked I could not sort out those legs. I was sure that Paddy M'Geady, our obstetrics lecturer, had not covered this eventuality, but there again, maybe I had been off to the races on the afternoon of that lecture. An occasional trip to Punchestown racecourse was a good cure for boredom, particularly if one had a beautiful young lady to escort.

George was looking anxious so I commented, trying to sound confident, "We have a problem, George. There are more legs in here than the front line of the chorus and they are not labelled as to which pairs go together."

By this time John had arrived to watch the show and I was once more beginning to lose self-confidence. After a couple of minutes I turned to George and said, "I could fiddle around in here for a long time and get nowhere, perhaps losing you a calf in the meantime. Do you mind if I call Brian in to help sort this out?. He has a lot more experience than I have."

They looked at one another knowingly and George went off to phone the surgery. John looked at his watch, muttered brusquely, "I'll be back in fifteen minutes. I must go and check, Blodwen, one of my sows, she is just starting to farrow". My heart sank. Knowing glances passed between the two friends and they both departed. Probably to complain to Brian when he arrives that his assistant is incompetent. I was in the bottom of a trough again! Time to have a quick word with my maker once more!

Within a couple of minutes John returned. "Can you give me a hand? Blodwen has only had two piglets, another afterbirth has arrived and now she has stopped. Her belly is still quite big so I think she has more to come."

Picking up my pail of water I followed him across the yard into the piggery and walked down the passage where I could see several sows lying down, letting their little pink piglets have yet one more meal. All was fairly quiet apart from the contented grunts of the mums and the odd complaint as one little person latched onto the wrong teat and was quickly put into his place. Blodwen's pen was at the end and as I glanced in I saw the most enormous sow lying at full stretch, grunting and wriggling in discomfort. John went in ahead of me and knelt beside her, scratching her ear, crooning and talking to her like a baby. So the hard man of the local business community had an Achilles Heel after all! "Do what you can for her Ned, she is my best sow."

I scrubbed up and slowly inserted my hand into her uterus. Because she was so large I had to lie flat on the ground, in a glorious cocktail of pig droppings and urine; not that it made any difference after my experience with Buttercup. At the full extent of my reach I could feel something solid. Quickly assessing the situation I realised that it was the hard back of a piglet that had come down one horn of the uterus, lost its way and entered the other horn instead of continuing into the body of the uterus. Most mammals have a Y shaped uterus and in the sow some piglets develop in one arm of the Y and the rest in the other side. On their way out they are moved onwards by gentle muscle contractions so that one side

29

empties and the others then follow. In this case, the piglet had gone over the cross-roads instead of turning right at the sign marked exit, blocked the passage, and prevented all his siblings from being born. I could just feel the piglet's tail and pulling gently I drew him out backside first. As I expected he was dead. I could imagine the communal sigh of relief as all the other little pigs continued their journey. We sat around for five minutes and two more piglets appeared, slithered in the goo and coating of afterbirth and staggered round to claim the best teat. Once they stake their claim to a teat they try to return to it every time.

We were interrupted by the sound of Brian's car arriving and hurried across to the loose box. As he entered, I explained the position and he replied for all to hear," You did the best thing possible Ned. I had a similar problem when I joined my first practice and they helped me out of my predicament. Let's both put an arm inside the cow and I will talk you through it."

Fortunately, Buttercup was just big enough to cope with our two arms and as we chatted I was shown which legs to repel so that I could pull on the legs that belonged to the head and with a little effort out slid a nice, pretty little roan heifer calf, still alive and active. The in-house situation had resolved itself and I could now straighten out both hind legs of the next calf and with a bit of traction number two arrived, a nice little brown heifer. The third problem child still had his head tucked down between his fore legs and once this was corrected he slid out easily. In the meantime George had been clearing the mucus from the nostrils of each calf and sticking a piece of straw up the nostril to make them sneeze before putting them in a bed of clean straw so that Buttercup could lick them with her rough, caressing tongue. This licking is so important to cow and calf to stimulate the calf, initiate milk flow in the cow and create a bond between them.

These earlier calvings in which I was involved always gave me a tremendous thrill and forty years later it still excites me. The entry of any young animal into the world never ceases to be a miracle and even the most hardened stockmen still accept it as one of nature's greatest bonuses. I can still sit and watch the new-born animal becoming aware of his existence. How does the maiden heifer or sheep know that she must lick the young and remove the choking afterbirth from the newly arrived animal? What instinct makes the new-born hunt for the teat or even attempt to walk? Scientists have put forward many logical explanations although the mechanics of this behaviour are still cloaked in mystery. Even the ability of new-born calves to absorb the antibody rich colostrum or first milk depends on a trigger reaction when the cow licks the calf's bottom. If the calf is orphaned a similar reaction takes place if it has the anus tickled with a feather.

I turned wearily, as Brian was washing himself, and said, "Thanks for the help. I would have had a lot of problems otherwise."

"It was no problem," he retorted. "If it had been twins you would have had no difficulty. It's always nice to have some back up. George can witness that you owe me a pint in the "The Jolly Farmer" expertly served by your friendly barmaid." With a chuckle and a wave he disappeared, having defused what might have been a problem.

The calves were now left to Buttercup to clean up as John dragged me away to see how Blodwen had progressed. When we arrived she was talking contentedly to her twelve babies who were either asleep or still suckling. One dead pig lay behind her. John rushed in and scratched her belly, testing each teat for milk or signs of mastitis. "Thank you Ned," he said in his usual terse manner, "you did a good job today. A nice, healthy litter of piglets and living triplets. I hope they all survive but no fault of yours if they don't. I respect you for having the common sense and humility to call in Brian for advice. He's a good chap. Now I must be off to a meeting." With that brusque comment he went off towards the house.

George came in and said, "You did a good job there, lad. Come in and have a cup of tea whilst you clean up a bit. You won't pull the girls smelling like you do. You did a right job with Blodwen and gained yoursel' a few Brownie points with John. Do you know? He thinks more of that old girl than he does of his missus. A good thing that you took off your shirt before you started otherwise you might have had some washing tonight. It's all in a day's work. Vera, here's a young man wi' a terrible thirst."

# Chapter 11

When Brian bought the practice from his predecessor, he kept Ruth on as housekeeper. She had run the household and practice very efficiently for Andrew Dawson over the years and he could see no reason to change. Andrew was a constant source for reminiscence with Ruth. Apparently, he had been held in great awe by his clients and insisted that if he was called out to a calving he should have a scrubbed table available in the cow's house on which there would be, neatly laid out, a bowl of warm water, disinfectant, soap and a clean towel. His pre-calving exercises, even in his seventies, consisted of stripping down to his waist, grasping the end of the table and standing on his head for half a minute.

Before he came to the island he had a friend, by the name of Jesse Boot, a drug salesman from Nottingham, who brought round various veterinary drenches and potions. If only Jesse were alive now, to see how his little business had flourished into a household name.

I had felt rather overawed by Ruth when I was a student. Stockily built and middle aged, she always seemed to wear a severe grey dress with white collar and sleeves. Her short cut greying hair and steel rimmed glasses, through which she peered closely at all and sundry, put me in mind of a prison warder. Despite these preconceptions she was kindness itself to all who came in contact with her.

She ran the practice with almost military efficiency and any erring clients or students were very quietly but firmly corrected. The Catholic priest, who called to remonstrate with her for not attending mass regularly, was firmly reminded that they both had a flock to care for and when she felt in need of confession she would call him! Not only did Ruth know every client in the practice, she also knew all their family histories, the dates that their fathers died, who was pregnant and the name of the father. She had been brought up on one of the big farms where her father had been the herdsman. When the owner, Lord Plunket, came on the phone requesting a visit for his horse she would visibly curtsey and mutter, "Yes m'lud. Right away m'lud." We always knew who was on the phone when she gave a deferential bob as she took the message. With all this local knowledge she was indispensable for directing new members of the practice to many of the farms.

Soon after my arrival in the practice I had a phone call from Ruth at 7a.m, summoning me to an urgent milk fever. I rushed into the surgery to collect the necessary equipment and was handed a wine bottle full of Calcium Gluconate, piping hot from the stove. I had always been used to using pre-packed calcium from a well-known drug firm, when I had been seeing practice in England, but here Ruth made it all by weighing out Calcium Gluconate and pouring it into boiling water, after which it was strained through a filter into a sterile wine bottle. It may seem old fashioned but it was very cheap and effective. "It's Mr Benson, up at Gob-na-geay farm. A six-year-old Friesian cow, calved last night in the field and they found her flat out this morning and bloated. I told them to sit her up and support her with bales so that she doesn't bloat too much and die. You went past the door yesterday. Off you go now and I'll give you a new bottle when you return. Mind you bring back the empty bottle, they cost money to replace!"

Still half asleep I jumped into the Morris Oxford and roared up the road, narrowly missing the milkman as I headed out towards the mountain. The road was wide and clear so it was less than ten minutes later that I drove into the yard.

32

"Gob-na-geay", or Mouth of the Wind, was a solid grey stone house built on one end of a row of equally low, grey buildings. They had been sturdily constructed to withstand the constant winds that battered it for much of the year. In the summer sun there was no better place to be, perched up on the hill with a great sweep of green fields running south towards Douglas and Castletown.

As I climbed out of my car I had to lean into the gale in order to remain standing. Struggling into my boots, I could see a group of men huddled beside the gate for shelter from the wind, which seemed to penetrate every loose part of clothing. Taking the precious bottle of calcium and the flutter valve in my hand I hurried across to the gate and the group separated for me to see the cow. They had done a good job. The patient was supported with straw bales along her sides so that she sat upright and a tarpaulin spread across her back for protection. Her head was stretched out along another bale with her tongue hanging out and a brownish discharge coming away from the nostril. She gave a regular low grunting noise and made no movement as I approached. As a matter of routine I muttered my diagnosis as I went along. "She's moderately bloated on the left side, no sign of ruminal movement. Dew like sweating on the back, no dung to be seen, dry nose and dilated pupils. Temperature is all right." I checked the udder and there was no sign of mastitis. It was certainly a fairly advanced case of milk fever, therefore no time to lose. I assembled my flutter valve by pushing the rubber cap end onto the open bottle of calcium and handed it to the cowman to hold. Using a length of baler twine from my pocket I tied it in a loop around her neck as a tourniquet and tightened it to raise the jugular vein. I quickly slipped the needle into the vein and a jet of dark red blood shot out. Addressing the cowman I said; "Turn the bottle upside down so that the liquid flows out and down the rubber tube" As it did so and cleared any air bubbles out of the tube I joined it up to the needle in the vein. The calcium was still fairly hot and I had to slow down the flow by nipping the tube periodically. Using my stethoscope I could monitor the heart beat constantly. Gradually the grunting grew less, and I could feel movements in the rumen as stomach muscles responded to the calcium. She belched, reducing the bloat and her ears started to twitch. After a couple of minutes her tail raised and a few dark, hard pieces of dung were forced out. As the last of the life giving calcium flowed into her neck I removed the needle and we stood around to observe her whilst she grew brighter by the minute. She raised up her head and unsuccessfully tried to lift her heavy body. The spirit was willing but the body still too weak to succeed. " Leave her here for a couple of hours," I said, "If she's not up by then let me know." Bill, the cowman, nodded, saying, "Oi didn't have time to interduce mysel' Mr Carson. Oi'm Bill Pitman the herdsman so we shall have lots of dealin's in the future. I hear that you did a good job at Mr Broughton's place the other day. I was 'avin' a pint at the 'Jolly Farmer' wi' George Andrews and 'ee told me all about it. Can you tell me, why cows do go off their legs with Milk Fever?"

"Thanks Bill," I replied, "It's always nice to know that my patients go on all right. Milk Fever is a funny old thing. It really isn't a fever at all but a mineral deficiency. When the cow starts to produce a large quantity of milk at calving time she transfers a lot of calcium from her body into the milk. When this is done too rapidly it greatly reduces available calcium in the blood. This calcium is needed by the nervous system to send messages to the body muscles and other organs. When you lower the calcium levels it is rather like reducing the power supply in a telephone exchange. The messages don't get through to the muscles, which cease to work; therefore the cow can't stand up, can't swallow, burp or pass dung. You've just seen what happens when the power is turned on again."

"Well," said Bill, "Thank you Mr Carson for comin' so promptly. There is nothing new in this world. Doesn't it make you feel humble to feel that all those wonderful things are happening whilst we look on? It will make a good tale to tell George at the Jolly Farmer"

# Chapter 12

One of the most distressing incidents of my time in this practice came about when I had to put my first patient to sleep. He was an ancient and much loved Labrador called "Mush" who had lost all pleasure in life due to blindness and a large tumour on his liver. Old Charlie Jones had been a widower for many years and was a well-known sight in the area, as he and "Mush" would walk for miles along the country lanes, taking great pleasure in each other's company. Gradually their rambles became shorter as they both stiffened up and ran out of breath. Instead, they would sit on a capstan at the quayside after enjoying a lunchtime Guinness at the Market Inn. Several times Charlie had said to me that one day he would arrive with his pal, hand me the lead and say, "Put him to sleep Mr Carson."

One Friday afternoon at the end of surgery they walked in together, he looked in the old dog's sightless eyes, and blowing deeply into his handkerchief, handed me his lead and walked away with his head downcast, sobbing quietly. I almost put my hand on his shoulder to acknowledge my part in sharing his grief but thought better of it. Theirs had been a very close relationship and I thought that he should be given his own privacy.

I felt that I was doing "Mush" a service as the quality of his life had gone, but I had also developed a strong attachment to this old retainer. I was able to sit Mush down and as I talked to him quietly he held out his leg with complete trust and acceptance and allowed me to inject barbiturate into his vein. He didn't even feel the tiny needle prick because after a few seconds he relaxed onto the ground as the anaesthetic acted, his life's work over. It made me realise how privileged I was to have shared some moments between these two old friends and in the end to have avoided a distressing end for "Mush."

I spent the evening wondering how Charlie was feeling after losing his only contact with his wife Rose, who had died four years earlier. Mush had filled the gap after Rose died and all his affections had been centred on the dog since that time. To arrive home to an empty room and have no one with whom to share his social hours would be devastating for the old man. I was beginning to appreciate that not only was my duty of care towards the patient, but also the owner in these deeply emotive situations. It concerned me so deeply that after work I wrote him a letter in a rather futile attempt to show that I shared his grief and suggesting that if I came upon a lonely dog, in need of a companion, I would contact him.

This reminded me of a similar incident some six years earlier when I was a student with Brian's predecessor, Andrew Dawson. Andrew was incapacitated with a fractured wrist and found that he was unable to put an old dog to sleep. He asked me to do the job for him. To make things worse for me, I had to use a mixture of prussic acid and strychnine that was the standard means of euthanasia at that time. I took the old dog aside and with great care injected the mixture into his heart. He fell over and went into a rigid spasm before dying. Death was very rapid and probably not as stressful to the patient as it was to the observer. After laying his body in the kennel I walked straight into the house and told Andrew that I felt that we should order barbiturates as not only was the prussic acid technique unfair on the animal but risky for the handler as well. Within a couple of days, half a dozen bottles of barbiturate arrived and we had at last reached the second half of the twentieth century.

My concern about using prussic acid stemmed from an incident that took place a week before I put the old dog to sleep. We had always handled prussic acid injection extremely carefully. It was supplied in a small brown poison bottle with a glass stopper. The reason for the glass stopper was to stop the prussic leaking out, as it would rapidly produce poisonous fumes that smelled of 'Pear drops', so popular with writers of murder mysteries. We were driving home in Andrew's luxurious Alvis Speed 20 after putting a dog to sleep at a house in Laxey. The bottle of prussic acid was lying in the glove compartment and must have rolled around until the stopper came loose and the contents spilled out. I was the first to smell the "pear drops" and screamed out to stop the car, as even the fumes are lethal. We both leapt out of the vehicle and left the doors wide open. Fortunately, there was a brisk breeze blowing, which dissipated the volatile fumes in a few minutes when we could retrieve the bottle, replace the stopper and drive home with all the windows open. Death follows very rapidly from prussic acid poisoning so we considered ourselves extremely fortunate.

I had always enjoyed seeing practice with Andrew. A grizzled old man with a bushy moustache, a pork pie hat and a bandy legged walk, he resembled a character out of a Western film. All that was missing were the spurs and holsters. He was extremely kind and a driving force behind my decision to become a veterinary surgeon. He enjoyed his life as a vet and patiently passed on his knowledge of the veterinary art to me. He may not have been an expert at veterinary science but he excelled in the veterinary art, which is basically bedside manner. As a teenager I placed him on a pedestal and felt that he could do no wrong. It is good for youngsters to have a role model but this one had one failing which I was to discover!

Andrew had been very quiet for several days and had even given up singing romantic songs as we drove through the countryside. He became quite depressed until eventually he confessed to me that he had been suffering from severe toothache for the past three weeks but he was afraid of visiting the dentist. Several times Ruth had made an appointment for him to have his teeth out and each time he would reach the gate, start shaking and return home for a stiff whiskey. Eventually, he became physically ill from his rotten roots and his doctor sedated him and took him to the dentist. He hardly spoke for three days as his mouth was so sore and he only had three teeth left in his head

We were returning home from a farm call about a week later when Andrew said, "I think that we should call in and collect my new teeth on the way home" By this time his mouth had healed up and he was once again his happy self. We returned home and he said, "ee Lad! He won't get me back in his chair again. Fetch me a whiskey lad and we'll drink a toast to these new teeth." With great ceremony he opened the box, lifted out the pristine dentures and placed them on the mantelpiece. Lifting up his glass, he shook his fist at them saying, "There you buggers - ache!" and started singing- 'Dancing in the Dark' to show that he was back on form.

# Chapter 13

Veterinary practice is not a bed of roses and the unexpected lies in wait for the unwary-calling upon your immediate survival instincts. A very frightening encounter occurred when Brian asked me to visit Mr Browning of Higher Rushen Farm to see a cow that was lame in two feet. I had already attended one lame cow there during the week so the thought of a repeat performance set my mind working overtime. Had I misdiagnosed the first case. Could this be the start of a foot and mouth outbreak? Foot and Mouth Disease is a highly infectious disease of cloven-footed animals such as cattle, sheep, pigs and goats. It is not normally present in the British Isles but, when it does appear, can spread rapidly across large areas of the country. It is an untreatable virus disease that causes extreme ulceration of the mouth and feet. The animals are in great pain, cannot eat and become very emaciated. The only means of disease control is to slaughter all in contact animals. Many prime herds, built up over a lifetime, have been lost because of this condition. Since that time there have been many attempts to produce an effective vaccine to control this disease and eliminate it completely. The current vaccines can control the spread of Foot and Mouth outbreak but have the drawback that they only last several months and some vaccinated animals will continue to shed the virus and act as a focus of infection.. Consequently, all vaccinated animals have to be slaughtered within twelve months of vaccination.

As I drove along the road towards Higher Rushen Farm all these thoughts ran through my mind and I had visions of all the cattle in the island being slaughtered and myself being exiled to work in Siberia or even worse, the Ministry of Agriculture. So soon after graduation I had not fully appreciated the full meaning of "Common things occur commonly" and Foot and Mouth certainly was not common.

On arriving in the farmyard I spoke to Mrs Browning who said that the men were in the fields and would be back soon. They had left the cow in the shed as she had difficulty in standing with her sore feet. I said that I would go and have a look and see what I could do in the meantime.

Entering the cowshed I saw a beautiful young Ayrshire cow, with a most impressively sweeping pair of horns, lying on the floor. My heart went out to her as I realised her acute discomfort with two sore feet. When I approached, she struggled to her feet with difficulty, put her head down and charged straight at me! A little voice in my head said, "Bulls always close their eyes and charge straight, cows throw their heads about." So it came to pass, that as I did a delicate pas-de-deux, to avoid contact, her left horn caught the crutch of my trousers travelled upwards and stopped at the waistband! My initial thought, as I clutched my stomach was, "Thank you God, I'm not disembowelled but am I going to have to call off the wedding? It shouldn't happen to one of such tender years" Discretion being the better part of valour, I escaped through the door to examine the damage. Everything appeared to be in working order apart from the fact that I was shaking with fear. There was the consolation that at least I could look forward to a rosy future. The tear in my trousers made me look positively indecent, but fortunately I had a brown dustcoat in the car. After a short rest to recover, I returned to the shed armed with a stick and rope. Whether it was the brown coat or the stick that acted as a sign of authority, the cow quietly walked into her stall and let me chain her up-quite content after her show of strength. She let me lift up both hind feet that were infected but not ulcerated. The painful swelling, inflammation of the feet, dead tissue and nauseating smell as I pulled my finger between her claws confirmed that this was foot rot. She did object to this probing and kicked out but fortunately I was holding her leg

37

high enough to prevent any damage. With some trepidation I opened her mouth and looked inside; it was a healthy pink colour with no sign of ulceration or salivation. Reaching into my case I took out a bottle of sulphadimidine and injected her, content in my mind that she would soon be cured. This injection was quite irritant and I always injected on the side away from me. On my first attempt, as a student, I had injected over the near side ribs and received a smart kick in the crutch as a thank you gift.

There had always been a few greyhounds on the island, often used for coursing and I used to treat quite a few for sprains and knocked up toes. It was a common sight on a Sunday morning to see men out walking their dogs to keep them in trim. One Sunday lunch time I was due to have a meal with Moira and had been off on a couple of calls before handing over the duty to Brian. I was just leaving the surgery when the phone rang, "Hello, Is dat de vit'. This is Liam Rafferty. I have an emergency for you. My running dog has cut herself real bad and she'll need some stitching. I could be with you in five minutes and there's blood all over the place," came the voice, pleading and verging on panic.

"Bring him right in," I replied, another minute and he would have missed me. I didn't know the man from Adam but the dog had to be seen fairly soon. Now what was I going to tell Moira when I arrived late for our lunch date?

Sure enough about five minutes later there was the roar of an engine, without a silencer, as a dilapidated green van pulled up outside the gate. Out stepped a couple of men, right out of the book of dubious characters and wide boys. With well greased, black hair hanging down over their eyes, open neck check shirts with rolled up sleeves, sad looking grey trousers that looked as if they were in deep mourning, scuffed black shoes and fags hanging from their lips I instantly gave up all ideas of receiving any payment.

They opened the back door of the van and leant inside, reappearing with a body stretched out on an old length of carpet. Gently carrying their burden up the path to the surgery door, which I had held open for them, they carried a large brindle greyhound into the room and laid her on the floor. Both men were unshaven and tattooed on their arms, and the slightly shorter one of the pair was blowing his nose and wiping his eyes as if he had a bad cold-or perhaps, had been crying. They looked like a pair of desperadoes but the way they were caressing and talking to the dog belied their appearance.

The smaller one looked up at me appealingly, "Can you do anythin' for our Bella, mister? She was chasin' a hare and went right through a gateway. Then we heard a scream and she must have run into some rusty galvanised iron, 'cos when we found her she were pouring blood from her side and looked like 'dis."

At which point, with the air of a conjurer, he pulled off an old cloth that had been covering Bella. It was a most amazing sight. Bella's side had been unzipped from the base of her neck to the top of her hind leg. Greyhounds in pursuit of prey become completely divorced from time and place. Their entire being is concentrated on the chase and nothing else matters. In the excitement she must have run along a sharp edge without realising the problem for a few seconds. Despite her problems, Bella looked at me soulfully with her liquid brown eyes. She might have been saying, sorry; but I almost caught that hare! I could see that this was going to be a mammoth suturing operation, so my first instinct was to check her heart and also her mucous membranes for evidence of shock or excessive haemorrhage. I didn't fancy her chances with prolonged barbiturate anaesthesia, particularly as I had no help. I opted for morphine, as an alternative, which was very suitable for the situation. I went to the dangerous drugs cupboard, dissolved some morphine in water and injected Bella whilst Liam and Kevin, as I later found out, talked to her. "Keep talking," I said, "I shall boil up some instruments and collect equipment whilst she dozes off. It looks like a long job, but with care Bella should be completely healed in three weeks.

"I hope so, mister, she's very special to brother and me. Sure we'll never let her chase hare's again."

"I don't believe it," I said, "It's part of her nature and it would be unfair on Bella to keep her on a lead. By the way, where did she have the accident? There aren't too many wild hares around at the moment?"

The brothers looked at one another rather sheepishly. "Oh, just a mile or two down the road there's a bit of parkland-good for running the dogs. As you say, it would not be fair to keep her tied up."

Bells started to ring in my brain. "I see. It wouldn't by any chance have been the parkland at Ballaronan?" Knowing quite well that the sporting rights on the farm were jealously preserved, I wondered whether a bit of poaching might have taken place.

Dead silence and exchanged glances as a guilty blush spread across Liam's weathered features. "Well, you could say that the dogs strayed across the boundary a little bit and entered the back fields in Ballaronan. It is sometimes impossible to control them entirely when they're followin' a hare."

"Right lads, lift Bella up gently onto the table here and Liam, if you would just talk to her quietly I shall give her a bit of local anaesthetic and clean the bits of grass out of the wound."

Using a pair of curved scissors, I clipped the hair along the edge of the wound, constantly washing any stray hairs and grass away. Peroxide was then poured over the wound to freshen up the tissues, which were then washed well with acriflavine. Carefully, I checked the wound for deep tissue damage. Fortunately, the cut was not too deep, as the sharp object seemed to have bounced off the ribs and only gone in deeper above the shoulder blade and on the hind leg.

No permanent damage was evident so, after scrubbing my hands well I commenced suturing the long gash. The broad-spectrum antibiotics were not freely used at that time and asepsis was of paramount importance.

Slowly and laboriously I went along the long wound, describing the process as I went to these amiable rogues, whilst pulling the underlying tissues together, closing those parts that might form air pockets and delay healing. This also enabled me to check for, and remove, any fine hairs left in the wound. These sutures were of catgut and would dissolve in about three weeks, whilst the skin sutures were made of linen and would remain there for at least ten days before removal.

So engrossed was I in my labours, that I failed to keep an eye on Bella's owners. The surgery was small and cramped so I was not surprised that after twenty minutes, Kevin turned to Liam, saying, "I'm going out for a breather and 'ter get some fags." The response was a grunt from Liam, and about five minutes later he gave a gentle sigh and slid gracefully to the floor, looking slightly green. After another five minutes Kevin returned, saw his brother sleeping on the floor, muttered, "Mother of God!" and promptly collapsed beside Liam. Of course, I was unable to help them and went on with the job, and then put in another layer of skin sutures to close the wound. After I had finished, poor old Bella resembled a piece of embroidery with over seventy stitches holding her together. All this time, she lay there motionless, doubtless dreaming of psychedelic rabbits!

Eventually both my sleeping helpers aroused themselves, just after I had finished the operation. Two rather tough grown men sitting side by side on the floor, like Tweedle Dum and Tweedle Dee, was a sight to remember. It always amazes me that the roughest and toughest of men are really teddy bears at heart. I gave Bella an antidote, for the morphine and as she recovered, told them that my fee on a Sunday lunchtime, which I had just missed, was ten pounds. Yet again, they glanced at one another as Kevin reached into his pocket, pulled out a large wad of notes, the like of which I had never seen before, peeled off twenty and gave them to me. "You're a gentleman, mister. We're ever so grateful. I hope we can help you sometime. You won't say anything about Ballaronan, will yer? God bless you, sir". Pocketing my hush money, I replied, "No that's between these four walls. Unless you have any problems I hope to see Bella in ten days to take those stitches out. Only exercise her on a lead and here's some tablets in case she becomes infected."

Moira was not entirely delighted when I arrived for lunch two hours late. Almost in tears she produced Yorkshire pudding that had collapsed, roast potatoes to challenge the teeth and roast beef that was rather dry but very tender! It took all of my powers of persuasion and flattery to entice her out for tea during the afternoon. "This is all part of the job when you are in a caring profession", I said humbly. "As a vet's wife, you will find that I can make you no promises that I shall always be on time for meals!"

Kevin and Liam returned in twelve days to have the stitches removed. After such an injury I had fully expected to see them before that time with infection in the wound.
It was with some trepidation that I checked the site and to my delight it had healed completely, save for one or two stitches. Removing seventy stitches was quite a long drawn out business in itself but the boys kept me entertained with anecdotes of their coursing adventures.

Bella stood there patiently whilst I checked each suture. Liam commented, "I really tink dat Bella knows that you're doing her good. If she could speak she'd be thanking you"

"Indeed," I replied. "She's a real lady. I wish that they were all like her." Sure enough she left me a thank you present. When I had finished tidying up I found that she had casually left a bottle of Jamieson's Whiskey sitting on the mantelpiece!

# Chapter 14

Half way between Douglas and Ramsey on the East coast of the island Laxey sits comfortably in the valley bottom as it runs down from Snaefell. This valley was carved out over the ages by the Laxey River that tumbles and chuckles its way down to the sea.. Long ago the river held a stock of salmon, hence the Norse word Lax, a salmon, to describe the river. After the onset of mining for gold and silver during the nineteenth century the fish stocks disappeared owing to pollution. A permanent monument to those prosperous times is the "Lady Isabella", the largest waterwheel in the world which was constructed to pump water out of the mines

There were many people in Laxey who ran smallholdings to help to eke out a living and keep a well-stocked larder. The lower paid workers had a great deal of independence and pride before the insidious cosseting effect of the welfare state created too much reliance on others. Many of these small cottages had long gardens and back yards whilst the owners would also grow vegetables in nearby allotments. This was an era when many people in towns still had close contact with pigs and poultry and had the ability to rear and slaughter them for home use. Chicken runs and lean-to pig sheds were commonplace and it was not uncommon to be called to an address in a terrace of cottages to treat sick pigs.

Bernie Kewin was the night watchman in a nearby mill. In all weathers he wore the same garb. The jacket and waistcoat from a suit, a pair of breeches, well-polished brown boots and gaiters gave him the appearance of a bandy legged pixie! He had been laid off from the electric railway after a tram had crushed one of his legs and rendered him unfit to work. He was a small wiry character whose sheer determination had enabled him to overcome his severe lameness and with the help of his wife Betsy, who was as round as he was thin, made sufficient income to rear their six children. Bert worked at night and half of the day whilst Betsy helped to run a green grocery shop down the street. Whenever I saw Bert he was always working, with the odd break to fill his well-chewed pipe with some rubbed shag tobacco. When he was not tending his allotment or caring for the animals he could be found pushing a four-wheeled trolley containing pigswill collected from around the village.

Late one afternoon I was asked to drop in with Bernie on my way back from a session dehorning a herd of cows. I pulled up at the front of number seven Mine Cottages, a nondescript terrace of dinghy grey stone cottages, which all looked alike save for the gleaming brass house number on the front door. Pride of possession was also reflected in the golden glow of the well-burnished door sill and handle, shouting out to all and sundry that this was a well cared for establishment. It was a public announcement that the house belonged to an upward looking working family with high standards and aspirations. Walking up the path to the front door I was impressed by the well-maintained flower beds and shrubs in the tiny front garden. I rapped twice with the freshly painted black dolphin door knocker and after a sliding of bolts on the inside, Betsy Kewin, clad in a clean floral overall looked up at me, "You'll be Mr Carson, the vet. We're so glad to see you. A litter of young pigs we bought the other day have been squitting all over the place and a couple are looking really poorly. Normally, Mr Scanlon comes along the back lane, as it's easier to get into the yard. I see that you've got your case so you might as well come through this way."

Having been politely put in my place, I almost tiptoed across the sitting room, down the passage with its shining linoleum and rag rug, in case I left muddy footprints in this immaculate house. It was evident that the family spent most of the week living in the warmth of the comfortable kitchen. On either side of the glowing kitchen range stood two armchairs, upholstered in red moquette over the backs of which hung ornate antimacassars. A heavy copper kettle stood on a trivet beside the fire, flanked by a brass coal scuttle and a basket of logs. Above the range, out of reach of young children, was the mantle shelf, guarded at both ends by orange china dogs with spotted noses. All the oddments in the house lay between these ornaments, a black and gold tea caddy, Bernie's tobacco cabinet, boxes of matches, a ball of string and a letter rack.

Out through the scullery and into the cobbled yard I followed Betsy. Bernie was just coming out of the hen house with a bowl of eggs, which he presented to his wife, saying, "So you're the new chap. I'm glad to meet you. Can't help but be an improvement on that last drunken Scotsman. I had to drag him out of the pub a few times. How he managed to get home sometimes I don't know. Come and have a look at these poor little things. They were doing ever so well up to a couple of days ago and now they've got the squits."

Bending low, we entered a small dark wooden shed with a galvanised roof. Ten little, grunting piglets scuttled away into the corner and as I looked around I could see patches of grey diarrhoea on the floor. "Can you catch that one in the corner with the drooping ears?" I said to Bernie. He reached across and took hold of the piglet by the hind leg. It squealed, a very high-pitched note, and a jet of diarrhoea shot out of his rear end.

"Now look at this chap, Bernie. His ears are thickened and going purple, he has a strange squeal and diarrhoea. This all adds up to a condition called bowel oedema. I'll lay odds that you had these pigs about fourteen days ago, when they were weaned. Since that time they have really tucked into their grub and done well. Too much good feeding given suddenly meant that they could not cope and the diarrhoea started. The bug in the gut causes a lot of waterlogging of the bowel wall, the voice box and the ears, ending in death. Now we must try and reverse the process."

"You're right, Mr Vet," said Bernie, "We've had them fourteen days tomorrow. What do we do now as I cannot afford to lose 'em?"

"First of all I want you to empty and clean out the trough. Wash down the pen with clean water, as the dung is infectious if it is licked up. Give them ample water to drink and I would add a teaspoonful of Epsom Salts, per piglet, to the drinking water for the next forty-eight hours. That should reduce the water logging and make them feel better. No food for twenty-four hours and then starting at quarter rations, gradually build it up so that they get accustomed to it slowly. I shall inject them all today to kill off the infection and may have to see them tomorrow if they are not improving. Don't forget that all sick animals respond to tender loving care so I would suggest a good bed of straw and a warm pig lamp tonight."
"Well," said Bernie, after we had finished. "I've learned somethin' today. Thank you Mr Whatsit - sorry I never was good at names. Come int'er house and I shall pay thee. Mr Scanlon and I have an arrangement- A dozen eggs a call and if he wants more he lets me know. He's a right good man. As you've been so helpful, have half a dozen for yourself "

He shook me by the hand and sent me off home, content that I had made someone happy. As I looked back I could see this little figure in gaiters waving at the roadside.

42

# Chapter 15

Brian had been brought up on a farm in Ulster and horses were part of his life. In his younger days he had been a member of the Route Hunt and a very competent point-to-point rider. He had a couple of horses stabled out at Abbeylands, where he spent much of his free time at weekends. On Friday afternoons he would be very restless and eager to tie off any loose ends of work in order that he didn't have to appear the following morning.

With his attractive Irish brogue and outgoing manner, he had developed a cult following amongst the local horsewomen, so that he was never short of company when hacking across the hills. Sometimes the pressures became too great when he found himself being pursued by several ladies simultaneously, who saw him as an escape from a stale relationship.

Like many men of great charm he appeared to be naively unaware of his attraction. He would enter a room full of people, a gangly six-footer, golden blonde hair swept back in waves. Within minutes, heads were turning and many ladies would be sidling across the room in his direction, drawn by his indefinable animal magnetism.

John Davies and his wife Megan were acquaintances of Brian and the two men sometimes rode out together on the hills. When John casually mentioned that he would be away in England on business for a week, Brian offered to take Megan out hacking on the Saturday morning. This suited them, as the two Davies boys were boarders at King William's College and Megan would be at a loose end. Megan had hunted in the Welsh Marches some years earlier, before her figure had become more rounded and comfortable.

""I hope that you won't be needing me in the morning, Ned," were Brian's parting words as we finished Friday evening surgery. "You see, I promised John that I would take Megan out for a wee ride in the morning."

I gave him a meaningful look and chuckled, "Perhaps I should be praying for your safe return, Brian. You are dealing in hot property. No doubt you realise that the pert Mrs Davies is known locally as 'Delilah'"

"Absolute nonsense, Ned. You Manxmen are all the same, you've been listening to too much local gossip. She's a delightful lady and I'm sure that John would be very hurt to hear you say that," was his swift rejoinder.

Megan duly appeared in the surgery at nine o'clock next morning, looking very attractive in breeches and a bottle green polo neck jersey. Her halo of brown curls sparkled as they peeped coyly out from beneath her riding hat. "I hope that I don't make a fool of myself, Brian." She said disarmingly. "I haven't been on a horse for so long that I've almost forgotten which end to feed. Do tell me if I make too many mistakes!"

"Don't worry your head," replied Brian. " I'm sure that it will come back to you quicker than you think. You'll be going at full stretch before the morning's out," he added prophetically.

They drove out to Abbeylands where Brian had his loose boxes in a yard attached to a cottage. After they entered the loose box, Brian tied up the horses, saying, "Now you take

'Jade.' She's a quiet wee mare although she can be skittish at times. I'll ride the big grey 'Baska,' as he is inclined to be a bit wilful. Take the rug off, clean out her feet and give her a good brush down. Don't forget to oil her feet. There's a jar of Neat's-foot oil in the window."

Megan fell into the routine as if it were a daily occurrence. The all-pervading smell of horses and leather took her mind back to her carefree days in Wales. She fumbled a bit with the bridle and asked for some help with the martingale. After saddling up she set to, tightening the girth and adjusting the stirrup leathers.

"Take her outside and let me help you to mount," said Brian, making a step with his hands and helping Megan into the saddle. "How does that feel now?"

"Just wonderful," replied Megan, adjusting the reins and standing up in the stirrups. Suddenly she tipped sideways as the saddle slipped and flung her arms around Brian's neck. "I say this is an unexpected bonus. Much more fun than riding," she continued without attempting to extract herself from Brian's firm embrace. "Oh dear! I couldn't have pulled the girth up tight enough, thank goodness you came to my rescue."

Alarm bells rang as Brian realised that things were not going according to plan and he gently but firmly put her back in the saddle before adjusting the girth.

Megan smiled, realising that she was a bit premature. With a wicked twinkle in her eyes she added "Sorry! I rather enjoyed that but we must get on with the ride."

After a couple of turns around the field to warm up they broke into a canter towards the gate bordering the hill pasture. Megan felt the thrill of the chase as the wind swept past her face and Jade comfortably kept pace with her stable mate. She glanced aside to watch Brian sitting effortlessly, almost arrogantly, astride Baska. Excitement, almost forgotten over the years, surged through her body at the sight of his complete mastery over the horse. She could feel her heart thumping as her whole body tingled in anticipation.

Jade was sweating a bit but evidently enjoying the outing as much as Megan. As they stopped at the moor gate, the little mare was shifting from foot to foot in eagerness but Megan had her well in hand. Megan felt a pulse throbbing in her temple; she was also over excited. With flushed cheeks and eyes sparkling she laid a hand firmly on Brian's arm and coquettishly dared him to race to the far end of the field.

"If you're up to it," replied Brian, jestingly. There are a couple of banks to clear towards the far end. Be careful, as there is a ditch full of water before the second bank, over yonder, by the gap in the thorn hedge. Jade will probably leave this old war horse of mine miles behind."

With a whoop of exultation she set off towards the far bank, intent on creating an impression. Jade was in her element as Megan gave her her head and stretched out at full gallop with Baska in full pursuit. Faultlessly clearing the first bank she was well ahead with the heavyweights thundering along behind. With just the hillside and sky before her Megan was ecstatic and held on for dear life as she neared the second jump.

Fate decreed that, at that moment, a scatty young chaffinch flew out of the hedge into the path of a marauding sparrow hawk. Innocent of his fate, he was snatched by the talons of the hawk as it burst through the gap in the thorn bush, in an explosion of feathers. Jade's concentration snapped as she cat-jumped sideways and bucked Megan straight up in the air.

Some twenty yards behind, Brian watched as the whole scene took place in slow motion. There was a half formed shout as Megan performed a graceful parabola and disappeared slowly into the ditch with a most impressive splash.

Leaping off Baska, he rushed to the rescue just in time to see the attractive Megan, all passion spent, break surface. Controlling his laughter at the scene he held out his hand to her as she crawled out of the stinking morass, covered with mud and a halo of Canadian pond weed.

Determined not to give way she sat disconsolately on the bank, tears running in rivulets down her muddy face, repeatedly shouting, "Bloody bird, bloody bird! I hope you choke on it!"

It was a sad little party that trudged back to the stables. Brian had wiped her down and cleaned off the mud as best he could. He was mounted on Jade whilst Baska, on a lead rein carried a very unhappy Megan. Brian drove her home as in the depths of despair all she really wanted was to steep in a hot bath and forget her romantic inclinations.

# Chapter 16

Sometime after the incident with Megan, I had been called out to Dick Maddrell's farm where I had spent the morning dehorning his herd of Ayrshire cows. Anyone who has handled Ayrshires will know what beautiful beasts they are with their rich red and white coats, wedge shaped bodies and delicate ladylike heads. Someone must have been inspired to create their shape with a design award in mind. To top it off they were endowed with a very graceful pair of sweeping horns. The downside is that they know to within an inch, the direction in which those sharp horn tips point, as I had already found out to my cost at Higher Rushen Farm. They are Prima Donnas, inclined to fling their heads around and in crowded conditions such as collecting yards or narrow gateways, they have been known to cause very severe tear wounds to each other by puncturing udders and vulvas. I had often thought that this problem was made worse when they were chained up by the neck against cement rendered partitions. The constant movement of their head meant that they were forever honing the horn tips to fine spikes. During the summer evenings, when the cows were walking up narrow lanes, and being driven to distraction by flies they would toss their heads to move the pests, and accidentally injure a neighbouring beast.

It is always a hazardous job dehorning cows when they are tied side by side. The one that is not being worked on keeps waving her head about and thumping one sharply in the back. Thankfully, my assistant was Dick's son Roger, a rather overweight young lad who had just left school and was working on the farm before going to agricultural college. Roger was a cheerful, baby faced boy, who didn't look tough enough for the rigours of farming.

Roger would grab a cow by the nose whilst I injected local anaesthetic behind the eye. This completely anaesthetises the horn area on one side of the head whilst the process is repeated on the other horn. We would inject about six cows and then start at the beginning to remove the horns. Before the operation we tied baling cord firmly around the head at the base of the horns to act as a tourniquet and prevent bleeding. A pair of "bulldogs" or nose grips were then fastened onto the cow's nose to enable the handler to control the animal more efficiently. The horn was then cut off just above the base using a butcher's saw and exposing a hole into the head sinus. The resulting wound was dressed with antiseptic powder and covered with a pad of sterile gauze in order to speed up healing. Dick and Roger were instructed to feed hay only on the floor until the hole in the skull closed over, to avoid the danger of chaff falling into the wounds and causing infection.

The only hitch occurred in mid morning when a tourniquet slipped and a jet of blood hit me straight in the face, covered my smart tie and soaked through my dust coat onto my shirt. Temporarily blinded, I staggered between the two cows, tripped over a bovine foot and measured my length in the wheel barrow- full of cow dung! Was it my fate to end up constantly smelling of 'roses'? Of course, Dick and Roger burst into helpless laughter. My only solace was that Mrs Maddrell brought me a cup of tea as a consolation prize whilst I was cleaning myself up.

Roger turned out to be such an efficient and strong assistant that we had finished his herd of forty cows by lunchtime. It was a great relief to us to finish so quickly as the work was strenuous. It had been a worrying time for the owners who had been very concerned about the operations on their animals. Each cow had a name and they were all part of the family so naturally this decision had taken a lot of heart searching. They need not have worried however as there was very little reduction in milk yield at the evening milking, a good indicator of any upset. All through the afternoon neighbours had been dropping in to see how the work was going, in case they might want to have their own cows dehorned one day in the future. The farming grapevine is very efficient means of free advertising.

When I met Roger in the market several days later he came across to me, smiling broadly, but sporting a lovely black eye. After the usual banter about falling out with his girlfriend, he said, "No Ned, to be honest it was not that at all. It was the funniest thing. At milking time, as the cows breathed in the cold air, steam came out of the holes in their heads. You see, none of them recognised each other, Rather like ladies spotting each other by their hats, the cows identified each other by their horns. There was quite a bit of head butting until they found out who was who. The "boss" cow who used her big horns very effectively to stay at the top has had a right duffin' up. It looks as if the peckin' order is now changin'. The Young Farmer's Club were all so impressed by tales of your performance that they want you to give a talk to us on the advantages of dehorning!"

"That's not a very satisfactory answer Roger," I replied, "You've managed to skirt around the black eye question!"

Looking a bit embarrassed Roger continued, "I hoped that you would forget that. I was a bit stupid, you see Well, it took us quite a time to sort out which cow was which, forgetting that we too had used their horns to recognise them. So of course we got a few cows tied up in the wrong side of their stalls and as you know they don't much like being milked on the wrong side. As I was putting the milking machine clusters on one of these cows she let fly with her hind foot and gave me this great 'shiner'."

I must confess that I saw the funny side of the story, realising that he would get some ribbing at the next club meeting. Watching my mirth he couldn't resist a smile. "I'll tell you what, Mr Smarty Pants Vetinry, if I should hear a word of this at the club I could let slip what happened to you in our cow shed! On the other hand I could forget about it when you give your talk to us about dehorning!"

# Chapter 17

Bulls on the other hand have a very maccho outlook on life. Their whole being is fired up by the hormone Testosterone, that creates the drive and dominance. Putting too much trust in bulls of any breed has cost many people their lives. Not only are they immensely strong and heavy, but the dairy bull in particular loves to flaunt his virility before all comers. When a bull of up to one and a half tons in weight tosses a person in the air, it is as if the victim were a rag doll. Few people survive being gored and then knelt upon after landing on the ground. Many bulls are kept in solitary confinement in a custom-built bullpen that makes them very frustrated and angry. Being able to fulfil his duties in a herd of cows keeps him satisfied and calmer until a challenger to his supremacy appears, and a fight for leadership of the herd ensues.

The first time I went to an agricultural show, it was shortly after the war, in the Isle of Man. I was so excited by the livestock display, the show jumping and the marquees with poultry, rabbits and vegetables on display. All of these were being lovingly attended by the exhibitors and brought up to a high level of perfection for the judges. I did not realise, at the time, the degree of competitive tension that builds up in showing, whether it be in vegetables or horses. The language and venom that I heard from one or two bad losers at that event put me off showing for a period. When I thought about the situation I realised, that whenever a huge amount of concentration and dedication are put into an interest, any disruption can cause an outburst of tension. I could recall examples from my own experience. When playing rugby I had been hit on the nose, deliberately or unwittingly, and but for the tears blinding my vision, I would have lashed out spontaneously at the perpetrator.

There is a magic in the air as the show day arrives. The air crackles with anticipation. Excitement, quietly increasing over the last few days, reaches fever pitch. A bright sunny morning is an added bonus that brings out smiling faces, greeting old friends and strangers alike. Many people have been out early, putting the final touches to the exhibits or walking off the effects of the previous night's conviviality.

I overcame my concerns when I discovered the great pleasure that most of the competitors get from preparing their exhibits for showing. Whether the produce be sheep or onions is immaterial. The amount of meticulous care that is put into each presentation is proportional to the enjoyment that they get on the show day. Everything must be right or there will be a lot of banter from your friends.

There is always a rush for the spectators to get into the flower and vegetable tents early in the day when everything is bright and fresh. The atmosphere is charged with the heady scent of thousands of pristine blooms, but as the day wears on, like us, they become a bit jaded in the heat and bustle of the crowds.

It is a time of appreciation and criticism of the finer points by the experts and also a time to reflect on the many hours of work put in by the competitors. In a few short hours it is all over until the next show.

The animal lines are never quiet. Row upon row of cattle, sheep and other livestock are lined up in their standings, complete with large wooden boxes containing white coats, grooming kit, rugs and medicines. Those immaculate creatures that parade round the show ring are the results of months of preparation. They have to be fed, milked, cleaned out and groomed with monotonous regularity. No svelte models on the catwalk are pampered and coddled with such tender loving care.

A couple of incidents occurred at that show that stayed with me for life. The first concerned a very handsome Cleveland Bay stallion, Charnwood Boyo, who was being shown in hand. I had known and handled him for several years and he had always been a perfect gentleman. More like a pet sheep than a stallion, as he would follow me around the loose box, nudging me for a mint. He had behaved impeccably all day and brought gasps of admiration from the crowd. As he was brought out to receive a Class winner's rosette and the judge turned away he must have scented romance in the air and promptly mounted the poor unfortunate man. Fortunately, the judge was only knocked off balance but he might well have been badly injured.

The band started playing to keep the crowd happy and distracted before the grand parade of winners in the cattle class. The proud owners walked in with their charges, the bull class leading the way. One particularly large Friesian Bull, "Jupiter," was led out by two handlers dressed in clean white coats as befitted the occasion. As he was so big, they walked one either side of him holding a bull pole attached to the ring in his nose. He was a sight to behold as the bright sun reflected off his immaculate black and white coat and the great muscles rippled on his enormous shoulders. Whether he also scented romance, we shall never know as he arched his great neck, shook his head and the two handlers were thrown through the air like ninepins and lost the grip on their poles. There was a deep gasp from the spectators followed by complete silence. Most people were just preparing to flee in panic, but at that moment Jupiter was distracted by the poles attached to his nose. A young farmer in the crowd stepped quickly out into the arena alongside the bull, grasped his nose ring firmly and pulled his head up in the air, giving the handlers time to struggle to their feet and regain their bull poles. A roar of admiration from the crowd was followed by loud applause for a very courageous act!

Strangely enough, rather like the human male, groups of bulls in Artificial Insemination centres or those being reared for bull beef get on very well together. The trouble always seems to be started by the introduction of a skittish young female to the group who flutters her eyelashes and rouses a few passions.

# Chapter 18

It was a cold wet morning and Ruth had sent a message on to ask me to call in to George Collister, Ballaclutey Mooar, to examine a cow, which had died suddenly. George was not renowned for his generosity and felt that life was a hand to mouth struggle.

Ballaclutey had been built of granite, as if to defy the ravages of the prevailing winds that blew round it much of the year. It stood steadfastly, at the head of a valley, in front of a cluster of grey stone cattle sheds that after years of neglect were gradually becoming more dilapidated.

As I drove out across the Plains of Heaven I felt that they weren't living up to their name on such a ghastly morning. Beneath a bleak grey sky the bare trees stretched questing fingers skywards, creaking and swaying in obeisance to the blustery wind.

George was one of those Falstaffian characters who weighed in at over 18 stone and had a voice to match. A part time dealer, he was always to be seen at the markets, wheeling and dealing over a pen of sheep or calves. His whisky tinted features and Sherlock Holmes pipe, clenched between yellow teeth, seemed to be sandwiched between a greasy old hat and scarlet spotted neckerchief.

As I got out of the car, struggling into my waterproofs, George's big frame filled the shippon door. " Are you Mr Carson? I've been hanging around all morning waiting for you," he commenced belligerently." I've got a lot on and dead cows don't make any money. She's out here in the meadow. Do you want to see her or can you give me a note on the spot".

"Let's have a look at her," I replied," What happened to her?"

"Found her in the meadow this morning, at milking time," was the gruff response. " Right as rain last night. Mind you, there was a thunder storm during the night and she had to be the one struck by lightning. Best cow I've got, in full milk and carrying a valuable calf."

"Aren't they all?" I muttered to myself as we entered the field, heads down and leaning against the storm. My mind was racing. What was it that Prof. Kelly had said to us about sudden death in cattle? Lead poisoning, lightning stroke, anthrax, yew poisoning and grass staggers! It had to be one of them. That is, if somebody hadn't shot it!

Sure enough the cow was lying under the trees at the far hedge. There were no signs of struggling, therefore death must have been fairly rapid. I examined her carefully for signs of scorching or burn marks on the skin. Perhaps they would show up on post mortem. The absence of yew trees or a neighbouring churchyard eliminated the plant poisoning.

I turned to George and said, "Sorry, I can't find any evidence for lightning stroke, but before you move the carcass I must check it for anthrax to satisfy the Board of Agriculture, particularly as there's some very dark blood at her anus!"

As I watched George's face, it became a deep purple and his Falstaffian nose almost glowed as his whole figure appeared to swell, like an amorous bullfrog, and he shook with rage.

Visualising the insurance claim slipping through his fingers, he flung his arms in the air and shouted, "What's the use of sending out smart young buggers like you, who don't know nowt? Of course it's bloody lightning, anyone can see that. Bloody Scanlon can whistle for his money if this is the kind of service that he's offering."

Whilst I stood gazing into space, listening to this tirade, I couldn't help noticing the first snowdrops shyly peeping out beneath the hedge, and thinking;" Please God, don't let him have a heart attack until after I have left."

I made a cut in the base of the ear and as the dark blood welled up I made a blood smear on a microscope slide. I stood up, and said;" I'm sorry for the bother but this is important for the protection of you and your livestock. Can you cover the carcass with a tarpaulin and keep any other stock, including dogs, well away from it until you hear from the government veterinary office?"

"It's all bloody well for you smart guys who don't know what a day's work is, while I'm trying to scrape an honest living. Better get a move on. I can't afford to lose hard earned money, whilst you and those government chaps play around!"

Back at the surgery I stained the blood smear and examined it under the microscope. Clearly showing up on the slide were the incriminating chains of bacteria, each one cloaked in its own purple halo. This was positive for anthrax and was of immense public health importance. This was the first notifiable disease I had encountered in practice and as it was anthrax, could have widespread repercussions. I could hardly contain my excitement as I called Brian over to confirm the diagnosis. A brief glimpse and he immediately telephoned the government veterinary office and George Collister. Needless to say, I was delighted at the diagnosis of my first case of anthrax, and was on the crest of a wave! As a precautionary measure I was sent off to the doctor and put on a course of penicillin.

I did hear, from the locals, in The Jolly Farmer, that when his farm was invaded by police and government veterinary officers, all clad in black boots and black protective waterproofs, George was like a man possessed. Not only had his insurance claim gone up in smoke but his farm had been taken over by civil servants.

Anthrax is a "zoonosis" or disease transmissible from animal to man. It can very rapidly cause severe illness or death but as a Notifiable Disease is very swiftly controlled by the government veterinary service. When the real dangers were explained to George and the problems that would have ensued if he had sent the carcass to the knackers, he became mollified and almost thankful, although he did begrudge losing the insurance money.

Any discharges from an infected animal can contaminate the ground where the anthrax bacteria form spores that are very resistant to weather and can lie dormant in infected land for a generation. A single case can pose a threat for many years. Alkaline ground suits the spores that can proliferate in warm moist conditions following a period of drought until they are picked up by grazing animals. In hot countries, where disease control is not so strict, whole areas of ground may be affected. Infected material may be imported into this country with concentrated feeds or bone meal. It used to be known as 'Wool Sorters disease' as it could cause malignant ulcers or fatal pneumonia in people handling sheep's wool. For similar reasons the carcass cannot be sent to the knackers. Fortunately,

51

the disease is easily controlled in the early stages with the use of vaccines and antibiotics in infected animals.

This case was the first of many that occurred during the next few weeks. The main victims were cattle and pigs who had been fed with concentrated feed imported from Simingtons Mill in Liverpool. A cargo of groundnut meal had arrived in Liverpool and Simingtons had elected to buy the contents of the front hold, which unbeknown to them was infected with anthrax spores. We felt very sorry for the staff at the mill as not only did they have to undergo health checks but also the complete mill had to be stripped down and sterilised! After six weeks of tension we finally eliminated the last cases of anthrax by removing all contaminated feed. Simingtons Mill did compensate all their clients for any animals affected by the anthrax problem in a very generous manner.

The anthrax cases became so regular that we could recognise a positive case, by the purple glow on our microscope slides before we even put them under the microscope.

We had regular visits from Ieuan Harries, a veterinary officer of the Board of Agriculture, to discuss the progress of the disease. I always found him a bit daunting. A large, dour Welshman, he always appeared to have the worries of the world upon his shoulders. Clad in a long black overcoat, dark jowled and brooding he gave the impression that the end of the world was nigh. Indeed, he bore a striking resemblance to my uncle who was a Baptist preacher in the South Wales valleys and looked upon smiling as a mortal sin!. When I had the temerity to mention one day that my mother had also been called Harries, Ieuan turned his dying bloodhound gaze upon me and said in his measured, sepulchral tones, "Welcome to the family circle, bach! We are all bastard descendants of Henry Tudor." At that point I had to leave the room rapidly, before the next gem of wisdom was uttered!.

A few weeks later Moira and I were sitting in the snug of Jolly Farmer, enjoying a quiet drink, when we heard the booming voice of George Collister in the bar. As ever, he was holding forth to all and sundry. " It's been a hard few weeks on the farm with all these anthrax worries. They brought a lorry load of coal and a pile of logs on to the farm, dumped old Bluebell onto the top and incinerated her. At least they had the decency to dig a hole afterwards and bury her ashes; a truly fitting end for what was probably the best-bred and most valuable cow in the island. I doubt whether we shall see the likes of her again. It was a good thing I told young Carson that I thought that it might be anthrax. His prompt action cut the outbreak short. He's got a lot to learn but he'll do all right if he listens to his elders!" Probably, his audience included George Andrews and Bill Pitman who already knew the true story.

I looked at Moira and smiled at the pleasure that she was getting from the Collister interpretation of the facts. We were really enjoying being in each other's company but the thought of a showdown with George was too much of a temptation for me.

Quietly we walked into the saloon and sat at the other end of the bar, behind George. "I made the police and those government fellas clean up after them," continued George, "They were a scruffy lot but they did a good job in the end" At this stage George Andrews could not contain himself any longer and said, "Good evening Ned, Moira. Can I buy you a drink?"

George Collister, ponderously swivelled round on the bar stool, nose aglow and uncertain how much we had heard. "Oh! Oh! Mr Carson and a lovely young lady. You lucky man!" he blurted out, as all the others enjoyed his discomfort. " I was just saying. What a great job you did on that anthrax case. A smart young man you've got there, Miss! No. I absolutely insist that the drinks are on me tonight seeing as to how you helped get me that compensation." At this stage Bill Pitman had to leave the bar to control his mirth. "Mind you, it was a bit careless of Simingtons to buy a load of infected food!"

We stayed on and chatted with George Andrews for a little while. "We were glad to see you arrive. I thought that we'd never get George Collister to buy a round," he commented smiling broadly. "It's a funny old thing. Last week I went out into the back meadow, where there's a gateway into the copse field. There's a piece of galvanised sheeting lying by the hedge. It had come off an old barn in the last storm. There were one or two patches of blood on it but I couldn't find any sign of bleeding in the cattle. Could it have been a poacher's dog, I wonder?"

Glimpsing briefly at Moira, who smiled at me knowingly, I replied rather lamely, "It's possible, George, but there again it might have been a sheep."

"Possible, but not probable, because I found a couple of tufts of dog hair on the sheet," he continued, with a knowing look in his eye. " The gash would probably require some treatment!" As we drove home I was left with the uncomfortable, nagging thought in my mind as to how much he really knew.

# Chapter 19

Brian had offered to take over my Sunday duty as I had worked on Saturday in order that he could go duck shooting. As I was going out of the surgery, Brian called out. "Ned! I have something here that might interest you, after your eventful times in Dublin. I was sent a copy of the Belfast Telegraph to update me with the local news. Look at this headline on the death of a student". Under the headline of 'Mysterious death of young student in Dublin' was a short paragraph. 'The body of a medical student, Thomas Mary Noel Gleeson, was found in the River Liffey, below O'Connell Bridge on Sunday morning. He had recently been questioned by the Royal Ulster Constabulary in association with an explosion in Belfast. He had also been under surveillance by the Gardai in Dublin regarding his association with members of an extremist republican group. The deceased had head injuries, which could have been sustained by a fall from the bridge but the Gardai are keeping an open mind on the situation and carrying out further enquiries'.

A thrill of relief ran through my body as I realised that I could have been involved in the situation. "Thank you Brian. I feel that it was not a situation for me to be involved with. The unsolved mystery is, who did it? I only hope that the Plunket family are not under suspicion as I should hate Maeve to be involved."

I hadn't meant to take the call to Rafferty of Creggan Mill, but I recognised the name at once-Rafferty of the greyhound Bella, who had taken so much time to stitch up some weeks before! Surely there couldn't be two Rafferty families. I had never visited Creggan Mill before but the name seemed so out of context with the amiable roughnecks who came in with Bella, that curiosity got the better of me. Anyway, I had to let Moira see these larger than life characters!

It was a chill but sunny Sunday morning as Moira and I drove down the winding lanes towards Creggan Mill. One could almost hear the sap rising through the roots as nature prepared to rush headlong into spring. Looking out of my bedroom window I could watch the rooks, in the trees opposite, discussing their accommodation problems before settling down in earnest to the intricate task of nest building. They appeared to be nesting high that year, which bode well for a good springtime.

The name of Creggan Mill also stirred in my memory one of the romantic stories that had come down, by word of mouth, over the centuries.

When I was a youngster there were always the old fishermen in Port Erin, who loved to tell yarns whilst they were sitting repairing their nets or crab pots. I had always been told that you could never trust anyone from the North of the island. They were a shifty lot! Quite where that left the people in the middle, from Douglas and Peel, I wasn't told, save that they were no better than they ought to be.

"Mind you, yessir," continued Jack Cregeen, the grizzled old fisherman, who was narrating this gem of history. "It's now more than two hundred years since they made Douglas the capital instead of Castletown. Lickin' the boots of their English masters I call it."

Many times I had heard mutterings about Creggan Mill, just up from Rushen Abbey, as everyone except me appeared to know exactly what happened in those far off days.

Jack returned to repairing his nets and sucking on his pipe as he sought further inspiration. I watched his rugged face, cheeks crossed with a network of tiny blood vessels, his great shaggy grey eyebrows, almost big enough for a wren to nest in. He was always dressed in heavy, navy twill trousers and a navy knit polo neck jersey with RNLI written on the chest. He was coxswain on the local lifeboat and also hired out rowing boats in the summer season.

After a few minutes he knocked out the dottle on a convenient bollard and scraped the bowl out carefully. Very carefully he cut several slices of tobacco off a block and rubbed them between his hands to break it up. The ritual of filling his pipe had almost developed into an art form for Jack and it was several minutes before he tamped down the tobacco to his satisfaction. Out came a box of Captain Webb matches and after striking one he was haloed in a cloud of blue smoke. Oftimes before I had watched these smoke clouds drifting upwards and wonder where they disappeared too!

Picking up the net he started to work once more. "Look at that great hole, boy! It got caught in the rocks and torn. A never ending job is repairing nets." With that he picked up his wooden netting needle and commenced weaving in and out and tying knots so skilfully that the finished job was as good as new.

"There was a family living up at Creggan Mill, in by Rushen Abbey. He was George Arlott, steward to the Roundhead, Colonel Fairfax. But for all that he was a decent church going man and his family were well liked. Now his son Garth was a good young man so they tell. Full of fun and very popular with the locals, particularly some of the young wenches in the village."

Jack laid his net down on the ground to inspect his handiwork and give him time to relight his pipe. The problem was that he always used his pipe like a conductor's baton when he spoke to you and inevitably it went out.

"'Twas at the Tynwald Fair that he met Edwina Hanson, the daughter of Charles Hanson, a merchant up Ramsey way. Young Garth fell hopelessly in love with this Titian - haired young beauty and she returned his affections."

By this time I was sitting on the thwarts of the boat enjoying the tale. Jack was just getting into his stride as he loved a good audience so, he continued:

"Now, Charles was a great supporter of the Royalist cause and objected very strongly to this young man courting his daughter, as he had hopes that she might marry into the aristocracy. It was like trying to mix oil and water. It would never work!

As lovers will, they found ways around the situation and used to tryst secretly in Sulby Glen, aided and abetted by one of her servants. Sooner or later these affairs become public knowledge and her father had Edwina attended constantly by a chaperone. He did not however, realise that Edwina was already carrying Garth's child. A distraction was arranged for the young woman's chaperone and Garth rode off with her to Creggan Mill, where she was made welcome and they were married shortly afterwards. The feud became even worse when the child turned out to be a son, very diplomatically christened George Charles Arlott!"

55

There was a short break whilst Jack tamped down his pipe and lit up again.

"Charles Hanson, who openly sought preferment in Court circles, in the hope of a knighthood, was enraged and organised a posse to carry his daughter back home. When he arrived at Creggan Mill he found all the local country folk determined to protect the Arlott family and he and his supporters were put to flight. On his second venture down South with a band of his supporters he ignored the advice of his men, who were locals, and chose not to wish good day to the "Little People" as he passed over Ballaglonney Bridge. This upset the Fairy Folk who made his horse rear, throwing him to the ground and breaking his leg. So much for the men from the North," commented Jack scathingly.

"There were many skirmishes between the families over the years with the Northerners looking forward to a battle with the perfidious Southerners. As time healed the wounds, the combats became limited to the football field or darts competitions although they were always fought out with great tribal zest. A favoured venue for these confrontations was at St. Johns, which boasted a sports field and a public house."

I had been so absorbed in the story that I hadn't realised the time and excused myself, as I had to be at home for lunch. Everyone likes an audience so Jack told me to return for the rest of the story in the afternoon.

I couldn't get back quickly enough and when I returned he was rubbing down the paintwork on one of his boats. "Look at this boy," he said in his deep sonorous voice. "Never waste anything from a dogfish. Feel that rough old skin that I'm using to rub down the paintwork. They're not bad to eat and you can always use them as bait in the crab pots."

As he washed off the paintwork, he continued, "It's still the same up North. Ramsey is where all the "comeovers" live and they fancy themselves as being a cut above the rest of us".

I knew nothing about role models but, at that moment, I felt that I would like to be a fisherman when I grew up and tell old tales to small boys in search of the truth!

# Chapter 20

Creggan Mill lay in a shallow valley, bordered by lush water meadows and patches of woodland fringing the higher ground and silhouetted against the evening sky. In the early summer it was a never-ending source of delight to us to wander along the lanes and riverbank when the may blossom was in its glory and the hedges were a tapestry of colour. We could sit outside "The Cross Keys", enjoying a drink and peacefully chatting, whilst below us the fat trout cruised back and forth in the bridge pool quietly sucking down their a-la-carte supper.

Following directions from Ruth, I came upon a high brick wall and half way along turned into a cobbled yard surrounded by neat redbrick outbuildings. This was much too neat for any farmyard and I wondered if the old mill had been converted into a private dwelling and smallholding, with the outhouses and surrounding fields being used for livestock. As I got out of the car a young girl of about seventeen years old came out of the doorway. Her slim figure was clad in overalls, which highlighted a pretty face with twinkling blue eyes, framed by hair as black as a raven's wing. She walked across the yard and with a disarming smile said in a soft brogue, "You'll be Mr Carson? I'm Roisin Rafferty. You met Liam and Kevin, those two wild brothers of mine some weeks ago. I hope that they didn't plague you too much with their beloved Bella. Hold on and I'll give brother Finbar, a shout. Annabelle the sow is his property."

In response to her call, a well-built young man appeared. Equally dark as his sister, with shining, wavy black hair, he was the type to set the girls talking. "Ah, Mr Carson, am I glad to see you. Annabelle, one of my best sows, produced twelve nice little bonhams, you would call them piglets, last evening. All went well, and she settled down and let them feed, but this morning was another story. She is off her food and staggering round a bit. I'm not at all happy about her. I only have six sows and as weaner pigs are fetching a good sum. I must look after them."

He immediately led me into the pig house, where the warmth and comfortable grunting of contented sows greeted me. In the second pen along the passage I could see a Large White sow lying at full stretch, unsuccessfully trying to pass dung although there were a couple of hard droppings behind her. I checked her udder for mastitis and also for any discharge from her uterus. All was clear but as I took her temperature she staggered to her feet, splaying out all four legs for support. She was frothing at the mouth and swaying unsteadily.

Finn hurriedly guided the piglets into a corner to safety, with a piece of corrugated sheeting, lest Annabelle should fall down and crush them.

" It looks very like milk fever to me. I'll inject her with calcium before she gets any worse. She must be producing a lot of milk to feed that hungry horde."

I injected a large volume of calcium on either side behind her ears and massaged it in well. "This is a difficult technique in healthy sows as the solution is very irritant", I said to Finbar who was supporting her, "Fortunately, she is not very aware of her surroundings. Keep the piglets penned and I'll stay here for a few minutes as this is the first case I've seen and I want to keep an eye on her".

At that moment the door opened and a thickset man in his late fifties walked in. With short cut greying hair, and well-trimmed moustache he gave the impression of being neat and well organised, which indeed he was!

"Good morning Mr Carson, I'm Brendan Rafferty, Finn's father, and I have taken the liberty of inviting your young lady to come in and watch. What's the problem with Annabelle?"

I explained that I was going to wait for a few minutes for my injection to take effect on the sow.

"In that case, come on into the house. I'm sure that my wife, Nuala, will have the kettle on the hob ready for morning tea."

Walking back towards the house, Moira remarked about several wrought iron sculptures positioned around the yard. Several were very artistic pieces and a pair of attractive exterior lamp brackets must have illuminated the entire yard at night.

"That's the work of Liam another of my sons," explained our host proudly, "He has his mother's artistic temperament, combined with my love of working with metal. If we can only get him to settle down he has a very promising future."

As we passed through the back door it opened into a bright and airy kitchen. As Moira later commented, "Created by a real homemaker with a talent for decoration". In the centre of the room there was a large scrubbed table; dominating the end wall, a black cooking range squatted in an inglenook. Several water-colours of Irish country scenes hung on the light-cream painted walls.

When we entered the room, Nuala looked up with a welcoming smile as Brendan introduced us as Ned Carson, Bella's vet and his young lady, Moira,. "Welcome to you both. It's lovely to see new faces." She was a slim, neat person with a fresh complexion and shining mass of silver hair. She impressed me as one of those very active, can't-stay-still-for-long people.

Brendan asked if the kettle was on the boil as we all had a terrible thirst. "I see that you were having a good look at Nuala's paintings. They remind her very much of home in the County Tipperary", he said. In no time we were settled around the table with a plate of freshly made Irish soda bread and a great pot of tea. Moira asked Nuala where she had learned to paint. " At home in Cashel, County Tipperary, we had a very gifted schoolteacher who felt that I had some talent and gave me tuition. I had my future all planned out to descend upon Dublin and open a gallery when this soldier man of mine carried me off across the water. I ran a tea-room combined with a small craft gallery, outside Melton Mowbray for several years. The gentry would call in for afternoon tea and oftimes depart with one or two paintings"
" You certainly have a gift with light and colour," said Moira, who was quite interested in art. "I'd love to come in again and look at your pictures" "You'll be as welcome as the flowers in May," laughed Nuala, delighted with the compliment. "If you come down some time when you're free and Ned is working, we might just have an afternoon painting beside the river." It was this chance meeting that was to develop into an enduring friendship, that lasted long after we had moved on.

Roisin and Finn joined us for a few minutes to report that Annabelle was much better, before rushing off to see the bullocks. As they walked out Brendan commented, "Finn is very keen on his livestock, and is entered in the agricultural college, starting next term, so I shall be stockman during the term. He follows after my father who has a farm in Enniscorthy."

We discovered that Brendan had recently retired from the Royal Army Veterinary Corps as a Farrier Sergeant Major. They had taken over a smithy in Ballasalla for Brendan and the boys to run. Both Liam and Kevin had started off repairing farm machinery in the smithy and as mechanisation increased so did the demand for their services when they had to start carrying out repairs on the farms.

Nuala said, "Those two boys are the worry of my life. I made them smarten up a bit when they visited the farms, as it would never do to go around the country looking like tinkers! What would granny O'Malley in Cashel say if they were going round like a couple of down and outs?"

Nuala and Roisin had ideas of opening a tea-room and craft shop in the village once they were fully settled but they still had a lot of work to do on the house before that took place.

We found that we had very much in common; Brendan and I had been in the army together, whilst I did my National Service in the Veterinary Corps in Melton Mowbray, although we had never met. We also had many mutual acquaintances amongst the vets and horsemen in the west of Ireland. Best of all, he was a dedicated fly fisherman and we spent many happy evenings together casting a dry fly on the river.

"Liam and Kevin are full of your praises for saving Bella," continued Nuala as we rose to leave, "They are terrible fond of that dog. Pity they could not find themselves nice girls and settle down. Aren't children a worry?"

We were shown around the house to admire Nuala's paintings. There were also some very attractive planters and wrought iron candle sticks made by Liam. Every few steps Moira would turn to me and say, "Should we have something like that in our house?. I do like the colour schemes" It gave me great pleasure to see that she was developing ideas for our own house. Even though the wedding date hadn't been set and we had not announced our engagement to the world!

We left the house and walked across the yard to the piggery. Sure enough, Annabelle was much more content and standing at the trough making up for lost time. Waving our farewells we drove off in search of a nice quiet lunch in a country pub.

# Chapter 21

With thumping heart and tense with excitement, I stood on the banks of the River Lennon, in the County Donegal. The straining rod was almost bent double and the taut line cut slowly through the peaty waters. It felt like a very big fish. Paddy McGettigan, our delightful ghillie, walked over with the net, ready to land the catch. "That's a great "Fush" indeed sor!" I could just see the dark outline of the salmon as it came nearer.

"Ned, you've slept through your alarm-breakfast time!" Mary Careen's urgent tones shattered my dreams and lost me the biggest fish of a lifetime. "And what's more we've had some snow. Better get going"

I was aware of that sense of stillness and tranquillity that that comes with snow. The usual early morning sounds were absent as, shivering, I struggled into my clothes. I had developed a technique, in the cold weather, of taking off my shirt, vest, and pullover, all together at bedtime and laying them between blankets and eiderdown so that they were warm next morning. In the army, we had slept with our socks on, but in the interests of hygiene, I had given it up. Even the glass of water at my bedside had been known to freeze overnight. Looking out of the window confirmed my suspicions. There had been about four inches of snow since I went to bed and winter had clad the world in its bridal finery.

I rushed through breakfast, full of excitement and trepidation as to how I would cope with my first day's work under winter conditions. Previously, I had always been the student, who carried out the donkeywork without any responsibility! How were we going to get around?

Warmly clad against the elements in a parka, gloves and two pairs of socks inside my boots, I cleared the snow off the front path for Mrs Careen and then set to and cleaned snow off the car windows before checking the radiator for ice.

Fortunately, the streets were very flat as far as the surgery where we kept the snow chains and I was able to drive cautiously along the road. There were very few people on the streets and the only vehicle that I passed was an electric milk float that appeared to drift noiselessly on its journey.

The pewter sky was overhung with snow clouds and a few snowflakes still drifted aimlessly to the ground. I was very conscious of the black and white world into which we had been plunged. People and animals all seemed to be almost black against the strident, almost cruel, whiteness of the snow. The stark outlines of the rooftops and the winter trees, stretching their gaunt fingers in supplication to the sky were transformed to a gently rounded world where everything was covered in white marshmallow.

Maybe people were too busy coping with the snow because the phone remained stubbornly silent all morning. After fitting the snow chains, we were warming up with a cup of steaming hot Bovril when the phone shrilled stridently demanding instant attention. As I lifted up the handset a disembodied voice at the other end said, "Good morning, Mr Carson. I'm so sorry to bother you on a morning such as this but Charlotte's pony has gone very lame." Instantly, I recognised the low, husky tones, causing a tingle down the back of my neck, as those of Marjorie Blair-Hume from Cooil Vooar.

Marjorie Blair-Hume was a naturally attractive lady, in her mid thirties. Married to John Blair-Hume, a Liverpool industrialist some twenty years her senior, she was gifted with an intangible tingle factor, which attracted young men like bees to nectar. What made it even worse was that she seemed to be blithely unaware of her allure. I made an instant decision to take the call instead of Brian, who might at his age, have become overexcited and suffered a heart attack in the process! Anyway, the thought of overcoming blizzard conditions to visit Charlotte's pony appealed to my romantic spirit. A request for a call from Marjorie in this weather was very much a call for help from such a down to earth client.

The Blair-Humes lived in a small estate towards Santon, comprising Cooil Vooar and Cooil Veg. They kept a few horses and enjoyed riding when John could get away from the family business for a few days, and their daughter Charlotte was very involved with the pony club.

Normally, they had little problem with the horses apart from the odd sprained ligaments that we treated with rest and liniment. Some horse practices used to carry out firing or blistering over the tendons. Firing consisted of applying a hot iron to the skin over the tendons in the hope of promoting scar tissue to give support to the affected parts. This put the horse out of action for many months, which meant that they must be rested. I often wondered whether the intention was to take the horse out of use to let healing take place naturally as many horse owners would have them working too soon and compound the injury.

As the car scrunched quietly over the snow into the yard I could see a pile of used straw lying outside a loose box and parked beside it. The blonde pigtailed head of Charlotte looked out as she opened the door for me. "Hello, Mr Carson, I'm glad you could come to see poor Poppy today as she is in a lot of pain." Charlotte took after her father in looks and I could see that it would not be many years before Charlotte's almost Nordic attraction would be competing with her mother's dark beauty.

Poppy was a very pretty little grey show pony of about twelve hands in height and could hold her head up in any ring. Normally she was a very bright, inquisitive little, animal but today she was a picture of dejection in her loose box. Her head drooped and the right foreleg held up with just the toe tipping the ground. Horses seem to develop a definite expression in their faces that indicates pain.

She did not respond to my usual banter so I realised that her mind was elsewhere. I gently lifted up her extended limb and felt the foot, which was hot and tender. Even scraping the sole of the foot with a knife made her flinch. By squeezing the toe with a pair of smith's pliers I could isolate a sensitive area at the tip of the toe.

Paring away the sole I followed a dark track deep into the horn, whilst Charlotte kept tempting Poppy with pieces of apple and carrot. The black spot started to ooze and suddenly there was a rush of black, noxious smelling fluid out of a hole in the sole. Instantly the pony relaxed as the pressure inside the foot was relieved.

"It looks fairly clean to me, Poppy," I said, giving her a scratch on the chest. "You've either stood on a blackthorn or a nail by the look of it."

Turning to Charlotte, I continued, "That's a lot more comfortable for her. Can you give her a bran and Epsom salts poultice for a few days to draw out the infection? Make sure you clean out the foot each day. We don't want the drainage hole to block up."

Having injected Poppy with tetanus antitoxin and antibiotic, I promised to call in for a couple of days to keep an eye on her.

"Thank you Mr Carson," said Charlotte, "We are both very grateful. Mummy asked if you could call at the house before you go and have a look at Buster."

Buster was a smooth haired Dachshund, of great character, who insisted that he could rush across the fields, and keep up with their two black Labradors, Lady and Flight. Life was good, until two months ago, when Buster had run under one of the horses and had his pelvis badly crushed. We repaired him as best we could and he got around fairly well. That is, until he started to run when his front legs went forward and his wobbly hind legs went off at an angle so that Buster ended up in a tangle on the ground.

Striding up to the house I felt more than justified in taking this call. After all, I was the dog expert, and the sight of the delectable Marjorie might have been too much for Brian at his advanced age of forty-five years old!

As I rang the front doorbell there was pandemonium as the dogs hurtled up the passage and announced my presence. Fighting back the dogs, Marjorie let me in. "How kind of you to call Mr Carson. I want to have a serious talk with you about Buster. Come into the kitchen. I'm just making a cup of tea."

As she laid out the cups I felt that this is probably what I had studied so hard for all those years. Marjorie was clad in a black polo neck sweater and slacks that enhanced an already perfect figure, surmounted by a pair of green eyes and shoulder length black hair. How on earth could a chap be expected to talk seriously about a dog with wobbly legs when even the act of stirring her tea was a work of art? We can all dream!

" Right," I said, gathering my scattered wits together, " How is Buster progressing?"

"Oh, he's much better," replied Marjorie, delicately nibbling at a cupcake. " He always enjoyed chasing across the fields with the dogs and now he's like a demented crab. The spirit is there still but his aim is all wrong. We don't expect any wonders but it would be lovely if he could keep up with the others."

I had been listening carefully to avoid any distraction and an idea stirred in my mind. "I've read very recently about someone whose dog was paralysed in the hind quarters. He had a little trolley made to support the rear end, which gave him a new lease of life. I also know a man, Liam Rafferty, who is a very proficient metal worker and is extremely fond of animals. I think that with his skill and a set of wheels we might get Buster racing again!"

"Oh! Mr Carson, we'd all be delighted if this works. Where can we contact him?" exclaimed Marjorie, in great delight.

" Well," I replied, "You'll find him down at Creggan Mill, just up from Ballasalla, where his parents live. His name is Liam Rafferty and he has a way with metal work. Don't judge him by his looks. They're a nice family. Let me know when you have spoken to him and we'll work on the design together."

As I arrived back at the surgery Brian was just returning from a Milk Fever at Ballavaish Farm. "How did you get on at Cooil Vooar?" he said in a rather slighted manner. " I could have taken that in on the way back from my Milk Fever. I'm sure that Marjorie would have loved to see me."

"Don't worry," I replied, "Her skinny little daughter showed me the pony. Too young for you."

I watched his smile of satisfaction as he thought that I had missed out on seeing Marjorie.

"There was another little job that entailed supping tea in the kitchen. It was rather a technical discussion on dogs that would'nt have interested you!

Excuse me but I must hurry into the surgery as Captain Hunt should be waiting for me with his dog." I hurriedly escaped before his curiosity got the better of him.

# Chapter 22

Jasper Hunt was extremely tolerant and well behaved for a Pembroke Corgi. He was the focus of attention for Captain Hunt and his wife. They were both keen walkers and as a result Jasper was well known from the Trossachs to the Welsh Marches. He was quite heavily built and could have gone to fat but for his strict exercise regime. Walking the hills in the island only represented a training exercise for the more taxing journeys on the mainland. As becomes a dog who has assumed the responsibility of caring for a couple of slightly eccentric, hill walking humans he never left their side and was like an amiable sheep dog in charge of a pair of giddy lambs.

He regarded me with equanimity, as a friend of the family, brought in to placate his owners, who became very distressed when he was off colour.

I had examined him the previous week with a swollen gland at the back of the jaw. It had appeared to be quite painless so I assumed that it was a mild infection and treated it twice with antibiotics. Neither time had it responded but slowly grew larger. This wasn't in the textbook and once more I started losing confidence in my diagnosis. As a last resort I might have to lance the gland under anaesthesia. The day loomed ahead when Captain Hunt would be asking for a second opinion which would be a blow to my self-esteem. Better to have a word with that great advisor in the sky.

It pays to worry over one's problems. The answer came to me as I was enjoying a social pint in the 'Jolly Farmer' with George Andrews and Bill Pitman. After a hilarious few minutes carrying out a post mortem on George Collister's skill at diagnosing anthrax the subject turned to summer mastitis. Bill Pitman was complaining about the labour involved in stripping milk from an infected udder when George commented that he always used a liniment on the udder if he thought that there was an abscess developing.

That was the answer! Possibly, there was something inside Jasper's swollen gland that was triggering the problem, and all my antibiotics were merely holding back the development of abscess.

"I'm glad you brought that up George. It's given me an idea for treating a dog. If it works I'll buy you a pint."

In came the Hunt family and as I examined Jasper I could see that the swelling was a bit larger. " It's getting larger," I said, "And he's a bit uncomfortable. I'm afraid that these wonder drugs are only holding back the condition. We should be going back to basic principles, and either warm bathing or poulticing this abscess, to bring it to a head, when we can lance it and let it drain. Look, it's already coming to a head and a bit of warm bathing from you will sort out the problem. Are you willing to have a go at it?"

They looked at each other for a moment and Mrs Hunt smiled and replied, "Of course we'll have a try. Can't let our old friend down. It won't be very easy to poultice so we'll warm bathe it about four times a day. We shall come and see you in about four days time. We do appreciate the thought that you are putting into Jasper's problem and I'm sure that he's very grateful."

As they left I opened the consulting room door and called, "Next please." Out of the corner stepped a familiar figure. I stared momentarily and recognised old Charlie Jones, whose dog "Mush" I had to put to sleep soon after I joined the practice. Not only Charlie but also a lovely Border collie by his side.

"Come in Mr Jones. It's lovely to see you, and who have you got with you? She is a fine looking bitch!"

"Well, Mr Carson. After I lost Mush life was'nt the same. I 'ad no reason to go out walkin' and when I went into the Market Inn for a pint of Guinness it just was different. No old nose nuzzlin' into my hand at closin' time. That dog meant everythin' since my Rose passed away. I didn't know what to do until one day there was a knock on the door and there was a young man standing with this bitch here - Meg! His name was Bert Harris and he told me that his mother had just died and left Meg behind. He couldn't bear to see such a beautiful creature put down so he rang you. You told him to come and see me, so now she's come in for you to check up."

I looked at him in admiration. "I don't know about Meg  but you arrived in here looking so young and sprightly that I reckon you'll both outlive me."

He called the dog and she leapt up onto the examination table with paw outstretched to greet me. She had a lovely gloss on her coat and for an eight-year-old animal I could find no fault with her. "She's in tiptop condition Mr Jones and a credit to you. How long have you had her now?"

"We've been walkin' together for about six weeks now, thanks to you. It was love at first sight you see. She's got the sweetest nature you could find, though she was a bit overweight and had a dull old coat when she came. We soon walked the weight off and a drop of Guinness every day works wonders for the coat. Come to think of it, Mr Carson, your hair might benefit by it!" he continued with a twinkle in his eye and calling Meg to heel the two friends walked off in the direction of the Market Inn.

It was not very long before I saw Jasper once again. Two days later Captain Hunt phoned to tell me that the abscess on Jasper's neck had burst and his pristine white chest was smeared with blood.

"Bring him right in and I'll see him before I go on my rounds," I replied.

Ten minutes later Jasper arrived, wrapped up in a travelling rug, Captain Hunt placed him on the table. Jasper, of course was above getting excited about the visit and demanded his usual titbit of a yeast tablet before consulting me. The abscess had become itchy and burst after he scratched it. As I cleaned it all up and washed out the wound with acriflavine my cotton wool snagged on something. Carefully searching the site I caught a glint of silver and, using forceps, pulled a sewing needle out of the wound. Triumphantly holding the culprit in the air I said, "There had to be some sort of irritation causing the problem but how did it happen?"

There was a stunned silence for couple of minutes as everyone considered the matter. Suddenly, Mrs Hunt gasped and said, "Kenneth, that old woolly toy that Jasper plays with

65

might be the cause. I must have dropped a ball of darning wool with a needle in it and he picked it up in his mouth to chew. Goodness me! It could have killed our little shepherd dog. Oh! Mr Carson, I do apologise for the problems that we have caused."

"Don't worry. Problem over. Let's look to the future. Bathe that wound regularly and it will heal up in no time. Very soon you'll all be back in the hills."

A great problem facing new graduates is being able to cope with their patients who can develop varied defensive techniques ranging from being quite obnoxious to life threatening. Animals under stress can revert to the jungle very rapidly if not handled properly. I felt that as I had seen ten years of practice before I qualified, my chances of being assaulted were minimal. Little did I realise what nature had in store for me over the next forty years!

One of my first lessons was that "Those who turn and run away, live to fight another day." I am a self confessed coward when the opponent is many times my weight.

One of my earlier episodes occurred in my pre-college days. I was helping in the surgery, when Andrew asked me to help him castrate a mature tomcat. The normal procedure for a cat in those days, when being neutered, was a local anaesthetic injected into the testicles. There were various ways of restraining the patient for one's own protection, which included putting him down the leg of a wellington boot, up the sleeve of a jacket or, if you were up to date, in a custom built wooden box, with a hole in the end through which the hind quarters protruded.

My job as the menial student was to hold the cat's legs whilst the operation was being performed. The cat, of course, regarded such restraint as an affront to his dignity. I was just telling the vet that I was ready, when pussy struggled and squirted his strong and evil smelling urine all over my face, hair and clothes. I should have learnt to keep my mouth shut in such circumstances. To an amorous she cat this smells like "Old Spice" but to a young man who had a date that evening the romance was somewhat tarnished.

Soon after qualifying, I was presented with a young Alsatian, Karl, who required an injection. He was quite a nervous dog, suffering from Alsatian "angst" and his owner had great problems in restraining him. After a struggle, we pushed him against the wall to control him, at which point he panicked and tried to bite the nearest person. Quickly, I carried out the injection only to find, to my amazement, that Karl and I were firmly attached. In the excitement he had bitten my wrist and his canine tooth was embedded up to the gum in my flesh. I hadn't felt a thing at the time but the scar is still there today!

This came as a salutary lesson, and the fault was entirely mine as I had not taken enough time to chat up my patient and calm his fears. Later on, I went through a phase of muzzling unreliable dogs but found that this process only made them harder to handle on the subsequent visits. I found that I could interpret the body language of a dog as it enters the consulting room and respond accordingly.

# Chapter 23

One bright spring morning Brian asked me to call into a smallholding owned by Matt Munslow, who had a sow that was not letting her piglets suckle. It was one of those exhilarating days towards the end of March when, after a grey and wet, month the sun shone and the wind blew hard to dry up all the puddles. Blustery weather makes cats have giddy spells when they run around like March hares. It also affects the crow family who have a great sense of fun, and as I drove down the lanes past St Marks, the rooks would zoom over the hedge on the wind's uplift, swoop down into the road and up again, until the wind caught them and flung them into the sky, like rag dolls, as they appeared over the hedge top once more.

I watched this continuous aerial ballet with pleasure, but my mind was working overtime as I drove along the lane towards the farm. What conditions would make a sow reject her young? Professor Kelly, where were your medicine notes at this critical hour? I recalled that agalactia, i.e. no milk, could be a cause, panic in a young gilt and also very painful mastitis. As I entered the yard I could smell the pig swill cooking, and see rows of dirty looking dustbins around the lean-to sheds, covered in rusting corrugated sheeting.

The whole yard was a rubbish tip. There were used planks of wood piled up at the side with weeds growing in front of then. In one corner I could see an old chipped bath with a couple of Belfast sinks beside it. An ancient galvanised hip bath stood in as a water trough for a pair of scrawny ponies who stood with drooping heads, contemplating the chaos.

Picking my way through the scrap and splashing through pools of black, stinking mud, I had to stoop down as I entered the dark shed, lit only by a couple of cob webbed electric bulbs. Matt came waddling up the passage with a couple of pails of swill.

Fat and forty was an apt description of Matt. I could never remember him in a change of clothes. It was always a collarless striped shirt, exposing a grey vest to the waist, with a thick belt supporting a pair of shapeless corduroy trousers. Pieces of dirty sacking were tied around the bottom to act as gaiters. A toothy smile in his unshaven, florid face spoke volumes. Even his pigs took evasive action because he smelt so badly! With his overall aroma and dress sense he was never going to find a wife.

"The 'owd sow's down here vetinry. She's not very smart. Pity, 'cos she's the best one I've got."

I followed to see this prize beast. There in the corner was a Large White sow shuffling uncomfortably as the hungry, squealing little pigs tried to suckle. As I opened the pen to go in she sat up and gave a loud bark that plainly said beware! Struggling to her feet in the wet and slippery bedding she headed towards the door, as I hastily backed out. When threatened by 400 pounds of bad tempered sow, who could break your arm with one bite you concede victory.

"Hold on," said Matt, "I should've told yer that she's a bit touchy. I'll just get some sheeting." With that he disappeared into the passage and returned with a walking stick and an eight-foot sheet of corrugated roof sheet. As he entered the pen he held it in front, as a shield, and gently poked the grunting sow into the corner. "Now you can look at her in comfort Mr Carson."

I cautiously leaned over the sheet and took her temperature. Whilst doing so I could see that she had a whitish discharge from the uterus and I slid my hand under her belly and the udder was rock hard and very hot. The 'owd bitch', as Matt called her, resented my handling of her very painful udder and but for the sheeting would have chased us both out of the pen. "She's got farrowing fever Matt. No wonder she's bad tempered. You'd feel the same. Don't go away. I'm going to inject her behind the ear with quite a large quantity of stuff that will sting, so hang on." she shrieked and complained but fortunately Matt's solid, smelly, seventeen stone figure held her firmly in the corner.

Once outside the pen I turned to Matt and said, "She's picked up infection that has caused farrowing fever, possibly because the pen is dirty. Clean pens will help to prevent it."

"I can't possibly do that Vetinry. I've got little enough spare time as it is running a business. Any help that I get on the farm never seems to stay very long. Mark you, I do pay a substantial wage."

At that stage I felt I had to give up, he would never mend his ways. Probably, most of his farm workers left because they had a sense of smell!

About four weeks after this incident I went on a routine call to castrate a couple of litters of pigs for Finbar Rafferty. We did a lot of this work and I was becoming quite skilled at the operation. It was believed at that time that castrating piglets at this age resulted in an increase in growth rates. It also avoided taint in the meat as they grew older.

As I pulled into the yard I found Liam awaiting my arrival. "I just dropped in to give Finbar a hand with these bonhams," he said. "They're a lively lot. I've just been up to see Mrs Blair-Hume and Buster. You sure know how to pick them, she's some lady, that one. I fancy that I can make Buster a nice little jaunting cart. I could have the prototype ready by next Thursday. Maybe we should meet at Cooil Vooar and give the lady a demonstration."

Finbar stuck his head out of the piggery window. " Can anyone join in the conversation? You'd be much more help in here than talking. I've got the sows out of the pens so the little ones are ready for us to get to work!"

We walked along the passage in the piggery, pushing past the two rather disgruntled sows. Like all good mums, sows get quite upset when parted from their nearest and dearest. Entering the pen I found that Finbar had already brought in a bale of straw to sit on and also a pail of water. Whilst he sat on the bale, holding the piglets, I would castrate them and Liam would put them over the wall into the adjacent pen, as well as chatting up the sows to keep them happy.

At least that was the plan of campaign if you ignored Rafferty's Law that clearly states that all plans are great until you put them into action.

As Finbar sat on the bale, it split open and he fell onto the pail, which spilt across the already slippery floor. The little pigs squealed in alarm, the sows grunted uneasily and one even stood on her hind legs and leant over the low wall to assess the situation.

An interval of ten minutes elapsed whilst we restored our operating theatre and gave the pigs time to settle down once more.

We castrated the first couple of piglets, squealing with indignation, whilst the sows ran back and forth making agitated sounds. Finbar was fully engrossed in holding the little pigs, whilst my time was taken cleaning up the operation site and castrating. In the meantime, Liam was putting the piglets into the adjacent pen and fending off Annie the larger sow who was leaning over the wall, barking, with jaws champing. Gertie, the other sow was battering at the pen door with her snout in a state of great excitement.

Suddenly Gertie found the knack, lifted the door off its hinges and started to come at us. Fortunately, Annie had the same idea in mind and the two fat and angry sows jammed tight in the narrow entrance, like a cork in a bottle neck, and using the most atrocious language that meant only one thing - yum yum!

Pandemonium broke loose as we slipped and slid across the floor to reach safety, the sows calling the young and a complete scatteration of squeaking little piglets shooting back and forth like pink snooker balls.

Liam fell over the wall into the next pen, Finbar leapt out into the feed passage and I scrambled into the feed rack, a relic of cattle feeding days, with Annie's champing jaws close behind. As the rack started to pull away from the wall I clawed my way onto one of the crossbeams, amongst the cobwebs and chicken droppings, to watch the mums counting up their young ones. Although very frightened, I had time to give thanks for salvation as I visualised the headlines in the local paper, mourning the passing of a local vet on the threshold of his career!

As I waited for help I meditated on my graduation, when we were told that as young professional people we were embarking on a worthy and caring career, where no doubt, many of us would become pillars of local society. If only the Dean could see me now- reclining in a hayrack, adorned with feathers and chicken droppings!

When Liam eventually arrived with a corrugated sheet and guided the pigs back into their pens I descended and brushed myself off, a wiser man, with all semblance of dignity shattered.

# Chapter 24

The following week I met Liam at Cooil Vooar to try out Buster's jaunting cart. Fortunately, he was an extrovert animal and loved being handled. The trial event took place in the paddock where he had the opportunity to run and we could test the apparatus for any future modification.

It was one of those dreamy spring afternoons when the very roots of the plants have awoken from the winter's slumber to carry out their destiny of regrowth. The day had warmed up and the early blossom was seducing the droning bees with its languorous scent. It wasn't only the bees that had spring fever but also one ardent young Irishman and his assisting vet who found the whole ambience, with Marjorie in full bloom, to be a heady mixture indeed.

The prototype consisted of a wire cradle for Buster's body to rest upon. There were straps for the chest and abdomen to support it and a breast strap lest he ran out at the front end. On either side there were wheels, adjustable for height. His hind legs hung out at the rear, unimpeded by the frame. I had brought a roll of cotton wool to prevent rubbing between Buster and the metal framework. As we were to find out, much of our success rested on the wheels.

Buster was revelling in all the attention and the Labradors kept trying to assist him as he was fitted into the 'Jaunting car' as it was officially named. Once we had the patient strapped into the machine (It was suggested that goggles and a flying helmet would be appropriate for this Biggles of the canine world), Marjorie led him off across the paddock on a lead. It took him several minutes to get used to this new game before he started to use his legs properly and get into the rhythm. "You can let him go now," I said, when I saw that he had gained confidence.

We watched as he scampered across the grass, rejoicing in his new-found freedom. His Labrador playmates were somewhat bemused by this sudden burst of acceleration but kept up in the hope that a game would ensue. Just as suddenly, it was all over as the wheel caught in a furrow as he turned and dog and chariot finished upside down.

After we had rescued him we sat down to iron out the problems. The wheels were too small, causing bounce, and so narrow that they caught in ruts. If the wheels were two inches farther apart it would give a lot more stability. Liam arranged to attack these problems and would also make the ground clearance adjustable.

I didn't see Marjorie or Liam for some time as work was fairly intensive and wedding arrangements took precedence. We had arranged to marry in August and were somewhat unsure about our future. So much had taken place during the past year!

There was a little grocery shop, in a lane off Albany Road, where we used to buy liquorice shoelaces and other exotic sweets on our way back from school. It was a very handy type of shop, which served a social need before the advent of large stores. I was called out to this shop one winter evening, by the owners George and Daisy Kaighin, to see their aged Jack Russell Terrier, Danny, who was not well. Danny was very much loved by them and I had been involved with him as a student, when he was a puppy, 13 years before. George and Daisy were about 70 years of age and made a small but diminishing income as a neighbourhood store. I arrived at the shop and was shown into the back room by Daisy to find George listening to the radio. Daisy was quite small, round and jolly with steel rimmed spectacles, whereas George was equally small but thin, with a weather beaten face after many years spent as a council roadman. I could have cut the air with a knife in that tiny room. The heat from the blazing fire, combined with the fumes of the plug tobacco from George's pipe was enough to kill a donkey.

Danny was in his box by the fireside, well wrapped up in a blanket. "What's the trouble with our little friend tonight"? I said in a concerned manner.

"It's like this Mr Carson," said George. "You know how our Danny has been troubled with his walking over the past two years. Well, he's been getting slower of late and had a cough as if he had something jammed in his throat. Four days ago he went off his food and didn't want to go for a walk. Next day he lay in bed and lapped a little broth so we wrapped him up comfortably. Since then he's not wanted to eat or go for a walk so we left him a couple of days as we didn't want to call out a busy man like yourself over the weekend."

As I knelt down beside Danny he didn't make his usual move to greet me. I unfolded the covering blanket only to confirm my worst fears. Danny had been dead for possibly two days and his bloated body was already decomposing in the hot room. I was at a loss for words and went through the motions of examining him whilst I thought deeply. Turning round to face Daisy and George who were clasping hands on the sofa I said quietly, "I'm afraid, old friends, that Danny has just slipped away gently and quietly. At his age it would have been well nigh impossible to help him enjoy life as I suspect that he had developed heart problems and could never have been active again"

Daisy went over and sobbing quietly, stroked Danny's grizzled head whilst George blew his nose hard and set to re-stoking his pipe. Daisy interrupted the silence, "Thank you for coming Mr Carson, we knew that this day wasn't far off. I don't know what George will do as he used to take Danny to the Woodburn Hotel for a pint each evening. We have a little plot at the back where George can dig a hole in the morning."

I went home with a heavy heart. Had one of them realised that Danny had died beforehand and made no mention for fear of upsetting the other? After all he was the only child of this devoted couple and would leave a big gap in their lives. No matter how professionally we regard the situations that we encounter in practice, it is impossible to detach oneself from the emotions of the moment. Indeed, compassion is not the prerogative of the pet owner. Many farmers and horse owners are deeply affected by the suffering of animals in their care.

After being in practice for nearly a year I was very content to be working at the job I liked, in the land I loved and to be engaged to Moira. Moira had told me many times of her adventures in Africa and sometimes I felt that, like so many of my Celtic ancestors, the lure of far away places made me restless.

# Chapter 25

"The best laid schemes o' mice an' men,
Gang aft agley."
Robert Burns, "To a Mouse"

After the promise of an early spring, cold wintry spells kept returning throughout March, followed by rain in April that kept us busy on the farms. With the cold weather came Grass Staggers or magnesium deficiency, in the heavy yielding cows. Any undue excitement would trigger off the latent condition, when the animals would become nervous and twitchy, culminating in convulsions and death. At this stage the recumbent animals could be dangerous as they would strike out in all directions with their legs as they went into nervous spasms.

Ruth used to make up a concentrated solution of magnesium for injection into the muscle. The injection was very effective in treating the condition although it often caused abscesses. Today's technology would regard this as being very primitive but it served its purpose superbly during that era.

Eventually, I persuaded Brian to try injecting small quantities, slowly into the blood stream. This had to be administered very slowly, or the unfortunate cow could end up with a heart attack.

Early one morning I had to go rushing out to see Peter Bridson at Ballacannell. It was a crisp, exhilarating start to the day. The fields were white with hoar frost and the overnight ground mists were beginning to yield to the bright sun. It promised to be warm later on but it came too late for several of his cows.

The dawn had just broken and smoke from many chimneys was curling lazily upwards towards the azure sky. For several days we had been in the centre of a high-pressure belt with hardly a breath of wind to stir the conifers lining the farm driveway.

The ice crackled as I drove over the frozen puddles into the farmyard. Peter was awaiting my arrival impatiently as another of his cows was having a convulsion in the meadow behind the cowshed.

Warmly clad in a navy polo neck jersey under his brown dust coat he was rubbing his frozen hands together. He was an engaging character, a couple of years my junior, who was always full of drive and enthusiasm. This was his first year farming on his own after spending some time at agricultural college. Jennifer, his auburn haired wife was a sister at the local hospital and a valuable source of income in these early years.

His small herd was just starting to calve down and produce some income when disaster struck. Last week he had found one of his best cows lying in convulsions, in the field, bellowing and thrashing to such an extent that its feet had cut gouges in the ground. Unfortunately, it had died before we reached the farm. Brian's diagnosis was that it had been Grass Staggers.

Despite his worried frown Peter summoned up a smile and greeted me " Good morning Ned. Sorry to get you out before breakfast but we have been watching these cows closely since losing Daisy last week. Belinda has calved about a month and it looks like the same problem. Why is this suddenly affecting my cattle?"

" Let's have a look at her first, Peter. Then we can discuss the whys and wherefores after I've treated her," I said, as we hurried into the meadow.

Sure enough, there was Belinda, a handsome Shorthorn cow, lying in the lush grass of the meadow. She must have been there for some time as the ground was churned up by her feet and there was froth at her mouth and nostrils.

Peter interrupted, "Shall I sit her up as she is getting fairly bloated?

"No," I replied, "She could well have a touch of milk fever as well as staggers. Best not to overexcite her unduly as they can get very twitchy in this state. I'll mix some magnesium in with the calcium and inject it into the jugular vein. Can you sit on her head to keep her steady?" I slipped the needle deftly into the vein, inverted the bottle and watched the liquid running down the rubber tube into her neck, controlling the speed of flow, in order not to embarrass the heart; I could also watch her respirations in case there were any problems. At first Belinda gave a few convulsive kicks, but slowly, as the bottle emptied, I could sense her body relaxing. As she gradually improved there was a series of burps as her stomach started working and she expelled the bloating gases in her abdomen. Both ends moved into action as she cocked her tail and licked her nose simultaneously. She was recovering!

I sat on her rump to observe progress and said to Peter, "Don't be offended if I say that this is of your own making. We've both left college with all the latest knowledge, now we must gain experience! You've bought a lovely herd of cows, given them the best fodder so that they produce lots of milk and turned them out onto this lush well-fertilised pasture that has grown very rapidly. The growth has been so rapid, that the cattle develop diarrhoea on the wet grass and cannot absorb enough magnesium to keep up with that going out in their milk yield. Result-Grass Staggers."

As Belinda started to raise her head Peter suggested that we look over the rest of the herd. They moved away as we approached. "Watch Peter. Some of them are nervous and a couple are walking away quite stiffly with their heads held high. Those are the animals who could be the next victims. I shall inject a couple of them before I go. Put them onto old ley with a bit of fibrous grass and feed them hay before turning them out on to pasture. I shall also let you have some magnesium powder that you can feed them mixed with molasses."

Peter's face brightened up as he brushed back his mop of blonde hair. "I hope it works. Let's have a look at Belinda. I see that she's sitting up now. Jenny will have to do a few extra shifts to pay for this lot."
As Belinda was still a bit shaky and confused we left her to get up in her own time. Peter called in at lunchtime to collect the magnesium powder and let me know that she had fully recovered.

At the time I was not fully aware of the significance of this particular incident to my future career, but I'd just learnt my first lesson. During the wartime years the British farming

73

industry had to feed the nation, as the stranglehold of the U-boats threatened to cut off our food lifeline. The labour intensive farming of pre-war days, reminiscent of Hardy's rustic and idyllic Wessex had been swept away. The poppy covered cornfields were to become a thing of the past. Young men had gone to war, to be replaced by girls of the Land Army. Many of these girls were town bred, and set to with a will to meet the challenge unknowingly breaking the long family tradition of father to son as farm labourers.

This was the start of a revolution in agriculture when the whole system became more intensive and faster. Crop yields per acre increased with more intensive fertiliser applications and every effort was made to increase milk and beef production. The Ministry of Agriculture and Fisheries and many chemical companies were investing heavily into crop and livestock research. The powers of War Ag, the War Agriculture Executive Committee, were such that they controlled the development of agriculture throughout the country. There was a lot of local resistance to change when they introduced the heresy of ploughing up permanent pastures that had been in existence for generations. There was a war to be won and these pastures were required for growing food for the beleaguered nation.

War Ag. was made up of farmers, scientists and laymen, all dedicated to producing as much food as possible. Consequently, they developed nitrate and potash fertilisers to grow grass and crops even more rapidly. Chemical insecticides and herbicides were hailed as the answer to many of our problems. The thinking of the time was that if one eradicated weeds and parasites on the farm, there would be no holding back on production. Cheap and wholesome food for the masses was the bye-word.

The seething masses of refugees in post-war Europe were de-infested of fleas and lice with the wonder insecticide Dieldrin and its derivatives. Then we used these products in eliminating crop pests without much lateral thought to the long-term effects of their use. As a result the population of predatory birds plummeted, due to infertility, resulting from their diet of seed eating birds and mammals. The insects responsible for plant pollination were also destroyed by insecticides and lack of foresight of scientists. Despite these measures, a new generation of insects, which had become resistant to the current insecticides, developed. New generations of insecticides resulted, which, in turn, resulted in resistance, until mankind learned to use biological deterrents and cropping strategies.

The story of fertilisers is similar, with chemical products containing potash and nitrogen. These chemicals caused rapid growth of grass, resulting in lush green pastures and an early "bite" for cattle in the springtime. Unfortunately, there is little fibre in the grass at this stage and the cattle develop diarrhoea, as I have often found to my own discomfort. This lack of fibre results in the cattle becoming "bloated" when turned out to spring grass, unless they have a feed of fibrous hay beforehand. The action of this fibre is to stimulate the first stomach or rumen to work efficiently and enable the cow to belch, otherwise they can blow up like an inflated tyre and die.

The high potassium in the fertiliser is thought to prevent the normal intake of magnesium from the pasture, resulting in magnesium deficiency in the herd and cases of Grass Staggers. This is compounded by the use of herbicides, applied to destroy buttercups and nettles; both rich sources of magnesium. The way to prevent grass staggers on, a herd basis, is to provide free access to magnesium salts in powder or liquid form mixed with molasses.

The positive side of this story is that present day farming can provide the food, at the price demanded by the consumer. Intensive farming is the consequence of consumer pressure and if we wish to eat food grown in an extensive or organic manner, we must be prepared to pay for it. As in all things we must balance the advantages against the drawbacks.

# Chapter 26

Brian had asked me if I would like to attend the annual Southern Horse show as the Honorary Veterinary Surgeon. It was a friendly, local event, with show jumping and pony club events in order to make it a pleasant family day out. There was also to be a dressage display and an exhibition of sheep dogs being put through their paces at herding ducks.

It was a delightfully warm Saturday in May when the hedgerows were an intricate embroidery of interwoven colours, the pink of the campions intermixed with bluebells, buttercups and wild garlic. The pastures were at their sumptuous best. A rich green carpet dotted with daisies and dandelions. To mark my first public appearance at a show I dressed up for the occasion in my Donegal thorn proof tweed jacket and cavalry twill trousers. I drove there in my own resplendent Hillman Estate as the practice car was being serviced.

Brian had offered to stand in for me if I would cope with the morning consultations. Only a few clients attended the surgery. One of the first to arrive was Captain Hunt with Jasper, the amiable corgi, for a final check up before his first trek over the hills since his illness. The scar on his neck had healed up remarkably well and to show his appreciation he left me a box of chocolates.

Next on the list was a little fat Jack Russell terrier, called Rosie. She was round and jolly like her owners. They all ate too well and not too wisely. Exercise to burn off this surplus flab just was not in their scheme of things. Unfortunately, the obesity also contributed to Rosie's eczema, which was getting worse, particularly as she was now unable to scratch or nibble at fleas because of her girth.

I explained the discomfort that her condition was causing and persuaded her owners to embark on a strict diet with regular weight checks. After giving them a flea shampoo I remarked that my vegetable slimming diet was tailor-made for Rosie's portly figure. In her zest for food she did'nt appreciate that chopped up cabbage and carrot was being added to her diet in increasing quantities. Within a month her bulges were turning into curves. As every week passed by she was drawing more and more admiring glances from "the young dogs about town" as she developed that svelte look.

At the finish of consultations I rushed across to collect Moira from her flat. She looked stunning and had taken a lot of time developing that country show look. Dressed in a very practical pair of brown brogues and a Lovat Green tweed suit tailored to fit her trim figure she looked very much the country lady. She had been awaiting my arrival with a picnic basket already packed in case the catering facilities were inadequate. As it was still quite early for the show I suggested that we call in at the Mount Murray Hotel for a drink before lunch.

The lounge bar was empty apart from a man and woman, whom I vaguely recognised, sitting at a table beside the window with a large Golden Cocker Spaniel.

I nodded to the couple, who greeted me, and as I approached the bar I felt that the barmaid looked familiar. Then I recognised the dark beauty of Roisin Rafferty, cleaning the bar top.

"Hello," I said," I didn't know that you were working here. Could I have a pint of bitter please and a gin and tonic?"

" Indeed, you may," replied Roisin, smiling, "I didn't know that I worked here until half an hour ago. Bill Giles, the landlord, collapsed suddenly. He's a diabetic. His wife Gwen has rushed off to hospital with him and called me in at short notice. It's a good thing that I'd helped out Aunt Bridget in Skibbereen for a summer, so it comes quite easily. Fortunately, I'd not gone off to the show with father and the boys. Are you both on your way?"

I nodded in affirmation just as the Cocker Spaniel interrupted us-barking furiously as it backed away defensively. The owner laughingly apologised, "I'm sorry Mr Carson, but Hugo smelled your trousers and suddenly realised that you were the man who upset his dignity the other week by poking inside his ears."

Then I remembered Hugo. He was a very hysterical Golden Cocker and also a devout coward! He had most severely infected ears, which had required a lot of attention to remove a year's collection of wax. All the time that he was on the table he shivered and whimpered until eventually I sent him home with his ears shining like a couple of pink pearls.

I excused myself and returned to Moira with the drinks. As we discussed the weekend's activities I was pleased to see that Hugo had recovered from his panic and was sniffing around the table.

Suddenly, I had a most peculiar feeling in my shoe and looked down to see Hugo, with leg cocked, piddling over my brand new, ego boosting, cavalry twill trousers. I roared at him but without as much as an apology he trotted off to his owners with a smug "That's levelled the score" look on his face.

Hugo's owners wished they were somewhere else and hurried him, belatedly, outside to finish his performance. Moira, knowing how much care I had put into my appearance was chortling helplessly and Roisin lay across the bar, crying with laughter.

Any hopes I might have had of impressing the "County" owners at the show were dashed. I would have to arrive with my dry leg presented towards the public! I must have looked particularly helpless as Moira and Roisin, giggling with joy, cleaned me up and reinstated some of the dignity befitting a young veterinary surgeon in charge of his first show.

When we arrived at the show ground, cattle trucks and cars bordered the ring as the preliminary jumping rounds took place.

Feeling very much the part, I was presented with my Hon. Veterinary Surgeon's Badge and parked my car at the edge of the warming up area, where horses were constantly being ridden and taken over practice jumps. We were also to be provided with lunch in the refreshment tent. One of our greatest problems was extricating ourselves from the bonhomie of the hardened showmen drinking whisky and reminiscing around the bar. We made a graceful exit or it would have been drinks all round for the 'vetinry' and his young lady.

I was in my element escorting the most beautiful and elegant lady at the show, and knew that I must be the envy of all the other young men in the crowd. I had brought my shooting stick in case Moira wished to rest and watch the events in the ring, and my cup overflowed as I proudly introduced her to many clients whom we met at the ringside. It was an acute source of embarrassment to me that every second dog walking past came to sniff at my slightly damp trousers just to renew acquaintance with Hugo.

It didn't take long for the first problem to arise in the shape of a dispute about the height of a pony and its eligibility for one of the jumping classes. Rumours are always rife about height measurements, and if one listened to public opinion certain animals would change size, according to the weather. I had'nt brought my measuring staff so I arranged with Moira to telephone back to the surgery to ask if I could have the staff brought out to the show. A few minutes later Brian arrived with the measuring staff, smiling broadly and chuckling to himself. After Ruth had taken the message from Moira, she went to Brian and said that Mr Carson was being so thoughtful and wanted the staff to attend the show, but of course she was much too busy and had to do the shopping! After I produced the staff and carried out my duties a satisfactory agreement was reached between the owner and show stewards.

Height measurement in horses has always been beset with problems and the most reliable method of carrying it out is on a perfectly flat concrete surface. Even using this technique it depends, to some extent, on the position of the horse's head and whether the animal is completely relaxed or tensed up! As if these problems were not enough we had to measure them in a field, which may or may not be on a slope, therefore it was necessary to take the average of several readings.

As I returned to the stewards tent, an excited flurry of dogs passed me as Buster, with his Mark 2 Jaunting Cart, tore through the exercise area, closely pursued by Liam, cursing him in Gaelic and the Labradors barking encouragement. A long way behind came Marjorie who was not quite as fit as the rest of the field. She stopped to talk to us, very glad of an excuse to catch her breath. This was meant to be a test walk today but unfortunately Buster had other ideas when he found that the cart worked so well. She explained that John, her husband, had been so impressed with Liam's metal skills that he had offered him a permanent job as an engineer in his works.

As she rushed away after the dogs, Moira giggled, twitched her nose and said, "I can see that I'll have to check on some of the clients that you hurry off to see at every opportunity. What a very attractive lady she is and so full of life. She might even run away with you!"

We linked arms and were strolling towards the hospitality tent when a rather agitated steward appeared and asked if I would attend a horse that was bleeding badly after knocking a jump. I collected my bag and dust coat. At last a chance to prove myself to the "spavins and fetlocks brigade". We sought out the pony between a couple of cattle trucks. It was a nice, neat little pony with a plaited mane and tail to match her well-turned out rider. She had stumbled at one of the jumps and caught her near hind leg, making a cut in the skin and artery. Blood was pumping from the cut so I decided that it required a couple of stitches to pull the wound together. In retrospect, I felt that this was probably an error of judgement on my part. I asked the owner to lift the fore leg so that the pony would stand still whilst I injected local anaesthetic before suturing, which was an excellent idea - in theory. As I injected the solution it stung for a moment, the pony leapt in the air, knocking the owner over and my instruments onto the grass. As the crowd collected to see the fun, I gathered everything together and immersed my kit in a bowl of surgical spirit hoping that it would be fairly sterile. An old horseman came forward and offered his services to restrain the pony. He lifted the leg, talked to the pony and distracted her whilst I injected around the wound. It was a pleasure to see the effect that an experienced handler can have on a horse. After that it was a matter of three stitches and a pressure bandage to control any bleeding.

As I packed away my gear Moira looked at me and produced a mirror from her handbag. Those parts under my dust coat were protected but my face, shirt and beautiful new trousers were all freckled with little red spots. So much for the magnificent social occasion. Maybe a little humility is good for us all!

Strolling back through the warming up area, we could see a crowd of people standing beside my car. They appeared to be in deep discussion and looked up on spotting us.

Marjorie, her face flushed, walked out of the group and said, "Ned, I have bad news for you - Oh My God! What have you done to yourself? You're all red spots! Oh I see!" As Moira, laughing, explained my predicament. "I'm sorry," she continued, "But whilst you were away there has been a little accident to your car."

My heart sank. I had spent all my life avoiding accidents and as soon as my back is turned my faithful "Passion Wagon" gets into trouble! What a sad sight. I had spent many hours lovingly polishing her British Racing Green body to perfection. Now the wing, bonnet and door were all dented. Together we had shared many triumphs and disasters of courtship. I'm sure that my lower lip quivered.

Marjorie stood beside me very sadly and continued, "Sophie was exercising her horse on the grass, when Buster, on wheels, rushed past very fast and hit the pony's leg with his cart. The pony reared and went over backwards and Sophie fell onto the bonnet, followed by Poppy. It's a blessing that neither of them were hurt but look what it's done to your pretty car. Buster is definitely confined to barracks until we develop a braking system for his cart."

At that moment Liam, who had been helping to sort out the accident said, "Don't you be worrying now Ned. I may not be clever at mending animals like yourself but a bit of bodywork is no problem to Kevin and myself. Not only that but we are delighted to repay your kindness."

I was deeply touched that people were showing how much they appreciated my efforts. As I drove home with Moira I realised how fortunate we're to have such friends. It would be a long time before I had a day so full of incident.

# Chapter 27

I didn't call on Colonel and Mrs de Vere Pullen very often, as I was the junior member of the practice, and they were an old established family, who had arrived with the Normans!

They owned "Ballakilley", an estate containing several farms and the ancient Manor house. The big house was let out as a residence and they had built a more manageable abode adjoining the stable block and Home Farm.

For years the family had lived in Leicestershire and had been dedicated supporters of the Quorn and Belvoir hunt. There, they had maintained a stable of ten horses for hunting and point-to-point racing, which they passed on to their son when they moved across to the island.

Charles de Vere Pullen had a very distinguished war record, ranging from the Far East to Europe, where he had been seconded into the Special Operations Executive. He was a quiet and unassuming gentleman whose days were taken up managing the estate and helping his wife, Daphne, exercise the horses.

Daphne was made of sterner stuff and made sure that the estate and its staff functioned like clockwork. Chairman of the Village Fête Committee, secretary of the PCC and organiser of the Pony Club, she was brusque and energetic. The curt manner in which she barked out orders had earned her the nickname of "The Brigadier". I was only permitted to treat farm stock, dogs, and on occasion, to pass opinion on a horse, until I had established myself as "a good horse vet".

One evening, I was surprised to receive a call from the colonel to examine Marauder, a five-year-old bay mare. She was a steeple chaser, who had recently been returned to them as being "too hot to handle".

"I'm awfully sorry to disturb you," said the colonel. "Unfortunately, the damned fool got herself caught in barbed wire and panicked. Stitching job, I'm afraid. Mr Scanlon is off duty, I presume."

"Yes," I replied "He won't be back until fairly late but I'll pop out and see what I can do for you."

Rapidly gathering together all the necessary instruments for the job, I headed for Ballakilley in some trepidation. I felt as if I was about to be thrown to the lions and wasn't sure whether I would find Marauder or The Brigadier the hardest to handle.

The colonel was in the tack room when I arrived and we walked across the yard to Marauder's loosebox.

As we entered, I could see that she was still very nervous from her experience, and she shied away as the colonel took hold of her halter. Dancing from toe to toe, she did'nt make my examination easy. Most of the cuts were superficial, although there were a couple on the near hind leg that would benefit from a few stitches.

The mare became more and more worked up. Despite using the twitch to restrain her and lifting her foreleg, she wouldn't let me near the wounds. At this stage she became downright aggressive, striking out with her forelegs, threatening to cause damage to her handlers. After ten minutes of struggling the colonel gave up the battle. " It's no good. I shall have to call Daphne to assist."

Five minutes later Daphne arrived, surveyed the scene and pushed the colonel aside, saying, "Leave it to me, Charles," as she took hold of the lead rope, gave it a couple of twitches and shouted at Marauder. "Stand still, damn you, or you'll end up as dog meat!"

There was only five foot three of Daphne, and Marauder towered over her, but she stood there, visibly shaking, not daring to move lest flames issued from Daphne's nostrils! I was able to approach the mare in safety and inject local anaesthetic into the edge of the wounds. I must confess that I also felt rather intimidated.

Every time Marauder dared to moved as I sutured her leg, Daphne stared her in the eyes and brought out some more parade ground rhetoric, which has made many men shake in their shoes.

After I had administered tetanus antiserum, I stood back to look at the result. Daphne gave a brusque, "Thank you Mr Carson. A job well done. A good thing that you called me, Charles. She would never have let you handle her! Whilst you're here perhaps you'd look over an Arab filly that we've just bought at the sales. I hope that she's alright because we've just paid five thousand pounds for her."

She led a very pretty youngster out of the loose box. After the filly had been trotted up and down and I'd examined her legs and feet, I agreed that they had made a good purchase, but not to push her too hard to start. "I'd hoped that you would say that," commented Daphne. "She has very good breeding." It was then I realised that it was not the filly, but the vet who was being scrutinised to see if he knew how to handle a horse. I must have passed my fitness test as they never seemed to have reservations about me after that.

Driving home that evening, I mused on the absolute dominance that one person can have over a panicking animal.

# Chapter 28

The Isle of Man Board of Agriculture was then in the throes of initiating a Tuberculosis Eradication Scheme in cattle. Our situation on the island was ideal when compared with the embryo scheme being developed in the United Kingdom. We had no carriers of infection such as badgers, only about a thousand farms and all our boundaries were water.

One of the first problems to face the government veterinary officers was handling the cattle. Each animal had to be tattooed in the ear with an identification number. The hair on the neck was clipped and the skin thickness measured with callipers. Following these procedures a small amount of tuberculin was injected into the skin and any reaction checked in 72 hours. Rather like the Mantoux test that we all had at school.

There were no cattle crushes or raceways available in those early days so the farmers had to develop their own means of restraint. As this generally involved spending money form which they could see no material return, crushes were always at the bottom of the priority list. It was only later on, when cattle were being handled more often for worming, weighing and parasite control, that the necessity for a crush became more important.

For T.B. Testing, most of the animals were chained up or held loose in pens. Those loose animals were "scruffed" by grabbing them by the horn or ear in one hand and by the nose with the free hand. Wrestling with a twelve-hundredweight animal in a dung filled loose box with other cattle milling around in confusion is a very hazardous occupation and many people were crushed or trampled in the process. It was a job that had to be done despite the risks.

The vet's job was to carry out the test on the animal and read an indecipherable earmark as well as keeping a record on paper. Identity marking an animal involved rubbing black marking paste inside the ear, and with a special pair of pliers punching a number on pins, into the ear and then rubbing the paste into the holes with the finger. Much of this paste was transferred to the record sheets, which did not help the final interpretation. In the end we resorted to coercing a student or the farmer's wife to keep the records. Cows resented this interference and I often felt that young women having their own ears pierced must be very dedicated to the world of glamour!

It was at this time that I had my first skirmish with Josie Corkish! I had been brought up to believe that this was a 'do as you would be done by world', where other folk responded to your kindness. Not so Josie. She had been trained somewhere down in the bowels of the earth where every day was a trial by fire. I'm sure that at home there was a plaque on the wall granting her a B.Sc. from Hades!

Josie was chief clerk to Dick Cowley, the chief government veterinary officer, and protected him and her little empire to the detriment of all visitors. Her allegiance was to Dick, the Board of Agriculture, and those politicians who ran the Board and could affect her position of power.

We often used to wonder where her twisted outlook on life arose. She had been very belligerent when she attended Murrays Road school and managed to vent her spleen on the hockey field. She fought her way up through the civil service, leaving a trail of discord and ill will behind her. Eventually, she married George Corkish, a nice enough little guy who wouldn't say boo to a goose. They were happy in their way. He was out most evenings shooting in the rifle club or fishing during the summer months. Josie was into committee work or attending Board of Agriculture meetings.

Oh, but she could be nasty to any of her juniors in the office who offended her, or didn't do things as she liked them to be done. She had to dominate and bully all comers, and tried it out me.

I returned to the surgery one lunchtime to find a note asking me to phone Mrs Corkish.

"You'd better ring her now Ned," said Ruth with a hardly suppressed smile, "Or else she'll be on the 'phone every half hour. Don't stand any nonsense from her."

I picked up the phone and asked to be put through to Mrs Corkish. There was a pause followed by a rustling of paper as she assembled the damning evidence.

"Mr Carson. This is not good enough!" Came the staccato comment.

I paused to give effect before replying. "Is that right Mrs Corkish! Perhaps you can tell me what is not good enough?"

"Your TB testing sheets are untidy and in places unreadable. How do you expect me to interpret the results?"

"Not too easily Mrs Corkish as I had to complete the test outside in a heavy rainstorm. I'm sorry about that but I had neither shelter nor secretarial help."

"I'm afraid I shall have to put forward a complaint to Mr Cowley and let him sort out the matter."

"Yes." I rejoined with slight annoyance, but also remembering that I would be meeting Dick Cowley socially that evening, "It is a problem some times. Perhaps the Board of Agriculture would loan me a secretary for this type of test! By the way, isn't it Mr Cowley's duty to interpret the test results?"

At this juncture there was a click as she put the phone back on the receiver.

My first experience with T.B. testing was on a small farm at the North of the Island. I arrived at the premises early on a lovely summer morning. As I drove north from Ramsey I could smell the freshly mown hay and hear the birds singing in the hedgerows. The joy of this countryside and constant glimpses of the sea were a constant pleasure.

It was a very pretty smallholding with low whitewashed walls bordering the main road. The lime-washed house and out buildings were immaculate with no sign of the manure heap or rusting machinery as seen on so many farms.

Alured Quilleash was brushing the back entrance as I arrived, like a man who had little else to do. He was dressed in an old waistcoat over his white collarless shirt with rough fustian trousers neatly tucked into his spotless wellington boots. He looked every bit the retired farmer, neat and tidy like his farmyard!

He was a sturdily built man of average height and about sixty years of age. He must have had a good head of hair in his youth and what was remaining lay in regimented lines, like windrows, holding his ears together. A welcoming smile crept across his weather beaten features as he greeted me. "Are you Mr Carson? I'm glad to see that you're on time yessir! I've got everything ready for you. This is my second test. There are twelve Galloway yearlings tied up in the cow stalls."

As I dressed up in my waterproofs and belt, with holsters for my syringes, he told me that he had given up milking two years before and afterwards missed his animals so much that he decided to keep a few beef stock. "This way," he said, "I can go out in the field every day and take a look at them, without being bothered with milking or cleaning out."

" I bought them at St. Johns Mart, about a year ago," he continued. " They're so hardy that I only bring them in for testing. My neighbour, John Comaish, helped me to get them tied up before you came. They're a pretty lively lot but we managed in the end."

As I entered the low shippon I could see a row of woolly backsides; some dun coloured but mostly black. The shed was as clean inside as the yard. It was evident that Alured made good use of his spare time.

"Here you are," said Alured, with a bit of a twinkle in his eye. "I've got a list with each animal's sex, age and ear number, just as they are tied up. All you need do now is to test them!"

As I went between the first two animals they reacted to the injection and jumped around, bawling loudly. This developed into group panic and, as I went to the next couple, two pairs of hind feet shot out, hit me in the groin and spun me around.

"Funny old thing," chuckled Alured, smiling broadly, "I thought that they were a bit flighty this morning. Maybe they don't fancy you folk from the south of the Island."

Eventually, I worked out that if I leapt in between the yearlings quickly, it didn't hurt nearly as much. By the end of the test I was battered and bruised from calf to hip. Musing upon it afterwards, I can remember one of my tutors telling us that cattle can kick with only one leg at a time. Perhaps these ones hadn't read the textbook!

Margaret Quilleash appeared at the door and asked if I would like to come into the house and clean up a bit. After I had finished washing my hands in the kitchen, I walked into the front room to find a pot of tea and plate of scones on the table. " Just a little bite to keep yer goin' till lunchtime," added Margaret.

"You did a mighty good job this morning," said Alured, settling into his well - worn armchair. " The last man who came complained a lot and swore at the bullocks somethin' awful. Are you the doctor's son from down Douglas? I hear he's a mighty good man with eye problems. I hope he's a better man at dodgin' bullocks than his son," he finished with a mischievous smile.

I smiled to myself and guessed that most of the other tests wouldn't cause quite so many problems.

We generally knew what to expect on each farm before we went testing. The efficient farmers were eager to finish the test in the minimum time and organised themselves accordingly. John Corkill had a large dairy farm at Abbeylands. His father had been a farm worker by day and rabbit trapper by night and, by dint of sheer hard, work had saved up enough money to buy the land and run down buildings. More years of hard labour enabled him to build up his farm into a very efficient dairy and beef unit. For his own convenience he arranged the buildings so that he could tie up 100 animals under one roof. That made feeding cattle in the shed so much easier. Consequently, I could test the first hundred animals in an hour and a half, whilst the other fifty loose animals would take the same time.

Two days after finishing John Corkill's test I had another phone call from the Board of Agriculture. Josie Corkish was back with some more vitriol.

"Mr Carson! I am having problems recording your results from Mr Corkill's TB test. I wish you would try to get the facts right. Your record at writing up your testing sheets is very sloppy. Two or three times you have written down the breed as Ayrshire and put in the colour as black and white. What are these animals?"

This time I was determined not to let Josie upset me so I held the phone at arm's length to reduce the decibels. "No, Mrs Corkish." I responded wearily, " You are wrong. If I remember correctly, you were on the farm walk at Mr McClellan, Lower Nab, last week. I'm surprised that you didn't see several black and white Ayrshire heifers in his herd as they look very pretty."

There was a strangled hiss at the other end, followed by a curt, "No, I did not see them. It isn't natural. They were probably crossbred anyway. That does not improve the tidiness of your forms!" I could visualise all five feet of her, tense and tight lipped, clutching the phone in fury. With a curt 'good day', she went out of my life until the next complaint.

# Chapter 29

Lots were always drawn as to who could avoid carrying out Peter Quirk's test, when it was due, as it was a veritable disaster area. We had no problem with Peter, who was a nice enough chap, but a trifle slow. The main problem was the last will and testament of Uncle Ebenezer, who had left him his entire estate, which consisted of a very rundown farm and a room full of empty whiskey bottles. A condition of the will was that Peter must farm it, or the property would be sold and the proceeds donated to an orphanage in Fiji. This was a land where Uncle Ebenezer had spent several years of his misspent youth, so there may have been an intriguing story behind the gesture.

Peter had occupied the farm after spending much time and money making the house habitable. The farm buildings were a shambles with roofs, floors and doors that had fallen in. His first priority had been to reinstall power and water and then attempt to reinstate one building as a cowshed and dairy. All the other buildings had very makeshift calf pens, whilst his single suckling cows roamed in and out at will.

At testing time, the cattle were herded into the sheds, and all exits blocked with tractors, trailers or any suitable piece of farm machinery. The cattle were then roped or wrestled to a standstill in order to read indecipherable earmarks and administer injections.

As I came in the gate, I would normally expect to see the Mull of Galloway in the distance. Today I was lucky to find the farm! It was one of those foggy, drizzly, autumn mornings, when I arrived at The Lhergy to test. I could'nt have chosen a worse time or place!

Peter met me in the yard. " Sorry, but we've spent the last two hours trying to get the cattle in from the tops. You can't see a hand in front of you. Can you stand in the gap in the corner and help to guide the single sucklers and calves into the big shed? They should be down in a couple of minutes."

I picked up a stick and stood forlornly beside the shed, straining eyes and ears to detect the approaching cattle through the mist. After much squelching of feet and shouting from the drovers, the cattle hove in sight as shadowy figures in the mist. They drew near to find that the only avenue of escape was by going into the door of the shed. Slowly they ambled in through the entrance and filled up the building until one innovative animal discovered that it could walk out of a window where the dung was piled high. There were a few minutes of general panic as the escapees were rounded up and the window blocked with an old farm cart.

By the time we'd cut off all avenues of escape and actually started the test, it was 10.30 a.m. with every prospect of a late lunch. All my papers were on a clipboard and I had enough supplies to deal with all the herd. The lads of the village had come to join in the fun as it was good training for the tug-of-war team. The "A" team would grab a cow that was bogged down in a foot of wet mud and dung in the shed. They would read the ear number and I carried out the test and recorded all the details on my clipboard that I left in the window.

Then the "B" team took hold of the next animal whilst the first one was put outside the shed by the "A" team. All the time the cloying mud kept trying to suck my boots off; my hands were black with tattooing ink; wet from the cows' coats and the recording sheets were soggy and light grey in colour. Everything was in slow motion under these conditions but we,d tested thirty of the forty animals in the shed when I heard a gentle slurping behind me. Looking round I found that one of the cattle outside the shed, being curious by nature, had looked in the window behind me and was contentedly grazing on my completed record sheets. Fortunately, history does'nt record my comments to that cow as I was living in a very close Methodist community that did not approve of colourful language. The test eventually finished about two hours later than I anticipated. The one good feature was the feast of tea and rock buns provided by Peter. He did have the decency to apologise and hoped to improve things before next years test. Whilst we were eating he told us the story of how he came to own the farm.

In his young days it was always a holiday treat to go out to Lhergy farm and help with the milking and hay making. He really enjoyed the life and Uncle Ebenezer, who owned it, said that it might be his one day. Ebenezer had lived there with his two sisters when he was young. Sister Agnes had married and her husband, John, ran the farm whilst the other sister Irene, who was a well-endowed and attractive young lady, acted as housekeeper until her chance of marriage should arrive. Ebenezer set off to travel the world and ended up in Fiji on a coconut plantation. Life was very good for a strapping young bachelor in this Pacific idyll but fate deemed otherwise. He was very surprised, two years later when his sister Irene arrived on the plantation with the tragic news that John, the husband of Agnes, had recently died of consumption and so he must return to work the family homestead. Meanwhile, Irene would stay behind, wind up his affairs and follow him home on the next boat.

Against his better judgement, he returned home and sister Agnes went to live in town. He worked hard initially and the farm flourished. Twice a week he would visit the cattle markets in St Johns or Ramsey, either buying or selling. He was a tall angular man of an outgoing character and loved nothing better than to discuss current affairs or talk of those balmy days in the Pacific. At first he wrote regularly to Irene after she did'nt return at the appointed time. Indeed, he would have been deeply concerned, except that he received a brief note the following Christmas to say that she had made lots of friends and that they need not worry about her. That was the last news of her they ever received although there were a few tales brought back by sailors of a tall, well developed white lady who appeared to be a member of a local tribe!

His chocolate brown bowler hat could always be seen at the Mart, as he stood a good six inches higher than many of the crowd, whilst his deep stentorian voice would have set off the pulpit in the Primitive Methodist Chapel. Each day, after buying and selling he got down to talking with his cronies in the local hostelries and the chat would go on until late in the night, when each man would set off for home rather worse for the wear. Ebenezer would vaguely aim his pony and trap in the direction of home, and realising its responsibilities, the horse would carry him safely along the road, accompanied by the gentle crooning of his inebriated passenger. Sometime early in the morning Ebenezer would struggle up stairs and fall sound asleep.

Of course the next day was required for recuperating and, with two market days and two recuperating days, each week, it only left three working days on the farm. Then of course there was the Sabbath when no self respecting Manxman could consider working, "Six days shalt thou labour". This only left two work days in the week in which to go farming and in this brief time he could'nt repair the gates and hedges and do the ploughing and sowing like his more industrious neighbours. It didn't take many years for the place to fall into rack and ruin. Slates fell off the roofs and rain and snow soon probed their way into the buildings. Eventually, the doors and window frames all fell out and nature took over. In no time the farmyard was taken over by nettles and docks.

It wasn't so much the drink that finished poor Uncle Ebenezer off as the cruel hand of fate that carried him away in the prime of life.

He was riding his pony back from the St Johns Hotel one dark and stormy night when the rain had been pouring down for several hours, after the landlord had called a halt on a particularly good party. As he approached Ballig Bridge he saw lights shining and heard voices singing merrily under the bridge. Intrigued, and more than a little frightened by this phenomenon he rode up to the bridge quietly and peered over the edge, unsure whether it was poachers or the "little people" getting into some mischief. He'd heard tell that spirits and fairy folk were abroad on such nights.

Leaning sideways in the saddle, to get a better look, he slipped on the wet leather, lost his balance and clutching vainly at the horse's mane, tumbled over the parapet of the bridge into the torrent below. Next morning his body was found in the water, downstream, under St Johns Woollen Mills. Of course there was great consternation in the area at the untimely end of one of the local "characters" and there are still people today who won't pass the Ballig Bridge on a stormy night lest the "little people" should throw them into the river.

That is the story that Peter narrated to me and who am I to dispute it! It certainly brightened up a very depressing day, and reminded me that the Manx folk always enjoy telling a good tale to pass the time.

When I arrived back at the surgery, I confessed to Dick Cowley about the damaged   T. B. record sheets."It can't be helped" he replied. " I've tested Peter's herd before and we nearly lost one of the farm workers when he was trampled by a twelve hundredweight bullock. He was lucky that the dung in the shed was fairly soft as he only disappeared beneath the surface for a few seconds. It was a worrying moment but he looked mighty funny when this brown dripping figure stood up in the shed. His mother was a bit vexed as she had to wash his clothes afterwards!"

I was expecting Mrs Corkish to contact me. Next morning she was on the phone promptly at nine o'clock. "Mr Carson! What are these T.B. test sheets meant to represent? Some of them appear to be eaten. They are smeared with black marks and what may also be cow slurry."

"Good morning Mrs Corkish. I'm so glad you 'phoned as I was just about to call you to apologise to your young clerk for the condition of the sheets. Yes, you're quite correct. A friendly cow sampled some of the papers. It was impossible, under the conditions to keep them free of ink marks and I'm afraid that there was a lot of liquid dung in the shed. I have spoken to Mr Cowley and he recalls that his test sheets for Peter Quirk, last year were in a similar condition. However, with Mr Cowley's blessing I'm going to drop a big box of chocolates in for your clerk."

There was a strangled gasp at the other end of phone and the line went dead. I was quite concerned that Josie might have fainted.

# Chapter 30

William Bernstein was a wealthy County Court judge who, periodically managed to escape to the Island from his city chambers. He made such a habit of it that he eventually bought Ballamenaugh farm, which comprised the two farmhouses of Ballamenaugh Vooar and Ballamenaugh Veg, and a hundred acres of south sloping land, beyond the Braaid cross roads.

The big house at Ballamenaugh Vooar was approached by a farm "street" or driveway, from the St Marks road. It could be seen standing out like a white beacon, on the hillside, from several miles away, the farm buildings clustered around, like little chicks around a mother hen, in it's shadow. Beyond them was the smaller Ballamenaugh Veg farmhouse, where John Cretney the farm manager lived. A mature stand of trees, made up of oak, ash and beeches sheltered the house from the prevailing winds, which in the autumn and winter could blow long and hard from the South West. In front of the house the land dropped away to the South, allowing a clear view over Derbyhaven and Castletown.

William Bernstein, or Puffin' Billy as he was known locally, was a larger than life character. Weighing in at just under 20 stone, he loved to dress in an open neck shirt and a ghastly red spotted cravat with one of those navy blue blazers with shiny brass buttons so much loved by the sailing fraternity. True to his nickname, he was normally attached to a large Havana cigar and enclosed in a bluish aura of smoke. He professed to have little knowledge of farming and like so many people who have a great gift with words, had no great liking for anything that might involve physical exertion. One of his great pleasures was to entertain his friends from "across the water" and show them the simple joys of life in the island.

His wife, Audrey, the youngest of five children, had been raised on a farm. Her parents, Roy and Val Kewin had a mixed farm outside Peel and encouraged the children to work on the farm from an early age. She had quietly manoeuvred William into the idea of a house in the island, when they lived in suburbia, and he would return from town in the evening, tired and irritable. Now he was so delighted with the life he confessed to all and sundry that as it had actually been his idea, he had planted the seeds in Audrey's mind. After all, he was trained to be devious! As I swung the Morris 1000 into the farmyard I found it to be deserted, except for a pen of yearlings tucking into their morning feed. In the background I could hear cattle belving after being separated from their calves and a few Rhode Island hens on the top of the dung heap in front of the cow shed, scratched back and forth in search of a tasty morsel.

As I was looking over the shippon door I heard footsteps approaching and a girl of about sixteen years of age, hair streaming, came running round the corner. "Mr Carson, is it?", she said breathlessly, "Sorry to keep you. I'm Ann Cretney. Dad has had to go up to the big house to sort out Mr Bernstein's problems; a blocked drain, probably a gin bottle, as they had a party last weekend!"

She was an attractive young lady with deep, unfathomable brown eyes and a ready smile. Clad in green slacks, a polo neck jersey and a pair of wellingtons, she continued, "I'll give you a hand with the TB test until father comes. He shouldn't be long. Some of the animals are loose but we'll manage all right." I could see that I was going to have a rough time doing the cattle handling and T.B. test single handed whilst this slip of a girl did the book keeping, although I had to confess that she was pleasing to the eye. I had a lot to learn! I thought, momentarily, that perhaps I should postpone the test. John Cretney knew his stock and was well able to handle them.

" I've done the recording before and I've a stool handy to use as a desk. Let's start with the calves", she added in a businesslike manner," I know most of the numbers as I helped Dad tattoo their ears yesterday". I collected all my gear together and in no time we had tested the twenty calves housed in individual pens.

Next, came about a dozen yearlings who were rushing round the shed and trying to climb up walls. I'll swear that they had it all planned just to harass the vet; I gave a sigh of frustration, which was not missed by my assistant.

"Don't worry", she said, "We've worked out a system. If we drive them around the shed, there's a field gate tied to the wall at one end. Pull the other end out, chase a calf in behind the gate and you can jam him there for testing whilst I hold it from behind".

The system worked perfectly. We finished very quickly and then tested the main herd, which were chained up in the shippon. We walked across the yard to the next animal, a newly calved cow in a loosebox. As I entered the door she came at me, shaking her head with a very protective look in her eye. I bowed to her superior weight and slamming the door shut I announced to Ann that we had a problem. She smiled as she opened the latch, saying that Dottie wouldn't hurt a fly, calmly pushed the cow aside with her shoulder and chained her up.

With that little incident over I entered the next loosebox, only to see a large red, frustrated bull with head down, tongue out and deep-set neck arched. He was making a low, deep roaring sound as he pawed his bedding and threw the straw across the box. Slowly turning his head towards me he advanced with body language that said very clearly "I'm the boss here - you little worm!" My deeply ingrained survival instinct forced me to shut the door quickly and slide the bolt. Almost nonchalantly, I turned to Ann and said, "He's awfully big. How did you test him last time?"

"Watch this," she said, and opened the door to be met by the even more menacing top of the bull's head. In one deft movement she slapped him gently across the face, took hold of the ring in his nose and said, "Move over Sausage!" Whereupon, Sausage moved quietly aside whilst she chained him up for me to test.

By this time I was opened mouthed with amazement and admiration at her stock handling skills. "That's incredible, where on earth did you learn that trick."

"What trick?" she replied archly, fixing me with those deep brown eyes. "I just talk to them and they do as I ask. As for old Sausage. He's male and a bit slow but ever so gentle really."

Then I realised that she was a "natural" and did'nt completely realise the unconscious gift of communication that she had with animals. Three hundred years ago she would have been

90

regarded as a witch by simple country folk, who would be frightened by such inexplicable powers. In the Isle of Man, her punishment in those far off days would have been to be carried to the top of Slieu Whallian Mountain. She would then have been incarcerated in a barrel, into which many six-inch nails were driven, and rolled down the mountainside. If, by some odd chance she should be alive at the bottom, she must be a witch and was put to death. A most logical conclusion!

Ann was also a born stockman who had a deep understanding of her animals, which helped her to observe differences in their look and behaviour that indicated the early stages of disease unnoticed by the average observer. Such powers of observation are lost by those stockmen who are too busy to "stand and stare" although I believe that it is a latent gift that many of us possess. We had it drilled into us at college that you must learn to understand the normal before you can recognise the abnormal.

When John Cretney appeared she told him that we had finished the test and that he could take over as she was off to deliver the eggs. I commented on her ability and he told me that she'd always had this uncanny gift of being able to approach any animal without fear and they put complete trust in her. They seemed to accept her gentle discipline. So much for my doubts: with her skills and stockmanship she could go far in farming. I often wondered whether she would lose some of this ability if she were to go to agricultural college and fill her head with ideas of increased yields from stock and crops.

Women had been emancipated during the war years and realised that not only were they capable of working on farms as land girls, but were prepared to run their own units. They have a great feel for livestock and excel over men when it comes to raising young stock. After the war many women stayed on the land as herdswoman and those fortunate enough to have financial support went on to run very successful farms. Gradually, more and more places became available for women at agricultural colleges.

Just as I was preparing to leave, John asked me to have a look at a young cow that had "dropped her slacks" the day before but had made no progress since. In other words the ligaments around the pelvis had slackened off in preparation for calving. He went into the dairy and returned with a pail of warm water and soap whilst I collected my calving apron and ropes.

The cow was tied up opposite the door in the shippon, which was convenient for any helpers to pull at the calving ropes. She looked dejected with her ears flopped and back slightly humped.

"When I brought her in with the herd this morning she had been standing by herself but didn't appear to be getting on with the job", John said in a concerned tone. "She calved down all right last time without any assistance. I hope she's going to be OK as she comes from one of the best family lines".

I scrubbed up and covered my arms with one of the modern obstetrical lubricants that had just been developed. Previously we had always relied on soap and water or the vegetable oils such as linseed or rape. For many years we had made up "Lambing Oils" that consisted of rape oil and phenol, which proved to be life savers for many animals as the untutored

91

stockman, away from home, would insert his arm, including adherent faeces, into the uterus to carry out a delivery. We may squirm at the thought but must remember that we are only a generation away from the time when country doctors still had to carry out surgery on the kitchen table!

Gently inserting my hand into the uterus I could immediately sense that all was not well. I could feel a solid body at my fingertips. All the expected topographical arrangements were absent - no head, toes or even a tail could be felt. Then I realised that the back of the calf was being presented, creating an impossible situation where the calf certainly could not be born. Feeling on either side I eventually located a neck and ear forward in the uterus where the calf's head had turned back on itself instead of ending up in the pelvis.

I turned and looked at John. " It looks like a bit of a problem. I shall have to try and alter the position of the head and legs so they are pointing in the right direction. Probably the calf is dead but I hope that the cow won't suffer too much".

It was'nt an easy job rotating a large calf inside the womb, but the sun was shining warmly on my back, which was a bonus whenever I became tired. I heard voices in the background and then the unmistakable aroma of Havanas drifted past my nostrils. The scent of Havanas was a pleasant change after I'd had my arm inside Belinda's back end for half an hour trying to visualise and manipulate the position of the calf.

"Good morning Ned," came the greeting from the irrepressible Puffin' Billy. "What exactly is the problem with Lady Genevieve? My companion, Bob Collins, a city gent fresh from the fleshpots of London, is quite intrigued to find someone evidently enjoying himself in your unusual position. It's quite rare to see this type of thing in Gray's Inn!" What could I do but join in the banter? I closed my eyes, which is the best way to see which way the calf is lying, in the mind's eye. Feeling rather like an actor in a radio programme, I attempted to project myself to an unseen audience.

" Gentlemen", I extolled," The calf should be aiming to enter this world in a diving position but I think it is dead and the head and legs are facing back, towards the head end of the cow, with the calf's back jammed across her pelvis".

At this point Genevieve strained forcibly, jamming my arm between the calf and the sharp edge of her pelvis. Such was the pressure exerted that I almost waited for my arm to crack. I screamed out in pain, shouting, "God, give me patience!" much to the delight of my audience who guffawed with delight.
"Steady up Ned", chortled Billy. "My friend Mr Collins isn't used to people calling for divine guidance!"

"Don't worry old chap." interjected Bob, thoroughly enjoying the show. "Just the expression that I use in court on occasions after listening to some idiot barrister pontificating,"

"I now have my hand gripping the calf's head and am manoeuvring it up into the pelvis." Yet another scream as she caught my arm again as I reached for the forelegs, which brought more hilarity from the onlookers.

"I say Bob", interjected Billy, "You realise that this is all an act put on for your benefit!"

"It is now facing the right way and I am managing to pull the legs up, into the correct position".

I stood up for a breather whilst I fastened ropes on the calf's feet. Genevieve stood contentedly whilst Ann scratched her ear and whispered words of encouragement.

I turned to John, saying, "Take a hold on this rope and give her a hand. Pull each time she strains and we should soon winkle this one out!"

Genevieve pushed, we pulled and grunted with exertion, as the dead calf slowly eased its way into the world.

Suddenly I heard, "Good Lord, Bob, don't be such an ass. Oh dear, I'm afraid he's bitten the dust and fainted. Typical of these Thespian types, always seeking the limelight. What a lovely story to tell the chaps back in "The Smoke!"

As we finally delivered the calf I turned round to see the middle aged man, with well-tended iron-grey hair and neatly pressed grey flannels, sitting in a rather undignified position and leaning against the cowshed door. He was looking rather green and had a bemused and embarrassed look on his face.

"Sorry for making such a fool of myself. Must be the heat and all that blood and Yukky stuff. Good thing I didn't take up medicine. I'll never live it down when William's around. He's going to dine out on this for months".

We left him sitting on a milking stool, meditating on the joys of country life, whilst we went off to check on Genevieve's welfare.

# Chapter 31

After much excitement on the part of Moira and our respective parents I set off to Formby for our wedding. Unfortunately, I only had one day before our marriage, which was occupied with my best man, Bert, and myself, rushing around frantically making last minute arrangements.

All our family and friends arrived from afar to witness the event and, as the festivities were still twenty-four hours away, it seemed like a good idea to have a couple of drinks together before settling down to the serious business of married life. Once more Rafferty's Law ruled. After a very enjoyable evening with too many well-intentioned friends, Bert and I spent a long time walking the streets of Formby in an endeavour to clear our heads, in preparation for the next day. A good fairy must have been looking after me. I learned next day that the last pint I returned to the waiter contained six whiskies! I wonder how he felt?

The following morning, everything went according to plan. Bright skies prevailed until after the reception, and Moira arrived at the appointed moment. Even through her veil she looked stunning and my heart beat with joy as I realised how lucky I was. I was nervously watching my best man in case he had lost the ring after the previous night's adventures. Despite all my worries I was overwhelmed and comforted by the sight of my beautiful bride beside me. We had a quiet giggle when the vicar, a delightful old bachelor, gave us our marital advice, because we knew the rather sleazy pub where he stayed, in the Isle of Man, during his holidays. With a fleeting smile and twinkling blue eyes he finished his talk by confessing that he too had lived!

Our honeymoon in Cornwall went off perfectly, except for one minor hitch; In the pouring rain, dressed very smartly, I found myself attempting to untwist the wire binding a kipper to the exhaust manifold of my car. Thirty miles out of Liverpool we had been driven out of the car by that penetrating, and never to be forgotten kipper smell.

On our return home we moved temporarily, into a rented cottage in the centre of Peel. It was small and dark, which did'nt affect us greatly, as we were both working all day. I would collect Moira from my parents' house, when I had finished work, as we had no hope of being able to afford a second car. Our first confrontation occurred when I drove home one day, with my mind concentrating on a case I was treating and arrived at the door to find that I had forgotten to collect my wife! After rushing back to Douglas to collect Moira, I had to resort to humble pie once more.

Our landlady had, at some time in the past, acquired a job lot of satin, plus two packets of dye, one orange and the other pink. The orange cushions looked pretty nauseating but slippery pink satin sheets were a challenge for any newly weds!

Several weeks later we heard that "The Priory", Ballaquane, was available to rent, and we went up to inspect it that evening. We were delighted with the house, which had the added bonus of a yard and small garden.

In true Manx style, our milkman called at 8a.m. next morning and wanted to know when we were moving into the new house. News travels fast!

Living twelve miles away from the surgery did have some disadvantages. It often meant that I had a couple of calls on my journey back home after surgery, or that, I had to return to Douglas on my evenings on duty.

The telephone rang one Sunday evening during the early autumn. A rather distressed little boy was calling from Douglas. Could I possibly come quickly as they had a hedgehog that had swallowed a fishhook? I knew very little about hedgehogs, or how to handle them, so I set off with Moira's laughter ringing in my ears. This was not really how I had envisaged veterinary practice during my college days. As I arrived at the house and rang the front door bell. I was taken into the kitchen by the boy, Roderick, and his mother. In a cardboard box at the back door was a rolled up hedgehog, wrapped up in a pink towel in case he was suffering from shock! I picked him up and could see a length of nylon trace, but no head, which was lost in the spiny dell.

Apparently, Roderick had been fishing in one of my old haunts, "The Dubh" pool, and had stood the rod up outside the door with a worm still on the hook. This was an irresistible sight to a hungry hedgehog, who promptly devoured the worm and became hooked in the lip!

Never having handled a hedgehog I was in a quandary as to how I should proceed. I remembered reading somewhere that the average hedgehog had sixteen thousand prickles so I approached this case with great caution. Very carefully and with two extra helpers we wrapped both ends in a towel and exerted enough pressure to unroll him. Having achieved stage one I had to remove the offending hook. It was so sharp that it had penetrated right through the lip and emerged out the other side. I sent Roderick off to fetch a pair of pliers with which I snipped off the barb and managed to remove the body of the hook. After a shot of penicillin and a saucer of milk "Herbie" was released next day, apparently none the worse for his adventure.

Since this first episode I have many times had hedgehogs presented to me that have become tangled in fruit netting. After cutting the little spiny ball out of the net it is much easier to immerse him in a shallow bowl of water. He will immediately uncurl when he can be held gently using gardening gloves.

# Chapter 32

Jack and Joy Kaneen lived in Ballacreggan, on the road to Peel, near St Johns. They were very proud of their farm and kept it looking spick and span. The road walls and houses were always whitewashed and the garden in front of the house was a sea of colour, with bedding plants, roses and a large Cotoneaster spreading along the wall. They had about twenty Shorthorn cows that were their pride and joy and a flock of sixty Cheviot ewes. Jack was a very big, likeable man with a slow country manner and a great love for his way of life. Joy, on the other hand was a thin, hyperactive lady, who never stopped. She was actively involved in Parish and W.I. affairs and no matter how much she ate she could never put on a pound in weight. As John would say, "Slow down my girl. You're so thin that, when you stand sideways on, you look like a kipper!"

Jack and Joy had met at a Young Farmers Inter-Club sports day several years before. He had been taking part in several events and managed to break his collar bone, when Joy, a young staff nurse at Noble's hospital, and representing the Southern club, came to his rescue. Several bunches of flowers later, as so often happens in Y.F.C., a romance developed, and they eventually settled down in the family farm after they were married.

The care of the calves and lambs automatically fell to Joy, and the lambing season saw her out at all hours, helping the ewes with difficult lambings, or bottle feeding a faithful squad of orphan lambs who were constantly at her heels.

"Would you drop in on your way home?" was the message I received from Joy. "I've got a young ram lamb that's all stiff and wobbly and I don't want to lose him."

I had a fair idea what the problem was as soon as I saw the lamb. He was about two weeks old and as Joy put him on the ground he looked like a little rocking horse with stiff legs and froth around his mouth. I gave him a thorough examination and found that as well as being rigid he was unable to open his mouth and held his head back in a stiff and anxious manner.

"I don't much like this Joy," I said, "Your lamb has tetanus or 'lockjaw.' Probably introduced by infection entering the body from contaminated ground, via the navel soon after birth or it can occur with the slow healing wound if you use rubber rings for castration! The prognosis isn't good as he can't suck from his mother, so you could easily lose him."

" I know only too well", replied Joy," I helped to nurse a man who died of the disease several years ago. It was a most distressing case. We used Tetanus antitoxin and antibiotics in hospital for anyone standing on nails or with thorn pricks. Could we treat him? I'm quite happy to feed him with milk from a bottle.

" He couldn't be in better hands," I continued, delighted at the opportunity to follow up an interesting case which other owners might have given up. " There are several problems to overcome. If he can't swallow easily, he could choke unless the milk is administered very slowly. You'll have to inject him with antibiotics twice daily as well as antitoxin and relaxants to control muscle spasms."

Joy perked up at the thought of using her professional skills once more. " Leave it to me.

Just give me a list of instructions to follow. I can keep him in the kitchen and give him lots of attention, particularly when I'm listening to Saturday Night Theatre on the wireless or Book at Bedtime". "Nigel", the lamb held his own for several days, but he had reached the point of no return and died despite our efforts.

The following week Joy had another case, which she noticed at an earlier stage and as a result of her constant nursing, "Matilda" lived. It soon became apparent that the new land on which they were lambing was a "tetanus pasture". On certain land the spores of tetanus can exist for many years. After a further three cases that they managed to save, we injected all the new born lambs with tetanus antitoxin at birth to prevent the disease.

I called in one day to examine a lame cow for John. The cattle were inside all the time as the pastures were not yet ready for grazing. As I walked up the centre passage in the cow shed, between the two rows of cows contentedly munching their hay, I stopped as a heavy sweet smell wafted across my nostrils. Slowly I walked the length of the shed, looking behind the cows, in the dung channel. " You've got a sick cow somewhere John. I can smell it!"

"Can't smell a thing", he replied, "What's it like?"

"Joy's nail polisher remover, acetone", was my immediate response. "My mother has diabetes and I've become very sensitive to it as many diabetics produce it in their breath. Look over here! All the cow's have firm droppings but this one has very firm, shiny dung."

"Well", said John, "You could be right. She's been acting a bit daft and picky with her food during the past couple of days. Look at her now-she just keeps licking the wall. "

"Just watch", I said," whilst I test her milk in this test tube."

 I mixed powder with the milk and carefully added a liquid reagent to the tube. The purple ring that formed between the liquids confirmed my diagnosis that she had "Slow Fever" or acetonaemia".

John cocked his hat on his head, in amazement. " I'm impressed. Chemistry at school was never as interesting as this. Wait'til I get Joy out to look at it!" With that he rushed out into the yard and returned with Joy to demonstrate my bit of scientific magic.

"What causes the problem?" he continued.

"It appears to be a digestive upset after calving", I added, "Possibly tied up with feeding too much concentrated ground nut cake. They're less able to cope with these new, artificial foods than the herbage that nature intended. Give her a pound of treacle in a pint of warm water, as a drench, which should ease her constipation. I'll leave you a "slow fever" drench to give over the next few days. If it was a bit later in the season, I would suggest that you turn her out to grass and 'Dr Green' would cure her in a few days".

Concentrates such as groundnut, cottonseed, linseed and coconut cakes were being increasingly used for cattle feed as a high protein source, after having the oils extracted

97

from them by crushing. Other high protein feeds, such as beans and peas, were added to the protein side of the diet in order to increase milk yields and improve income on the farm. The agricultural advisers, journals and government scientists, were all encouraging farmers to increase their milk yields by scientific feeding, whilst cattle breeders produced bloodlines, particularly in the Friesian breed, aimed at producing greater quantities of milk in each lactation. The increased yields required more high protein foods and digestive problems were occurring more commonly, rather like ourselves eating Christmas pudding every day.

As I was driving out of the yard John stopped me. "I'm a bit concerned over this tetanus, vetin'ry. We seem to have sorted out the problem in the lambs. Does this mean that I shall have to vaccinate all my cows against the disease as well?"

"Not really", I said, "Normally, cows don't appear to be as susceptible as horses, humans and your young lambs, but it does occur. I've seen a couple of cases where rubber castration rings were used in a misguided attempt to dehorn yearlings. It was a very expensive experiment as the young bullocks were in pain and rubbed their heads in the hedge for relief. The wounds all became clogged with soil and he lost all three with lockjaw."

# Chapter 33

The following morning I called at the surgery just as Brian was finishing consultations. "Sorry I can't go on the southern run this morning." He muttered. " Do you remember that we saw Mona Brew's Irish setter, last month, after she swallowed a nylon stocking? She's done it again! Sometimes I feel that Setters are not gifted with a giant intellect! I shall have to operate before lunch but I have a couple of calls to do in Laxey just now. Perhaps you could take care of anything else that comes in."

As I was leaving, I happened to comment on the tetanus cases at Ballacreggan and mentioned that I'd left out a drench for the acetonaemia case.

Brian chuckled, "What colour was it? Red or yellow. Do you recall that we temporarily ran out of red colouring reagent for the drenches last month, and had to resort to the yellow colour. Since then there have been a few bottles of each colour sitting on the shelf. Several farmers have insisted that the "yeller" drench isn't a patch on the red one. It would appear that even our cows are colour conscious or people don't like change!"

My first call was to Jeannie MacTaggart, a delightful Scottish lady, at Ballakinvig. She had a dozen Large White sows and a flock of eighty Suffolk ewes. Her husband was agent for one of the large feed firms and spent most of his day selling on the farms, whilst she stayed at home to do the farming. She was a small woman with dark hair, streaked with silver, and steel grey eyes flecked with brown. She also had a very vital personality as a result of her store of pent up energy. " No." she would say in her lovely Stirlingshire lilt, "I never really had time to be thinkin' of children. Too busy lambing and feeding the pigs!" She used to imagine that I had a passing resemblance to Kenneth More, the film star, which I found very flattering. Half the time she referred to me as Kenneth!

Never despondent, she greeted me on my arrival with, "Och! Kenneth, I think that we may have a wee bitty problem with a couple of gilts. They were'nt very happy when I cast an eye upon them this morning and I fear that they may have 'The Diamonds.'"

Sure enough, as I entered the pen I could see a couple of young sows in the corner, well burrowed beneath the straw. They neither moved nor grunted as I entered which was a fair indication that they weren't very well. Gently sliding my hands over the skin I could feel small raised lumps and in the half-light could see the typical inflamed diamonds, typical of Swine Erysipelas. The thermometer confirmed that they both had high temperatures.

"It's no problem to treat Diamonds with antibiotics and they should be much better in twenty-four hours," I said, turning to Jeannie. "The danger is that erysipelas can leave pigs with heart defects that can result in them dropping dead in advanced pregnancy. You've reared a nice herd, and if you wish to sell gilts for breeding, I'd recommend that you vaccinate them against the disease, twice yearly. Reputations are hard to build up but easy to lose!"

I'd glimpsed Hamish MacDonald, the shepherd on my visits to Ellerslie Farm. His stockmanship was such that he rarely had need of our services. Wherever he went his Border Collie, Floss was at his side, bound to him by a reciprocal understanding.

He was a tall, craggy Highlander with a shock of white hair, shaggy eyebrows and deep-set piercing blue eyes, which appeared to glare down upon lesser mortals, like a Golden eagle surveying his mountain fastness. This assumed fierceness was allayed by his quiet lilting brogue.

In all weathers, he and Floss could be found tending his flock on the tops. Indeed, they were just as much her charges as she seemed to realise if one of the flock was missing and would set off to bring the truant home.

It was a regular sight, during the lambing season, to see him docking the newborn lambs. His tall figure would walk through the flock, stoop and pick up a new born lamb. Grasping it's tail firmly between his large, capable hands, he would rotate the tail at right angles, over a joint, give a sharp sideways movement and the tail would come away to leave a clean bloodless stump. The lamb was so surprised that he felt very little and it was soon forgotten, when he rushed back to suckle his mother.

Carelessly, the tail was thrown over the left shoulder to be expertly fielded by Floss, who had stationed herself in the right place. Every couple of hundred yards the feast would become too much and she would vomit all the tails up again. Refreshed once more she would set off on another tour of tail catching.

Today, Floss was not herself so I had a good feel at her tummy and fortunately she didn't have a stoppage caused by lambs' tails! "Weel," said Hamish, "She's vomiting and having terrible troubles with diarrhoea. What can the matter be?"

After I'd checked her thoroughly, we came to the conclusion that too many lamb's tails had actually created her problem, and that her intestines were scoured with lamb's wool and bits of bone. A few tablets, twenty-four hours starvation and a light broth soon put her on to the road to recovery.

We were discussing the merits of docking after the consultation and Hamish said, "I was ill for some weeks last year and the docking was neglected. As they grew fat in the summer the tails grew and looked very good. Unfortunately, we had a warm wet spell. The grass grew lush and they shot diarrhoea all over their tails. In no time they'd become fly blown and infested with a seething mass of maggots. I had to work very hard to cure them but I should'nt like to see any other lambs go through that suffering."

# Chapter 34

Ballavaish, where Jack Comish farmed, had always been one of my favourite spots. The land swept down from the hills to the gentler climate of the coastal plain where it met the rocky coastline. This was the haunt of the oyster catchers, piping their solitary call and shelducks busily shunting between their feeding ground and nesting sites on the shore. The coastal track between farm and sea was comparatively unused, save for courting couples seeking solitude.

Jack was not the easiest man to get on with. A gaunt and rangy six feet of energy and muscle as a result of fighting the elements over the years. His tanned, weather beaten features reflected the environment in which he lived and worked. The area could be idyllic and hot in summer but in wintertime the wind and rain could beat in incessantly over the rocky shore. He only employed one worker on the farm and expected them to keep up with his pace of work. Consequently, he had a steady turnover of staff as he didn't suffer fools gladly and could be brutally forthright, as I learnt to my cost early on.

"Oh! They've sent a boy to do a man's job, have they?" He grumbled at our first meeting, which once again dropped my self-esteem to an all time low. "Well, come on then. I can't be standing around all day. There's work to be done." I very quickly learnt to roll with the punches even though his manner was sometimes downright offensive.

The tender side of Jack was revealed to me when we met him with his family at the "Mhelliah" or Harvest Fair in Colby. There was this great big man gently escorting his tiny wife and two young boys around the stalls and displays as if they were made of Dresden china. Her every wish was his command. He stopped to introduce his family to Moira and me in a most charming manner. Moira could not believe that this was the hard man whom I had described. I had found his Achilles' heel at last and always made a point of asking after his family when I visited and his whole demeanour would soften.

Jack was a good stockman and had very little call for our veterinary services except for a few calvings and the odd case of "wooden tongue". Wooden tongue disease could be a problem on some farms that fed rolled barley. The spikes or awns on the grain would penetrate the mucous membrane of the mouth and carry the wooden tongue organism into the tissues where it would slowly develop into a series of abscesses, causing a hard, fibrous swelling in the tongue or cheek that felt like a lump of wood. As the infection spread, so the cow would lose the use of its tongue, could neither swallow nor graze and saliva would constantly run from its mouth.

Wooden tongue has been recorded for many years, since farmers started adding the higher protein grains to animal rations, in order to increase milk yields, as a supplement to the hay, turnips and cabbage fed in the winter. Even so, it's possible to develop the same problem when they're grazing on pasture containing wild barley.

Many cures have been used to treat the disease, including painting the tongue with iodine or injecting iodine into the jugular vein. Modern science had progressed and the current treatment was with sulpha drugs.

I had treated several wooden tongue cases during the springtime, and it came as no surprise to me when Jack contacted me one morning, to say that he had another case of wooden tongue in the cheek or possible "lumpy jaw". Lumpy jaw is a similar type of infection affecting the jaw, causing a deformity of the bone, and is virtually untreatable.

As I drove along the track to Ballavaish on this beautiful summer's morning I thought how fortunate I was to live in such a lovely spot doing the job that had been my aim for so many years. The sea was a dazzling blue, inviting all and sundry to come for a swim. I stopped off for a few minutes to watch the antics of a flock of choughs, playing and falling about in the sky like a troop of clowns. Their delightful chirring call is one of the joys of these wilderness places.

Jack was in the yard as I arrived, hopping from foot to foot, like a cat in a bed of nettles. I could almost hear him saying, "I can't wait much longer!" As I stepped out of the car, his border collie,'Jess', dropped a stone on my foot, as an open invitation to come and play. I threw it for her as I followed Jack into the cow shed. A wild-eyed shorthorn heifer was anxiously stomping back and forth in her stall, fed up with waiting as all the other cattle had gone off to pasture.

As she turned to look at us, I could see a large swelling on the side of her face. "It looks like another case, Jack," I said in a concerned tone. "That makes six cases this year. I'll just check her in case it's "lumpy jaw!"

Grabbing the heifer by the nostrils I slipped my hand up inside the mouth, between cheek and teeth. Looking round at Jack, somewhat uncertain of his reaction, I said, "This is one that you can tell your grandchildren about," as I pulled a rubber ball from her mouth.

Watching Jack's normally impassive features, I could see the full range of emotions as he struggled to cope with this new disease problem! Then he opened up and roared with laughter. "Just wait until I tell this to Dorothy. Those little scallywags have been out in the field throwing the ball for Jess.

Several weeks after this event I heard from Jack again. He sounded worried. "Have you got a metal detector, Ned? I think that one of my best milkers has got a nail in her stomach. I saw you operating on John Qualtrough's cow several months ago and this one seems very much the same. Can you have a look at her as she's is not very good!"

I had a word with Brian, and as we were'nt very busy, he suggested that we both went down, with Alan, to operate, if necessary. After Alan had sterilised the instruments and collected the necessary gear, we set off.

Jack was waiting impatiently for us to arrive. " It looks as if this could be my fault," he muttered glumly. " I've been putting down a new floor in the hayloft and a few nails dropped down into the cow shed. Doris has probably picked up a nail in the hayrack or manger."

"Doris" was a large Red and White Friesian cow and was standing in her stall with back arched, grunting spasmodically and looking decidedly unhappy. " She's right off her food, is very constipated and as soon as she lies down appears to be extremely uncomfortable," continued Jack in a despondent tone. His whole body posture suggested his guilt feeling as he stood with drooping shoulders and head hung low.

We checked her heart, lungs and abdomen thoroughly and stood back to watch her. Brian took her temperature and said," It's in cases like this that I wish we had a war surplus metal detector. That must be next on our shopping list! However, there's something about this case that doesn't ring true. How long has she been off her grub?"

"I noticed her first a couple of days ago," replied Jack. The first thing that made me suspicious was when she started losing her cud. I found quite a lot in the manger, which was a bit unusual".

"That alters the picture somewhat," added Brian. "We don't normally see "quidding" or cud dropping with nails but it would strongly suggest that there is a wooden tongue infection in the stomach. Now, I'm in a bit of a quandary as to whether I should treat her with drugs or operate. If there's a nail in the stomach, and we delay too much, she could die if it penetrates the heart!"

" Go inside and have a look," interrupted Jack. " Doris was one of our first cows and we owe it to her to look after her health."

Alan Ramsden broke into the conversation abruptly. " Right, if that's agreed Mr Comish, let's get organised and make things tidy for t' vets to operate. Can we have a couple of straw bales, covered with an old sheet to keep the dust down, that we can use as a table for t' instruments a couple of pails of hot water and some disinfectant, while you're at it?. We must look sharp as we don't want to be too late." Alan's smiling face, broad Yorkshire accent and twinkling blue eyes never seemed to raise offence, no matter how blunt he was.

Jack went off to fetch the bales and water, whilst Alan set to work clipping the hair from Doris's left flank behind the ribs. Brian and I collected all the kit from the car and once Alan had finished we went to work with local anaesthetic to deaden all feeling in the area on which we were going to operate.

At this juncture Jack arrived back with the water and soon we had the operation site shaved and sterilised.

To give her credit, Doris behaved like a real lady and stood like a rock whilst we made the vertical incision behind her ribs. It was a tense couple of minutes as we were'nt entirely sure of the outcome of the operation; would we find the nail that Jack said was in there, or was it going to be wooden tongue? I was standing by with sterile swabs as, with a gentle hiss, the scalpel entered the abdominal cavity, exposing the rumen or first stomach that is large enough to hold seventy gallons. Out of the corner of my eye I could see Jack moving from foot to foot and was'nt surprised when he walked out the door to seek fresh air. The blood dripping from the wound and his emotional tie with Doris were proving too much!

The only sound was Alan's chuckle, "Appen our Jack's not feeling too good! The bigger they are the harder they fall."

"Ned, put your hand in here and feel this," muttered Brian, smiling. " We weren't too far out."

I slipped my hand inside the wound, along the smooth surface of rumen and sure enough, as I drew near the bottom of the gullet, the surface became rough, hard and lumpy-a typical wooden tongue lesion. Extending my arm further forward I could'nt feel any evidence of metal penetrating the stomach wall towards the heart.

At that moment Jack returned, and as we told him the welcome news a great load came off his shoulders. " Thank God for that," he uttered," I thought I'd killed her. Excuse me whilst I go indoors to tell Dorothy the good news."

# Chapter 35

Monday mornings could always become a bit fraught as many people did'nt want to bother the vet on a Sunday for minor problems, and the calls all accumulated on the first day of the week.

I called into the surgery before heading northwards to carry out a small T.B. test for Jim Hudson at Barroose. Despite the fact that he only had ten animals he was never ready on time so I was in no great rush to get away. With a bit of luck I could be finished by ten a.m. and head back to a couple of calls at Patrick, on the west coast.

I casually lifted the receiver as the telephone demanded attention, whilst I was looking over the days work. A north country voice introduced himself as George Skidwell from Cornaa. " Could you come out this mornin' to see our Elsie? She's really poorly and has been throwin' up all morning. My wife, Doris is very upset as she's her special pet - Do yer see what I mean!"

"Hold on Mr Skidwell," I interrupted. "How long has Elsie been vomiting? You've not told me yet whether she's a cat or dog."

"Oh I'm so sorry. Do yer see what I mean? It's because we're so upset about it all. Our Elsie is an Anglo-Nubian goat, one of those with the big floppy ears. We got her last year to keep the grass down on the bank!" I could hear a catch in his voice as if he was almost sobbing. " Do come quickly Mr. Vet as she's so pretty and affectionate and we'd hate to lose her. She's standing there looking so unhappy with her droopy ears and all green around the mouth." This comment was again finished with another "Do yer see what I mean."

My mind was racing as bells rang - Inspiration please Professor Kelly? Goats have very catholic tastes - ranging from clothes pegs to spotted underpants. Then it dawned on me-it sounded like rhododendron poisoning!

"Does Elsie have any opportunity to browse on your garden plants Mr. Skidwell?"

"Not really 'cos we 'ave her tethered on the bank, which is separated from the garden by a dense rhododendron bush. It were getting a bit big so I trimmed it back yesterday and threw a small branch to Elsie as the grass is very short. Do yer see what I mean?"

"That's it." I interrupted his monologue. " She has rhododendron poisoning. Can you get her in a shed out of harm's way and I shall see her within the hour."

At this juncture Brian walked in and glanced at the day's calls. He looked a bit tired and explained that he had been up early on a call and spent some time at the microscope, carrying out a worm count on some dung samples.

"Och, Ned! I know that you had planned to head out west. Could you take on the northern route as I have a small problem to sort out? Anyway, Meg McCall up in Maughold has a lame pony to look at and she thinks that you're such a nice young man."

I always enjoyed going to see Meg, a large vivacious lady with a mop of riotous red hair and a voice that could be heard half a mile away. She was well endowed with common sense and never called without reason. Her husband was first mate on one of the Manx boats so she ran a small riding school to fill in the hours, when he spent most of his time at sea during the summer months. The boat from Douglas to Belfast would often call in at Ramsey en route and as it passed the klaxon would let out a loud blast of greeting. Meg would then pull her red flannel nightshirt up the flagpole in reply. Love knows no boundaries!

"You've persuaded me already Brian but I can't help feeling that you're being a bit devious. Just what is the problem?"

Looking rather abashed, he added. "Yesterday evening, I was called out by Graham Sutherland at Regaby. He had a batch of heifers that weren't thriving and had watery diarrhoea. In addition, the driving rain that we've had this last week didn't help, as they were chilled and unhappy. When I arrived at the farm he'd gone off with the tractor, in the pouring rain, to bring in one animal that was so weak that it could'nt stand up."

I was beginning to relish this story, as I knew the situation. Graham and Vera Sutherland had farmed for several years in Kenya, in the colonial era. Life had been very kind to them. Graham had worked hard and built up a successful farming enterprise with many natives helping him. Vera had led the expatriate existence with servants to do all the work in the house. A carefree life of tennis, croquet and coffee mornings had filled much of her life during the day with exotic dinner parties in the evenings.

After independence, they settled in Regaby where Graham worked all hours to maintain his farm with very little labour. Vera, on the other hand, found that her life had changed greatly. No servants, apart from a cleaner who came in twice a week, and coffee mornings were restricted to a much smaller social circle. She became extremely bored, and filled in her hours, in the isolated farmhouse, listening to the radio and sipping wine.

Brian's voice interrupted my musings. "Vera invited me into the sitting room to await Graham's return, sat me down on the enormous chintz settee and put a glass of whisky in my hand. Her high colour made her look quite attractive and I should have realised it was the 'Gin and It' talking. We chatted animatedly for a while and Vera was complaining that Graham was so busy working that it was a pleasure to talk to an intelligent man like myself."

When Brian noticed that I was chuckling to myself he became quite flustered and his Ulster accent became even more pronounced.

"Anyway," he continued. "The next moment she was along the settee with a rather predatory look on her face. Her voice dropped to a husky Lauren Bacall level and she laid her hand upon my knee. At this point I bailed out and retreated across the room; Graham is a big man to deal with! Next minute she had a hand on my lapel, ready for the kill. Thank God, I looked around and saw the chrysanthemums through the conservatory door. It was decision time! "Oh Vera," I said, "my favourite blooms". D'you mind if I look at them and fled through the door."

I was visualising the scene and had to sit down to wipe the tears from my eyes. "Tell me more or do I have to pay for the final episode?" I intervened, helpless with laughter.

"It's all very well for you," he said, seeing the funny side of it. "I thought I was going to be eaten alive - snapped up in a passionate embrace. There I was rushing from bloom to bloom, a case of sniff and run with a rather tipsy lady staggering in full pursuit. Fortunately for me, the headlights of the tractor lit up the room as I managed to rush out to in the yard."

"It must have made the examination of the yearlings seem a bit of an anticlimax. What were they like?"

"They were looking pretty whisht," added Brian. "All skin and bone so I collected samples to examine for worms and liver fluke. There were no fluke, but the worm egg counts were very high, so I think that you'd better take some worm drenches with you."

# Chapter 36

After my T.B.test I drove up the east coast road, through Laxey towards Cornaa. The sun was well up and the oil smooth sea seemed to stretch endlessly towards the Cumbrian hills in the far distance. Once again I felt that it was good to be alive on such a day and it was a great joy to be working at the vocation of my choice. If only everyone could be so fortunate!

Arriving at George Skidwell's house I found that they had managed to entice Elsie into a little garden shed after much pulling and pushing on their part.

The Skidwells lived in a little grey cottage on the road to Cornaa. The garden sloped away from the back door towards the small stream, laughing and chuckling as it bounced and splashed it's way to the sea.

Elsie was not a happy goat. As George said, "She feels as cold as a frog and keeps looking at her belly as if it hurts!" To prove her point she started vomiting up a green, frothy liquid which contained chewed rhododendron leaves. In a panic, Doris threw her arms around Elsie's neck crying out that she was dying whilst George, who had fed the leaves stood back looking suitably guilty.

I sent Doris off for a blanket and George for a bale of hay to scatter around and make a warm bed. In the meantime, I borrowed an old pop bottle and drenched Elsie with linseed oil, to hurry the toxic leaves out of her bowel.

When Doris returned, we piled hay over Elsie's back and tied the blanket around her to make a nice warm string vest.

There you are," I said, collecting my gear together. !" Fortunately, she has not had too many leaves and with a goat's constitution she should be as right as rain in forty-eight hours."

"Thanks Mr. Vet," said George, realising that I had placated Doris. "We're ever so grateful and won't make that mistake again."

My next stop was to call and see Meg McCall. It has always a pleasant drive down the narrow twisty lanes, through the little hidden valleys and fords, carved out over the centuries by the streams rushing down from the hills. I considered how one little stream could cut out a deep and broad valley over the years and yet the human race with all their inventions could feel so important! I generally paused at the entrance to her driveway. Leaning over the wall I could look for any freshly run sea trout in the stream below.

As I drew into the cobbled yard Meg's Titian red mop peered out of the tack -room door. "Morning Ned! I've got Abbie in the box for you to see her poorly foot. She's an old lady and should know better than to fall into rabbit holes!"

Entering the loose box I watched Abbie contentedly pulling hay out of her net, and resting a rather swollen fetlock. She flinched as I lifted the leg up and manipulated the joint. I could see some bruising on the skin.

"There don't appear to be any broken bones Meg. I'll let you have some liniment to rub into the leg. Only very little walking exercise until I see her next week."

"Thanks, Ned," continued Meg. "I put on a compress with Tincture of Arnica and Witch Hazel last night. This morning I hosed the leg down and now I feel she is a trifle better!"

As I was leaving Meg turned round with an impish smile saying, "I'm glad to hear that you've got rid of your rash. I heard that you were all covered with red spots at the Southern show and that you had a pair of lovely ladies showering you with sympathy. It didn't take long for the story to reach this end of the island."

"Get away with you Meg. It was all in the course of my duty to the sick, lame and lazy!"

At that moment the air was rent by the blast of a ship's klaxon somewhere out at sea. Meg was transformed, "Bye Ned," she yelled and raced up the garden towards the flagpole and her red flannel nightshirt!

# Chapter 37

Regaby Mooar farm lay in the fertile northern plain, between Ramsey and the Point of Ayre. This is essentially an agricultural region interspersed with small villages. The farmhouse was built on the site of a rather splendid mansion that had belonged to Charles Hanson, a loyalist merchant during the Cromwellian era.

Graham Sutherland had spent a considerable sum in restoring the farm to its former glory. It was an imposing, whitewashed building sitting, well rooted and firm at the end of a tree-lined drive. The house was separated from the farmyard by a well-stocked, walled garden. Vera supervised the plot but left much of the work to their full time gardener. Beyond the house, the lawn swept down from the French windows of the sitting room, towards a reed fringed lake. This was Graham's relaxation area where he could fish or wait for the duck flighting in the evening.

Graham was in the yard as I stopped outside the cattle shed. He was grim faced and non too communicative. " I'm glad that you've come because we lost a yearling last night. It's a bad job and I blame myself for sheer negligence. I spoke to Brian earlier and he told me that you were bringing worm drenches. I should have spotted it earlier! We have them all jammed in a shed with a couple of men to scruff them whilst you do the drenching. Anyway I want to speak to you later as I have some concerns about Brian!"

That comment gave me some food for thought as we administered the worm drenches. How much did he know? The cattle were too weak to give much trouble so it did'nt take us long to finish the job.

As we finished Graham said, "Come in and we can talk at leisure over a cup of coffee."

Full of curiosity, I followed him indoors. Was there a problem about last night? Did he suspect a relationship developing between Brian and Vera? I could see myself standing up in court to defend Brian's morality.

I sat down in the kitchen with Graham and Vera. She looked none the worse for the previous evening's escapade, despite Brian's graphic tale. She was still an attractive woman and capable of turning a man's head. Doubts flew into my brain. Was Brian the guilty party? Had he made up the story to cover his tracks? No wonder he landed me with this visit!

"Well," commenced Graham, "We're somewhat concerned about Brian. A thoroughly nice chap but when I met him last night he looked quite pale and anxious. Vera said that she thought that he looked positively ill and poured him a stiff Scotch to help him relax. That's part of the problem of being a widower. All work and no play. He and his late wife, Joy, were inseparable and I feel that he must miss her greatly. I think that what he needs is a good woman to take his mind off his worries!"

"Yes," I replied seriously. "He does work too hard. I must see if we can find someone suitable for him. He's a hard man to please."

I casually glanced across the table to Vera and as our eyes met, for an instant, she pursed her lips and gazed out of the window, possibly wondering how much I really knew.

Later in the day, Brian and I were in the Woodburn Hotel, chatting over a pint as I was'nt yet due to collect Moira from a meeting, in Douglas, before heading home to Peel. "D'you remember treating that old cow for the Misses Corteen at Lower Slieu Whallian, last week?" he commenced.

"Of course. The old girl had a touch of indigestion. She's all right isn't she?" I replied, slightly concerned. I should have been upset if she hadn't improved. I was fond of the two old ladies, who lavished all their concerns on their four cows, all of which were pensioners, somewhere in their late twenties.

Brian laughed. "Yes. They think you're a nice young man. You left them a bottle of medicine, to be given night and morning."

"That's right! It was the 'Stimulant and Cudding Drench.' Their brother, George, was going to give the drenches."

"Don't worry," Brian continued. "She rang me up this morning, highly delighted with the results. It didn't help the cow much, but apparently, her sister, Annie, who is an octogenarian and a bit short sighted, was suffering from constipation. She trundled down the stairs in the middle of the night for some of the medicine given to her by Dr Kelly. In the gaslight, she got hold of Daisy the cow's medicine by mistake and took a teaspoonful of it. She thought it tasted a bit funny but ever since then her "bowels is back to normal" and she feels ten years younger. Of course, because the drench contained strychnine, (which is a bowel and nerve stimulant in small doses), she felt great. If she'd taken a quarter of the bottle as is written on the label we could have been attending her wake."

"What a lovely story," I said. "Now I've got one for you. I called in at Ballasalla Mart today and met up with Henry Maddrell from the Eary Stane. You realise that every day with Henry is a Monday morning and life generally is ever so depressing. I thought I would cheer up his day and asked him if he was pleased with his cows since we dehorned them."

"Not very good," he said, fixing me with his "Why is life against me?" look. "They've dropped right down in their milk butter fat levels. You should have told me that they stored the butterfat in their horns. "

"Don't believe it, "I said. "Where on earth did you hear that story?"

"Oh, it's quite true. The fella's in the market told me!"

"It took me some time to persuade him that increasing their hay ration might solve the problem!"

I only heard later that a gang of drovers in the market had been stirring him up in the hope of getting a smile from him?"

# Chapter 37

It was August Bank holiday weekend, and Moira and I had spent a blissful Sunday afternoon having a barbecue on Gansey Beach with friends, and as we headed homewards the sun was slowly dropping down in the west. It was one of those glorious evenings with a golden light bringing a glow to the countryside and, as the dusk advanced the western sky was alive with pink and mauve embraced between the clouds and the majestic sweep of Cronk-ny-Arrey- Laa, a mountain that lived up to its name as 'Hill of the Rising Sun.' I stopped the car and we sat silently savouring the fleeting and magical moments. God was in his heaven and all was right with the world!

The telephone was ringing as we arrived back at the house, and I rushed inside, fully expecting to hear my brother-in-law announcing the arrival of their imminent baby. However, Brian's disembodied voice on the phone sounded very serious. " Ned, can you look after things in the morning if we're busy. I've not stopped all day and should be back on the farm soon after seven a.m. I'm fairly whacked now and would like to pass the phone to you tonight."

"Of course. What's the problem?" I replied, sensing the urgency in his voice.

"Walter Mylchreest at Ballaglanna has big problems. I went in to see him yesterday morning as he had a couple of his purebred Angus heifers off colour. When I saw him they were grunting, constipated and showing signs of colic. I suspected that they'd been poisoned and gave them both a purgative when, he told me that they'd been in a field where they'd been cleaning out ditches where there was hemlock growing."

"Was it hemlock or water dropwort?" I queried.

"That was my initial thought. I wish it had been," he continued. "I called back on my way from Castletown and we walked the riverside fields that they were ranging over. There was no sign of hemlock that had been grazed but there were two more cases-one completely blind and the other standing with its head in the hedge. Then, we found that they'd broken into the adjoining field with the yearlings!"

"Go on," I said, intrigued.

"We didn't have to go far. Walter had an old bus in the field that he used as a turkey house. It had a canvas roof that had deteriorated with age and the cows started licking at it and tearing off strips. Of course, cattle being curious by nature, they were all at it and chewing the material that was impregnated with white lead."

"What a disaster! A pity I wasn't at home to assist. Are there any fatalities?"

"Yes." said Brian, "I've just come from the farm. Six cows dead and quite a few more were ill. I carried out a post mortem at the knackers and found quite a bit of material in the stomach. As you know, a small amount of lead can be fatal! Our problem now is that we're running out of Epsom salts to treat them. The poisoning was so acute that the initial symptoms masked the classical signs of lead poisoning. I feel guilty that I hadn't spotted it quicker"

112

I joined Brian on the farm very early next morning. It was a heartbreaking scene. Eight more yearlings had died during the night, despite anaesthesia to control their convulsions. There were bodies lying in the loose box and the cow house. Three or four yearlings were recumbent on the ground, going in and out of convulsions, and a couple of heifers blundering sightlessly around the yard.

We felt so helpless! All one could do in that era was to attempt to neutralise the lead with magnesium salts and hope that the purging effect would remove some of the lead present in the gut. It was acutely distressing for us to watch these animals die and even worse for Walter to look on, despairingly, as the knacker's truck carried away twenty-two of his animals.

Walter had worked for years to develop a successful building firm but his aim had always been to return to his childhood roots and farm in his retirement. He had built up this herd from eight cows and a bull and then had to watch fifty per cent of his herd die within two days. He was fortunate to still be in business and young enough to rebuild from scratch. We headed for home in silence, having learnt a hard lesson on the dangers lurking around the farm. Looking at this incident retrospectively sets me thinking on what might have been the success rate if the incident had occurred 20 years later with the benefit of modern drugs.

His problem was not so much that his farming was slipshod as the fact that many farmers were opportunist as they had come through very bad times. The offer of an old bus, for next to nothing, was looked upon as manna from heaven and a lot cheaper than building a specialised turkey house.

People in those times did'nt suspect everything that they touched as being tainted, and certainly would'nt have considered that the roof was impregnated with lead. They had a much healthier outlook on life as they were'nt bombarded daily, by the media, with depressing news about the dangers of resistant bacteria, salmonella, BSE and the many problems facing mankind. There can be a very real danger in rapid communications. If we can stand back and look at these situations from a distance, they often fall into context as being almost insignificant.

I often recall helping my father make up the death statistics for Douglas. I used to wonder why so many people died of heart attacks. The answer was not hard to find. Medical knowledge was much less sophisticated and if the death could'nt have a label such as cancer, pneumonia or a ruptured ulcer, then it became a heart attack or natural causes. After all, we all have to die of something!

# Chapter 38

One of the periodic outbreaks of canine distemper was affecting the dog population on the island. Quite a few owners were now starting to vaccinate their dogs to prevent the disease, although, for many people, such a luxury was beyond their pockets. Now, a new variation of distemper, called Hardpad, was making its presence felt, and vaccines were adapted to counter this new threat. It was so called because the pads of the feet became very hard to touch and it was possible to hear the animal walking across the floor.

It all started with Mary Cowley arriving in the surgery with Jane, her young and very vivacious Golden Cocker spaniel. Mary Cowley had limited means and supplemented her war widows pension by doing dress making at home. She'd found it a struggle to raise two children and keep a dog, which accounted for the fact that Sally was not vaccinated.

"Good morning, Mr Carson," she greeted me in the consulting room, "I'm afraid we have a little problem with Jane. She seems to have caught a bit of a cold and is right off her food. She's just not like herself at all."

As I lifted Jane onto the examination table I could see that she was not very well. Her temperature was raised, eyes and nose discharging, and she looked very unhappy as she peered at me through her extremely inflamed and painful eyes. I felt the glands in her throat, which were quite enlarged, and she winced in pain and started to cough spasmodically.

" Things aren't looking to good for this young lady", I said, seriously. "It looks very like distemper to me. I'll treat her with antibiotics, which will deal only with the secondary infections, and we must hope that the distemper virus will be dealt with by the antiserum, which I'll give her. Meanwhile, much of the cure will be in your nursing. Spoon-feed her with nourishing foods like calf's foot jelly and chicken broth every hour. Also keep giving her teaspoons of glycerine and honey to ease her throat. Fortunately, there is no diarrhoea or vomiting - so far!"

Mary accepted the situation in a very common-sense manner. "Poor little Jane, we'll look after you. Fortunately, I work from home and I can use some of my nursing training from the war years. I presume that you'll want me to isolate her and keep her in the garden, like Mrs. Teare, who lives in the house opposite to me, had do with her dog?"

"Absolutely right." I replied, "Can I see her in a couple of days? Out of surgery hours to avoid spreading the disease."

As soon as Mary left, Alan and I got down to sterilising the surgery and consulting rooms, until the premises stank of Jeyes fluid and Dettol. "Pity", said Alan, "Remember the outbreak some years ago, when your dogs got it? Poor old Sally nearly died and went paralysed in her back end. It were only yer mother working hard wi' physiotherapy that set her up on her legs again. She's all right now isn't she?"

"Yes", I said, "Bright as a button, thanks to Brian's hard work. Her brother Shaun is also much better but he's been left with mental problems!"

When Jane came to see me two days later she was a bit better and the cough was less frequent but she'd started diarrhoea, which could result in dehydration and death. At this period in the mid fifties we were not equipped with intravenous drips to combat fluid loss. As a rapid result was required, we gave Jane regular doses of catechu and kaolin to stop the diarrhoea. This was so successful that within two weeks she was showing signs of improvement. Of course Mary was delighted but I warned her, from my own experience that anytime during the next six weeks she could develop nervous symptoms.

Word of the distemper outbreak spread rapidly, which meant that we had to hold extra clinics to vaccinate the dogs of those people fortunate enough to be able to afford such a luxury.

After a year in practice I was beginning to appreciate, more fully, just what it takes to make a good Veterinary practitioner. Apart from a strong degree of compassion for your fellow animals, one must be, above all, a good communicator with both animals and people. Many of the intellectual high flyers, whom I'd met in my college course, were destined for research or teaching posts. They could not cope with the vagaries of clients or animals, and found it difficult to translate technical conditions to the language of the layman. It appeared to me that the more highly educated they became the less able were they to cope with basic problems. I had always been concerned that students in veterinary college were being lectured by some graduates who had never spent any time in practice.

We all had to develop our own technique of coping with animals, as very few of us had the "gift" of Ann Cretney. I've always talked to my patients and owners quietly, and they accept this approach. Going in to them without warning, as I had done when testing the Galloways, is a recipe for disaster, and shouting and rushing around only produces an awful lot of cow dung! Likewise, direct eye contact can make a lot of animals very fearful.

I learned to sit on the floor and chat with my small animal patients, in preference to standing over them in a dominating manner that they regard as threatening. I found their reactions were a response to my initial approach. A hand descending from above was a threat, until a relationship had developed, whilst a palm coming up from below is submissive and friendly.

In my father's medical consulting room, the wall was covered with photographs of children (referred to by my mother as his illegitimates!), and there were tanks full of tropical fish to distract worried youngsters. He always had a drawer full of toys and a bottle of jelly babies.

Taking a leaf from his book, I've always found that a yeast tablet or treat makes all the difference to my patients. So much so that several dogs have tried to mug me for their rewards before being examined! The walls of the waiting room have a Rogue's Gallery, covered with photographs of everything from pampered Persian pussies to geese!

# Chapter 39

Eddie Christian was a baker by trade and a farmer by inclination. The second son of Willie Christian, who farmed at Ballakirkaugh, he had to find a job, as the smallholding could only support one family. Eventually he became a bake house assistant.

After a few years he started his own bakery, with the added bonus of having his sister, Voirrey, acting as housekeeper and general dogsbody in the bake house. This enabled Eddie to indulge in his true passion of rearing sheep. Each evening, after tea he would wander up to his thirty acre holding and potter around in his rickety old galvanised sheds, which were the headquarters of his farming empire. Of course, if he should find any problems, there was nothing easier than to pop down the road to the vetinry's house for advice or medicine. In spite of "the vetinry" trying to hide in the workshop, pub, or in the neighbour's house, Eddie's unerring instinct would find him and completely ruin his evening off duty. On a nuisance basis he scored seven out of ten. However, I couldn't help liking this jolly, little round man, who constantly bubbled with good humour and was always ready to be a good neighbour.

I was dreaming that the front door bell kept ringing, and I would rush to answer it, and there was nobody there. Several times the bell sounded, and I was becoming quite irritated, until suddenly I awoke as Moira cracked me sharply in the ribs with her elbow and brought me back to the real world. Moira made noises, which translated as "You go, *my* friends don't call at this hour!" As I staggered out of bed, the cold air caught me in its icy grip and I thought, "God! It can't be happening to me after the party last night."

I staggered to the window as the bell shrilled more demandingly than before. As I opened the casement, snow showered over me, followed by a sharp blast of arctic air. Summoning up my best professional manner, I stuck my head out into the gale and said,"Ugh! Who's that?"

I could just see an amorphous black shape, silhouetted against the white pathway, from which emanated Eddie's high pitched and squeaky voice. "Sorry, to disturb you, Ned. I've got a two-tooth ewe lambing, up the road, and the lamb's all twisted up. She's not far away. Can you help me?"

I mumbled, through my haze, "Down 'a minit," quietly condemning all late night shepherds to eternal flames. With teeth chattering, I pulled on my shirt and trousers on the top of my pyjamas to maintain some semblance of circulation, stubbed my toe on the foot of the bed and walked into the door, which miraculously, had not opened of its own accord. As I left the room a voice from under the blankets, murmured, "I'm glad I'm not a vet!" Heartless wench!

Clad in my waterproofs and boots, I found Eddie, sheltering under the porch, and gruffly suggested that he found himself a wife instead of wandering abroad at two o'clock in the morning.

"Follow me," he said, chuckling. "You'll really appreciate getting back into a nice warm bed."

It took five minutes to drive a hundred yards up the road to his sheds, which were rattling and banging in the gale. As we went inside, he lit the Tilley lamp and apologised, "Sorry I couldn't get her in off the hill but she won't walk. I've got some soap and a pail of cold water, so if you get your gear together, it's only across a couple of fields."

"Dear Lord. Why me?"

As we struggled against the blizzard, I was once again asking my maker what I had done to deserve being out on the hillside with an idiot farmer and a ewe, that would probably have lambed when I got there.

"She should be hereabouts, unless she's moved," came the disembodied voice in the dark. "I think I left her under the lee of this furze bush. Ah! Here we are, she's moved up onto the open hillside!"

As I knelt down in the snow beside the ewe I could see a leg protruding from her nether end. No sign of another leg or head. She was just lying down cold and exhausted. I then realised that I was a bit overdressed for the occasion and took off my waterproof jacket, thankful for the next line of defence, my heavy Donegal wool jersey. I found that soap didn't froth much with freezing cold water as I eased my hand into her womb. She had a very narrow pelvis, which complicated the situation, and the lamb's head was turned so far back that I could hardly reach the nose.

"We have a problem, Eddie. I think that the lamb has changed her mind and doesn't want to come out in the cold. I'm going to have to strip off to get at her head. Have you got a piece of binder twine to use as a head rope?"

Reluctantly, I stripped off to my rolled up shirtsleeves and started to shiver as the incessant cold probed its way into my bones and muscles. Eddy was holding the ewe as I looped the cord around the lamb's head, and gently pulled at the other end as I eased its head around to face the right way. Once that was achieved I gratefully slipped my freezing hand back into the warmth of her body and fastened another cord around the missing leg, which was bent at the knee. Two legs and a sizeable head required a lot of pressure to slide through the pelvis, and as the front parts of the lamb appeared he took a deep gasp in the cold air, which to me, made the privations of his birth worth it.

I gathered up my gear and the lamb in my arms and said to Eddie, "I've done all the work so far. You carry the ewe into the shed and we can give them a dry night."

I crept into bed at three a.m., after a wash; satisfied, cold and exhausted. I never did get a satisfactory explanation from Moira why she screamed, irately, as I tried to warm my frozen feet on her back! Sometimes I feel that the gentle sex are slightly intolerant!

Next morning, I looked at the devastation at the back door. Jersey, shirt and pyjamas lagged with mud, blood and yuk! Who'd be a vet's wife when he arrived back with all such mucky clothing to wash, sometimes twice a day?

It took me an hour to get into Douglas next morning through the winter wonderland. The sun was bright in the sky, causing myriad sequins to sparkle off the snow covered boughs and fields. There had been about four inches of snowfall but fortunately there were few cars on the road to become casualties of the weather.

As I drove slowly through the snow, I pondered on the problems that must face the new wives of vets in practice. The whole way of life must come as a rude shock. Moira had lived as an independent person for many years. Now she had been plunged into a life where she was on telephone call at home every other night, including weekends. This included receiving client calls, often in a strange dialect, using different expressions. She was meant to be able to instantly know that a cow "with her bed out" (a prolapsed uterus) was much more urgent than one that was "troublesome" i. e. in oestrus. From these messages she had to assess how urgent the case was and comfort the anxious owner until someone arrived on their premises. There was no such thing as car radio telephone to keep in contact although each village had a telephone box for us to call in after finishing the round and as few farms had the luxury of a telephone. Even when we were having dinner with friends, when I was off duty, I felt jumpy every time that the telephone rang.

After a busy day at work Moira would return home to prepare the evening meal, not really knowing when I would return to eat it. The midday meal has always been a moveable feast, which was generally started and finished in the span of twenty minutes before I departed again.

Coping with washing was also a nightmare. Sometimes I'd require a change of clothing each day. My clothing and overalls would smell very strongly of the farm and it all had to be washed by hand. The next problem was clothes drying in houses with no central heating or hanging space. Drying clothes, hung on the clotheshorse, in front of the fire, until the advent of the electric Flatley dryer.

The associated smells must be one of the most formidable challenges to overcome as a veterinary wife. Everyone is aware of the "hospital" aroma that lingers around the veterinary surgery and permeates the cars. Unusual, but not obnoxious.

To me, the most objectionable smell is the unforgettable, won't go away odour, of an "over ripe" cow's afterbirth that we're regularly called upon to remove. It's imbued with the gift of penetrating several layers of skin, taking up residence in the hair and hiding in every little crevasse and fingernail on the victim.

When I first graduated, there were no arm length plastic sleeves and obstetrical capes to provide protection. Calvings and afterbirth removal were carried out with bare arms and torso, using a rubber apron to give some shelter from any rear end discharges.
Consequently, I had an important smell disposal problem, which could only be achieved by dint of repeated baths and much scrubbing.

I felt that we'd made a great advance in the afterbirth or "cleansing" field when we replaced our acriflavine uterine pessaries with some made of iodoform. These masked the afterbirth smell admirably and left another strong smell, slightly less repellent. Gradually with the introduction of protective clothing and new deodorants this has ceased to be a problem. A great excitement of veterinary life is the uncertainty as to when you're next due to become a social leper!.

# Chapter 40

One of the saddest problems affecting cattle in my earlier years was "summer mastitis." Our main problem was to save their lives. The existing antibiotic, penicillin, and the new wonder drug 'streptomycin' were of little avail until aureomycin arrived and even that was only partly effective. It generally affected 'dry' (as opposed to milking) cows and heifers when the weather was humid. It was caused by a germ that resulted in nasty abscesses throughout the udder and several other bugs would join in to make a toxic cocktail. The udder became hard, inflamed and very painful, and all that could be extracted from it was a bloody serum or thick cheesy clots. The stench was atrocious and it produced lots of toxins that might kill fifty per cent of affected animals.

One of the first cases I encountered in practice, was at Alan Kermode's farm at Kerra Beg, up behind Grenaby. The last two months of June had been hot and humid. Ideal weather for holidaymakers. Douglas and Ramsey were seething with people. Driving had become a problem. The roads were full of coaches taking people on "Mystery Tours." By the end of two weeks on the Island they must have run out of mysteries to tour.

Alan had left the family farm in Santon about a year before and set up on thirty acres at Kerra Beg. It wasn't really much of a place, and hadn't been updated for forty years when the last occupant had moved in.

It had previously belonged to Charlie Moore, an old bachelor cousin of his mother. He had settled down on the farm with his new bride, Kate, soon after the First World War but it was a lonely existence for an extrovert young girl. Charlie was not very gifted with 'get up and go', so eventually it was Kate who got up and went, by running away with Tommy Costain, a fisherman from Port St. Mary.

Now, Charlie was quite upset about the whole business and resolved not to trust another woman again. He devoted the rest of his life to rearing pigs and sheep and became well known in the south of the island for his sheep dogs. Most days he could be seen out working his dogs and bringing on youngsters for sale in the Ballasalla mart. He enjoyed his own company and apart from his skill with sheep dogs very few people knew much about him. After a day in the market he always stopped for a pint and pipeful of tobacco before returning home but rarely joined in the general farming gossip, just preferring to sit and listen.

He was happy in his own way. He had his own plot beside the house where he grew potatoes and vegetables. For a change he would buy himself a few herrings to go with his spuds, otherwise it was mostly eggs from his chickens, which he kept in a derelict shed in the yard. Eventually, he acknowledged the ravages of arthritis and retired to a cottage in Colby.

When Alan took over the farm he found it needed a lot of work to bring it up to standard. Not that the place was falling to pieces. It just needed all the floors and windows replacing if Alan was to settle down with a family.

The sheds were just the same. Cobbled floors in the stables with very tired partitions and mangers that had run their span. The swallow's nests under the eaves were the only signs of modern building.

119

Since moving in, Alan had worked hard to make the house comfortable and had converted the old stables into a cow house to hold eight animals. He'd even installed a vacuum line so that he could milk by machine instead of the laborious business of hand milking!

When I arrived he was working in the yard converting one of the old pig pens into a calf house. He put down his tools and came over to the car. "I'm glad to see you, Ned. It's one of my two Friesian heifers I was hoping to milk. She's not due to calve until October, but is really off colour with mastitis. It looks like the summer mastitis case that father lost last year. I've managed to tie her up in the shippon."

As we entered, I could see that Alan had made a good job of the cow shed. The walls had all been whitewashed and the standings and partitions rendered in concrete.

The heifer was standing, uncomfortably with ears drooped and hind leg held out sideways to ease her painful udder. As I drew the bloody serum and one or two thick, cheesy clots, from the teat she winced in pain, although she was much too stiff to kick at me. The udder was so hard and inflamed that I didn't really need a thermometer to tell me she had a high temperature.

" You're right, Alan. It's summer mastitis, sure enough. You've got a very sick heifer here. Her nose is dry and she's sunken-eyed; also she's becoming toxic and dehydrated. If you're prepared to work on her we may have a fifty per cent chance of keeping her alive!"

" Look at it this way," Alan replied. " She represents ten per cent of my investment in this farm. I couldn't leave her in this state, looking so miserable. What else can I do? I've already rubbed embrocation into the udder and given her some ivy to eat but she's not very keen."

"First of all," I suggested. " Get her into a loose box with a good bed of straw. I would like you to massage her quarter with udder cream every hour if possible. Milk her into a pail of Jeye's fluid to prevent the spread of infection. Always have a pail of drinking water available, with a couple of handfuls of salt in it, and encourage her to drink. Feed her lush grass and greens if she'll take them. I'll inject her this morning and call in tomorrow. Can you give me a ring at five p.m. today?"

As I drove on to my next call, I felt a bit depressed, both for the plight of the heifer and also for Alan, who was struggling to build up his herd. I resolved to read up the latest information when I returned home. Looking back on the situation forty years later I can realise how much our knowledge and treatment of the condition has improved.

My next call was to examine a cow that was starting to calve. The cow belonged to Andrew Anderson, who had just returned from farming in Africa. Just in case he missed his life in the bush he'd brought some of it back with him. He would wander around the farm in company with his pet chimpanzee, George, who fancied himself as a trainee cattle dog. It was'nt unusual to meet the occasional ibis or stork as I entered the yard, or even George, who loved sitting on the warm car bonnet. Rumour had it that he also had a vivarium full of snakes in the house although fortunately we were never called to treat any cobras or mambas.

Andrew and his farm manager met me in the yard and took me into the large airy cowshed where the cow was standing with a calf's head and legs already protruding from her rear end.

"Sorry, to drag you out," said Andrew, "But the old girl has been messing around all morning and everything is happening in slow motion. I'm afraid that we might lose the calf. She has calved uneventfully about five times already."

I brought in my calving apron, pessaries and a large tube of the latest obstetrical lubricant, which I placed in the windowsill. After scrubbing up and smearing my arms with the lubricant, I examined the cow and calf. There was no obstruction, so after fixing ropes on the calf's feet we started pulling gently to ease it out of the pelvis. At this stage, I felt a splash on the side of my face and wiped it away, presuming that it was condensation from the roof. Again it happened and I looked upwards. There was George, the chimp, sitting on the roof trusses, with a happy smile on his face, squeezing all my super-duper hi-tech lubricant out of the tube onto the workers below.

It was an unusual farming scene as the calf entered the world. A chimp jumping up and down on the trusses and screaming with delight, Andrew was shouting some very unkind words in Swahili, (which I understood indicated that George would very soon end up as monkey stew,) whilst we just sat on a straw bale roaring with laughter.

Once things had settled down and I accepted the loss of my lubricant, I set to work and examined the cow further to investigate why she was so slow about calving. She was starting with the early stages of milk fever and recovered very rapidly after a calcium injection.

As Andrew and I watched the cow, now fully recovered from her milk fever, she inspected the calf, cautiously at first. The new-born calf lay on the straw, looking very pathetic with drooping ears and matted coat. He kept snorting through his flared nostrils in order to clear his airway of clogging mucous, and take in the life giving air. The eyes appeared to be inordinately large as the head appeared smaller when the entire coat was wet.

After a few preliminary sniffs the cow commenced to lick the calf all over, caressing it roughly with her abrasive tongue. Navel, bottom and tongue were all subject to her compulsive licking, stimulating the calf into action. Soon he raised his head to examine this strange new world and after a little while he sat up on his chest, flexing his limbs in preparation for the next stage of life. Having orientated himself, the rear end was launched up in the air and after some hesitation, and a bit of scrabbling he stood up on all four feet. Rather Bambi-like, with legs sliding in all directions he eventually tottered around, gradually becoming more balanced.

Having achieved stability he obeyed the most basic rule of life, a search for food. That innate drive forced him to move into the shadow of the cow, seek a teat, and announce his arrival with a dunt of the head into his mother's udder. At this stimulus, and the suckling motions of the calf, she let down her colostrum or first milk, for his initial feed.

The colostrum or "beastings", as it is termed contains high levels of nourishment and antibodies so essential for the existence of the calf. This first drink must take place within six hours of birth after which the calf 's stomach is unable to absorb much of the antibodies.

"This bonding process between cow and calf always leaves me slightly in awe and full of wonder," said Andrew. "It is pure instinct and a delight to watch the reaction of the calf. How does he know where to find the teat and start suckling, without a book of instructions?

I've seen exactly the same reaction with giraffe and elephant calves in the bush."

"It's all imprinted, somewhere in the brain," I replied. " I get a kick out of every birth. Somewhere, there's a great template in the sky, which tells them what to do."

# Chapter 41

At about this time the island was suffering from an influx of overseas repatriates as colonial independence progressed.

The Manx people normally classified the new residents from the U.K. as "Come Overs". After centuries of being occupied by Vikings, the other Celtic nations and the English, and yet maintaining their own identity, all foreigners have to carry a label. Many of these ex-colonials had lived the good life and were accustomed to entertaining and jolly parties. They quickly became known as the "When I's" and the "Whatillyuse", which is a loose translation from "When I was in Kenya" and "What'll you have old boy?" Many of these immigrants stayed on and became part of the community whilst others could not cope with our slow pace of life and returned to their own native soil, where things appeared to be much better.

It was a rainy Sunday morning and I'd just returned from a couple of rather hectic farm calls, which left me with a distinct farm-side aroma. I was enjoying a well-earned cup of coffee and looking forward to an early lunch, when the phone interrupted my reverie.

"Good morning. Is that the veterinary surgery? Dorothy Willman-Jones speaking," came the rather demanding and imperious enquiry.

"Good morning, Ned Carson speaking, can I help you?"

" Oh! Good morning, Mr. Carson. Do you know anything about dogs?"

I was somewhat taken aback by this rather ill-mannered assault on my dignity and could only reply, "Yes, madam. Of course. I am a well-known authority!"

" Thank goodness, Mr Carson. I am so desperately worried about darling Mitzi, my little cairn terrier. Could you come and see her for me?"

Always willing, I replied, "Certainly Mrs. Willman-Jones. I'll call in on my way home, later this morning. What is the problem with Mitzi?" In my mind I was visualising Mitzi gasping her last breath.

"Oh! She's been scratching for several days and is so distressed poor little baby. She has such tender skin that I am afraid that she will bruise badly. I would be so grateful if you could come."

Realising I'd been caught out I tried to excuse myself on the basis of my smelly clothes but she would have none of it and was most insistent that I should call.

Dotty W-J, as she was known, lived in a rather nice house in a select area of Douglas. The house was one of eight large pebble dashed houses built in the nineteen thirties. At that time it was very avant-garde to live in a four bed roomed house with a large bow window, fitted with a metal framed casement, looking out onto a well manicured lawn. She was the widow of a Vice-Admiral, who'd gone down with all hands in mid-Atlantic. I drove slowly from the surgery, delaying the confrontation as long as possible. I was still feeling somewhat affronted and trying to work out my best approach to the situation. I had difficulty in finding a parking spot in the crowd of vehicles parked in the road. Evidently, it was "drinkies time" on the avenue and the socially elite had gathered together for the festivities that could probably have been heard a mile away.

The door was open but the doorbell could not compete with the noise. A navy blue blazered type, complete with "Wizard Prang" moustache, wandered through the hallway, carrying a cocktail glass. "Come in," he said. "Are you the vet? Dotty's expecting you, old chap"

I was ushered into the kitchen, where Dotty was pouring gin into a large bowl full of a reddish liquor and tossing in Marachino cherries after it. A voluminous, beautifully coiffured lady, with wide blue eyes and bottle blonde hair, she looked unforgettable in a large floral dress, adorned with enormous, predatory looking, purple clematis clawing their way over her ample bosom. In her frightfully plummy accent, she burbled, "How nice to see you Mr. Carson. Mitzi is hoovering up the potato crisps in the front room. Reggie, darling, can you finish mixing the witch's brew?"

" Shall we look at her in the peace and quiet of the kitchen, Mrs Willman-Jones. I'm not really dressed for a party," I muttered.

"Oh. Don't worry," she replied in a patronising manner. "We have one or two friends in for cocktails so you must be my guest."

Feeling very self conscious, and aware of my accompanying aura, I followed her into the front room. She bulldozed her way through the crowded room, calling, in a rich soprano, "Mitzi, Mitzi, darling."

A rather chubby little cairn, veteran of many cocktail parties, emerged from the crowd, still chewing a couple of potato crisps. She exhibited the resigned demeanour of one who had so far, survived the overbearing attitude of her owner. She was instantly scooped up by Dotty and thrust into my arms.

I knelt down on the floor, still holding Mitzi, making the examination easier for both of us. We shared a small oasis in an everchanging sea of legs and chatter. I felt rather like a sardine drifting in the ebb and flow of a restless tide. No one was taking any notice of us, and from that level I had the opportunity to have a cairn's eye view of a cocktail party.

We were surrounded by trousers of many hues, from the knife-edge navy pin stripes to rough, matter of fact tweeds that must have belonged to a pipe smoker. I wondered whether all the mirror-like "spit and polish" shoes belonged to ex-army types. Undoubtedly, the RAF johnnies would be dressed in suede and brogues, possibly might even belong to country types such as tea-planters!

Ladies' legs kept moving around our world, all clad in sheer hose with shoes to match the outfit of the day. I was studying the legs, which came in all shapes and sizes. There were skinny legs, hockey legs, elegant and stumpy legs. Then a pair of legs hove into view, which instantly brought an Irish country expression to mind - "Beef to the heels like a Mullingar heifer!". I raised my eyes and sure enough they belonged to Dotty!

Hastily, I turned my attention to Mitzi, who looked at me as if to say, "For goodness sake, don't leave me with this lot!" I carefully checked her belly, anal glands and back but as I reached the head and neck I found the culprit!

Dotty's voice intervened and a pink coloured cocktail, with a cherry swimming around in it was thrust into my hand. She boomed out over the cacophony, "What is your diagnosis, Mr. Carson?"

Wishing to maintain client confidentiality, I replied, "Shall we discuss it in the kitchen, Mrs Willman-Jones?"

The high powered Dotty came in once again with all guns blazing, "Oh no. We are all dying to know what terrible problem is afflicting my dear little Mitzi." As if in accord, the whole room went silent, in anticipation.

There was a breathless hush as I felt two dozen pairs of eyes fixed upon me, awaitng my words of wisdom. " Huh! Well, it should be fairly easy to overcome with shampoos, but Mitzi has a heavy infestation of LICE!"

Somewhere, ice clinked in a glass and a throat was cleared as the crowd discreetly melted away into the next room. Even Dotty was stunned into silence and appeared to have visibly shrunk.

I produced the necessary medicaments and bid farewell to my host. As I made my strategic exit I passed Billy Bernstein, the High Court Judge, who muttered, "Well done Ned. It hit her right in the Plimsoll line. Maybe I could use that ploy to clear the court someday!"

# Chapter 42

One Friday evening feeling a bit hot and bothered, but looking forward to a pleasant weekend off, Moira suggested that after the evening meal, we might go for a walk on the cliffs, overlooking Peel bay with St Patrick's Isle and the castle in the background. I felt that this would be a very pleasant way to start the weekend and maybe a drive down to the harbour later in the evening.

I was banned from the kitchen while the meal was being prepared. After practising her culinary skills on me before our wedding Moira had improved in leaps and bounds. The delicious smell coming from the kitchen was tantalising. I was appointed to silver service and given the arduous job of laying the table and fetching a tablecloth and serviettes from the cupboard upstairs. This had to be a feast of some sort?

I arrived downstairs to find the table already laid with candles lit. So it had been a diversion and I had fallen for it! A bottle of Castletown Ale, a glass of orange squash and a bowl of flowers completed the décor. The chef marched in with steak, roast potatoes and green peas - my favourite! She then sat down, looking like a cat who's just had the cream off the milk. As I poured out my drink, she announced, "The toast this evening is to our firstborn, confirmed by Dr Kelly, just this morning!" Of course I was over the moon with delight as this opened up a completely new chapter in our lives. We spent the whole evening planning inconsequential things, such as clothes, cots and perambulators since it was a long way off. Too soon to tell grandparents as they are inclined to get overexcited and think of knitting booties and things in all the wrong colours.

After the meal we went for our stroll on the headland looking out to sea. It was one of those magical evenings, when the sea is a mirror and a red carpet is laid across the surface from the setting sun. Framed far in the west were the Mourne Mountains, standing black against the sky and as we looked to the north, beyond the Point of Ayre, we could see a plume of vapour as a train worked its way along the Mull of Galloway. It was a moment of supreme happiness for us!

After two years in practice I was becoming confident and enjoying life to the full. The continuing academic challenge and physical effort involved were an endless source of pleasure.

We had just acquired some furniture from my parents' house. I was in the process of negotiating it through the doorway when disaster struck. There was the most excruciating pain in my back and I fell to the floor.

Next day, my father diagnosed a slipped disc and referred me to the consultant. As was the custom in the mid-fifties, I was given an anaesthetic and put under traction - (A polite term for stretching you on the rack) then put into a plaster cast extending from my chest to my crotch, with a pointed extension at the bottom to restrict my movement! This life saving piece of technology was to remain on me for nine weeks. It caused untold problems over this period as it necessitated a very long scratching stick to relieve all my itches inside the plaster.

I was finding it hard to reconcile the fact that I might have to give up large animal practice if my back did'nt improve. I could be faced with a life working in a laboratory, or even worse, as a lackey of the Ministry of Agriculture. Having met Ieuan Harries in the anthrax outbreak, the prospect of joining the Ministry did not fill me with much enthusiasm. I had always had a horror of working for the government where political expediency could overrule my veterinary ethical code.

I soon found that I could get about in my plaster. Life became tolerable once I was able to get around the farms once more. In fact it became a positive social asset. All my friends in Round Table wanted to write little messages to Moira across it and, at one very formal function one of my "friends" ordered a second helping of turkey dinner for me which, in turn, prevented me from eating a delicious sweet.

As a result of the pointed extension on the cast, I was unable to bend forward to reach the gear lever in my Morris 1000. My very versatile garage mechanic made me a curved extension to the lever, which enabled me to drive to work fairly normally.

I was feeling so good that I entered into a Round Table treasure hunt and car trial. Moira's excellent navigation and my knowledge of the roads on the island helped us to win the first part. I knew that the second part would be difficult as my Morris 1000 was up against several sports cars. We fell behind somewhat in the speed and acceleration trials, but undeterred I entered one competition, that involved reversing, at speed, around a pole. Moira opted for me to enter this competition alone, as she was heavily pregnant. I reversed up to the start and finish line, pulled the steering lock hard round and accelerated backwards. I did very well by equalling the record. Unfortunately, centrifugal force flung my rigid frame across the seat so hard that I became impaled on top of the gear shift and could'nt get off! To everyone's amazement, I circled the pole three times before I could put my foot on the clutch and switch off the engine. This was a major part of the entertainment and I was carefully lifted off the gear stick to be given the appropriate prize, of an inflatable rubber cushion!

I felt rather like a tortoise for the next eight weeks - protected from the world but somewhat ungainly. At the start of each day Moira would roll me out of bed so that I landed on my hands and knees. From this position I was able to stand up and amble about rather like an automaton.. I was very grateful for my shell at one stage, when a young Ayrshire cow swung her pointed horns around and hit me on the chest. She was extremely surprised when I did'nt falter at her aggression but kept on coming, grabbed her by the nose and injected her, prior to dehorning her.

# Chapter 43

Rafferty's Law always comes into force when the boss goes on holiday. I was'nt particularly looking forward to taking full responsibility for the practice in his absence. Fortunately, the lazy days of summer were upon us. All the cattle were at pasture and the lambing season had long finished. He told me that nothing much happened in July and August.

The following morning I called in to see Alan Kermode's heifer which was suffering from summer mastitis. After twenty-four hours she appeared to be slightly improved as he had been massaging and stripping the quarter every hour during the night. He had actually sat up with her, in the loose box, and made sure that she had nourishment and fluid every hour and removed clots and toxic fluids. This was'nt the only sign of success. There was evidence that an abscess was about to burst on the rear of the quarter that would aid drainage from the infected gland.

" Where are you keeping your heifers at pasture, Alan?" I enquired, "Summer mastitis is now thought to be transmitted by flies. Are they in a place where there are a lot of them?"

"They're in a six acre pasture down by the Silverburn," he replied. "There are certainly a lot of midges down there amongst the trees in the evenings."

"If this idea is true, I'd get them out of there and put them up on the top fields where the breezes are strong and no self respecting fly would dare to go," I replied. "The sooner you move them, the less chance of another case."

He'd used the TLC factor to the utmost in that he'd tended the heifer throughout the night, very mindful that she represented ten per cent of his herd! Modern farmers, although equally caring, could'nt give that amount of time for one individual in a herd of two hundred cattle.

I'd been asked to call in to see Duggie Kerruish on my way home. He worked at the local woollen mill and kept a few cows at home, 'to keep the grass down' on his small holding on the Poortown Road, called Keillsluaig. He'd phoned the previous evening, as he was a bit concerned about one of his cows that seemed a bit over full and had become picky with her food.

As soon as I entered the shippon I knew that we had a problem on our hands. Ruby, was a slightly built cow, but now she was enormous. Her abdomen was greatly distended on both sides and she looked very uncomfortable.

"I thought she was having twins," commenced Duggie as I examined her thoroughly, "Now it looks like triplets. She's due in three weeks, but I doubt if she'll go full time. As I examined her internally my concerns were confirmed. Here I was, faced with my first caesarean, which had to be a hydrops calf. 'Professor M'Geady, why hadn't I listened more intently to your obstetrics lectures?' A small calm voice in my brain seemed to reply, "Ned, you're on you own, so get on with it"

"She's a very sick cow, Duggie. There are no triplets inside of her. Only an awful lot of fluid and probably a dead calf. Hydrops is a very strange condition, where a lot of fluid

128

builds up in the womb and keeps on increasing. It generally ends up with a dead calf. We don't exactly know the cause. Unless she calves, she could eventually die of heart failure."

"Hold on", interrupted Duggie, urgently. "Are you telling me that I should have her shot? Is there no chance for her?"

"No," I responded, "I do think that her chances aren't very good, but if you're willing, I'll have a go at saving her with surgery. It all depends on her constitution. It's a twofold operation. First of all, to remove the fluid slowly, so she doesn't suffer too badly from shock. If we let it run away rapidly she could die very quickly. The second stage is a caesarean to remove the calf."

"Well, it doesn't leave me much choice. She is not worth anything at the moment. Let's give her a chance."

"We mustn't stand around, "I said, "She's deteriorating all the time. I'll go back to the surgery to get the instruments sterilised and get Alan Ramsden to assist. This will be stage one. Stage two - the caesarean will take place after twelve to twenty-four hours. When I return can you have a couple of straw bales ready to put the instruments on and two pails of hot water.?"

I rushed off in the car towards the surgery, only stopping to phone Alan, to get the instruments and a length of rubber tubing sterilised. I entered the surgery yard to be greeted by Alan's smiling face. " Now's the time to show t'boss that we can manage whilst he's away. Anyway, I'll come and hold your hand. Come to think of it, best remove thee wedding ring now before 'owt appens!" and off he went, chortling happily to himself.

I knew just what he was thinking. One of my colleagues had gone off to calve a cow, late in the evening. It was a hard calving, in a mucky little loose box. As he went to wash his hands after the job he noticed that his wedding ring was missing. Back inside the womb went his arm, searching vainly amongst the fluid and afterbirth for the elusive ring. The adage, "Searching for a needle in a haystack," took on a whole new meaning. He and all the farm staff went through the bedding and cow dung with a fine toothcomb. Eventually, he disappeared homewards, after extracting a promise that they would remove nothing from the loose box, each day, until he had examined it. He even laid the afterbirth out on the floor, like a blanket, in order to search for this ring. We could only surmise that his wife was not best pleased by the loss of the wedding band and we teased him unmercifully. The time eventually came when the cow went for slaughter three years later, and he was there, knife in hand, carrying out a thorough autopsy. Alas! To no avail.

After this little incident, I chose the easy way out of such problems, or a similar situation might have arisen. I took off my ring, putting it into Moira's jewellery box for safekeeping and there it lay for many a day.

We returned to Keillsluaig to find that Duggie had not wasted his time. The shippon had been brushed out, the bales laid tidily in the walkway and he'd even driven a nail into the beams on which to hang a Tilley lamp, as a source of light for the operation.

"This is stage one," I explained, whilst Alan was clipping and sterilising an area on the left flank. "Push her tail straight up over her back while I inject her with local anaesthetic over the operation site. I forgot to do this with my last operation and I ended up with a very painful kick in the crotch." Poor Ruby was too ill to notice the injection and didn't give me any trouble.

"If you want to watch I'll talk to you as I go. Look here! I'm making a small incision through the skin and muscle to expose the swollen uterus." As the scalpel entered the abdomen there was a hiss of gas and the wall of the uterus filled the space.
"Now I'm stitching the uterus to either side of the incision. Between the two lines of stitches I am now making another small cut into the uterus." At that moment there was a minor interruption as a jet of uterine fluid shot out under pressure, under my arm, and hit the opposite wall.

"This is just what I didn't want as it could cause too much shock," I continued, as Alan handed me the rubber tubing, which I immediately pushed into the hole, and a much smaller stream of fluid came out the other end. "Now I'll anchor this tube in with a purse-string suture so that the liquid can flow out during the next few hours and reduce the pressure slowly."

Ruby was standing quietly as the pressure slowly decreased. "I'll leave you now, but keep a close eye on her and I'll call back after tea to check her and decide whether to operate tonight or tomorrow.

On the way home I called in to see Mrs. Cashen's two Siamese cats who were suffering from cat plague, commonly called feline enteritis. The Cashens were a childless couple and their world was centred around the cats, Ping and Pong. They were devastated when both cats ceased to take an interest in life and spent every possible moment lying on the cold stone floor. This disease had occurred for many years, affecting cats between three and twelve months most severely, and resulting in many deaths. Indeed, there'd been an outbreak in the town during the past month.

Fortunately, Ping and Pong were over a year and not affected quite so severely as young animals. They were so thin that it was easy to feel their swollen bowel wall. I'd been treating them with one of the new wonder drugs, Chloramphenicol, which appeared to have helped their condition. In the meantime Mr. and Mrs. Cashen had been hand feeding them with broth and calf's foot jelly to keep up their strength. When I'd seen them the previous day they'd shown some signs of improvement by struggling across the floor to find a lap to rest on.

Mrs. Cashen answered the doorbell and I could see by her smile that she had good news. "Oh, Mr. Carson, the boys have started to eat today. Only a little but they did it all on their own. We tempted them with sardines and raw egg and they've had several teaspoonfuls each."

As I sat down on the floor to talk to the cats, they responded to being stroked and after a bit of coaxing, started into some chopped raw liver. They weren't very handsome; emaciated and wobbly, but I could see that they would rapidly regain their strength.

"I'll pop in and see them later in the week Mrs. Cashen, but I think we're winning the battle."

" Thank you so much Mr. Carson. We can't tell you how much these two ragamuffins mean to us." Slipping an envelope into my hand Mrs. Cashen continued,
"We should like you to accept this as a token of our appreciation of your kindness."

Rather taken aback, I protested weakly that a gift was entirely unnecessary and thanked her profusely for their generosity. As high-minded young students we had many times discussed the ethics of tipping or presenting gifts to young professional people. When it actually happened I realised that there was nothing demeaning about it; these people genuinely wished to show their appreciation.

As I drove back to the surgery my heart was singing with pleasure. I opened the envelope and inside were three one pound notes. What riches! This was equal to one quarter of a week's salary. I could even afford to take Moira out to dinner!

# Chapter 44

There was a small surgery after lunch. I could hear the clients chatting in the waiting room as the intervening door stopped a couple of inches from the floor. Clients in veterinary waiting rooms become quite emotional due to underlying concerns for their pets. Some find a release in talking about their animals and their ailments, whilst others become so pent up that they become very rude and aggressive; sharing a common basis with road rage! This not only affects owners but also their pets at times, although, on the whole, the pets are very well behaved.

My first patient came bounding in with her mistress, both full of life. Mary Cowley and her Golden Cocker Spaniel, Jane, had arrived in for a check-up after her recovery from distemper. Jane looked bright eyed and fit with a glossy golden coat. The disease had left its mark however, and about two months after the distemper, she developed chorea or St. Vitus dance. This is a continuos nervous twitch, which can affect any part of the nervous system. In her case it was restricted to the muscles on the scalp so she spent her life with the ears moving up and down.

I looked into the waiting room as Mary and Jane departed. Only two more people inside. One was a very large man of about twenty stone, in working garb and heavy, cement stained boots. The other client was a tiny, bird-like old lady, dressed in black, trimmed with lace, who instantly brought to mind "Arsenic and old Lace."

The large man clumped in with a rolling gait. He had a rather fat little Jack Russell terrier clamped under his arm like a rolled up newspaper. He was quite bald, unshaven and had a reddish, beer tinted complexion.

"Good afternoon," I said, writing up a record card, " What's your name and address, please?"

"Jack Quayle, Shaw's Brow, and this is Mouse," came the gruff reply. "What d'yer want to know that for?"

"Sorry to give you the trouble Mr. Quayle, but we must keep a record of your dog's problems, in case we have to see her again."

"You probably won't have to see her again," came the swift retort.

"What appears to be the problem with Mouse," I asked politely, realising that one of Mouse's problems was overweight.

"That's what I bloody well brought her here for - you're the vet!"

"That's correct," I commented drily, whilst I popped a thermometer into Mouse's rear end, looked at her ears, eyes and teeth - Yuk!,( awful teeth) and also listened to her heart. "'Er! Is she having any diarrhoea or waterworks problems?"

"'Er poo's all right but the other part is where the trouble is. She keeps passing blood in her water and straining - poor little darlin'," came the gruff response with a slight tremor in the voice, as he wiped his eye with a dirty sleeve.

My mind went into a mild spasm again as I sought a possible diagnosis. Sounds like a cystitis and urethritis. I hope so! I couldn't feel any bladder stones through all that fat - Please God! - Don't let it be stones, as I've never operated on a polony before!

I carefully explained everything to Jack Quayle, who by this time had become quite pallid. Particularly when I added, "If she doesn't respond to antibiotics Mr. Quayle, I might have to open her up to check for bladder stones. In the meantime I'll inject her and give you some tablets for her."

That was the last straw. Jack pulled out a grubby handkerchief and wiping his perspiring forehead, groped his way to the door and went to sit down in the waiting room. Poor little Mouse was abandoned on the table awaiting her fate. I quickly injected her listening to the dialogue in the next room.

Arsenic and Old Lace lady, anxiously, "How is your little dog?"

Jack, snivelling quietly, "They're going to stick a needle in its ass, ma'am."

Old lady, "Oh dear me! I hope they give it gas!"

Suppressing a smile, I returned Mouse to her owner and arranged to see her in three days time.

"Next please?"

In tottered the old lady, of doubtful age, but probably having enjoyed eighty summers! In her hand she was clutching a shoebox.

"Mr Carson," she commenced in a very precise manner, "I am Mrs. Cynthia Frensham and I live in Demesne Road. I hear from my niece that you are very good with little birds. You see, I have a canary called Billy Boy."

"How nice of your niece," I replied, feeling quite elated. "Now, can I see your little bird. Is he in the box?"

"Oh yes," said Mrs. Frensham, at last relinquishing her hold on the box and laying it on the table.

Opening the box carefully lest the bird should fly away, I looked inside and there was Billy Boy, lying still and very dead. He'd been delicately laid out on a piece of the finest red, crushed silk.

"I'm sorry to tell you that your little bird is dead!"

"Oh dear! I'm so sorry, I should have told you that when I arrived, but I was so disturbed at the thought of dear little Mouse having to undergo that dreadful operation, and of course his owner was being so awfully brave. Well, you see, it's my husband, Fred. He's over eighty years old and sometimes I feel that he is becoming senile and almost childish. He gets very irritable and actually argues with me! When I found dear little Billy Boy, lying dead in his cage, I suspected that Fred had slammed the cage door shut and frightened the poor bird to death. Can you tell me if he caused him to die as I shall have to speak to him severely?"

As I picked up Billy's frail little body, I asked, "How old was he, because I feel that I should carry out a post mortem examination to find the cause of death?"

"Quite young," was the reply. "We only had him for fifteen years."

"If you would like to go home Mrs Frensham, I'll telephone you after the post mortem, to put your mind at rest."

"Oh Mr. Carson. You are so kind." She rushed round the examination table, gave me a big hug and trotted off home.

Ten minutes later I was able to 'phone her up and say that Billy Boy had died of natural causes. Fred could be forgiven and I had arranged with a friend to leave her a replacement canary.

We returned to Keillsluaig late in the afternoon and Ruby almost looked like a normal cow. Her girth had decreased appreciably, her ears were cocked and she was looking much happier. I spent some time weighing up the pros and cons and eventually decided to operate there and then.

We went through the routine of an anaesthetic nerve block on her left flank, and scrubbed up and sterilised the operation site.

Fortunately, I was able to extend the original flank incision to expose the uterus. Then, using a similar technique, I was able to enlarge the uterine incision and remove the drainage tube.

The hind feet of the calf appeared at the opening, clothed in the foetal membranes. I cut through the membranes and Alan and Duggie pulled the dead calf out backwards, whilst I held the edges of the uterus. The membranes themselves had separated away from the uterus so I was able to remove these very easily. Before closing up the uterine wound I put in antibiotic pessaries to counter any infection.

Suturing up the uterus, muscle and skin was probably the longest part of the operation. I was rather pleased with the result as the skin suture, finished off with a blanket stitch, looked very neat.

I suddenly realised just how tired I was. It had been an eventful day and I was ready for an early bed. Thank goodness Brian was coming home tomorrow.

# Chapter 45

I never knew what to expect when I visited Willie Kinrade. He was a delightful old rogue who always came out with the unexpected. At seventy-five years old he was getting a bit infirm and spent much of his time sitting in an old Windsor chair beside the open fireplace. It could be a lonely place for a gregarious old man, so he always left instructions that I must "cast a sight" upon him before I went home. He had chewed tobacco all his life, and when he was sitting in his chair there would be a 'kaak' and a 'fsst' as he aimed a tobacco spit into the open fire or a large brass spittoon which guarded the fireplace. His sheer expertise with a wad of tobacco had long ago earned him the nickname of "spittin' Willie". Always he had a tale to tell about someone or something and the thought of letting the truth interfere with a good story was foreign to his nature. I very quickly learned not to pass on any information that might be changed into mischievous gossip.

Ballakissack had been the home of the Kinrade family for over a century. It was situated north of Douglas, on a headland looking out towards Cumbria. The family had improved the original farm buildings so that they formed a square around a central courtyard with the traditional dung heap in the middle, for convenience. This design was also a much-needed protection against the elements as the farm buildings were in a very exposed position. Over the years the farm had diversified from solely beef and sheep to include dairying, pigs and turkeys for the Christmas market.

One of my great delights whenever I arrived on the farm was to watch "Fly", the Border collie. I've always regarded this breed as one of the smartest in the canine world. She had never forgotten that one of my first visits to the farm had been to examine a batch of lame ewes. Subsequently, each time my car arrived in the yard, all available sheep would be rounded up at the nearest gate, for a quick check over, with Fly lying patiently behind, awaiting my next instructions.

This time it was the turn of the sons of Fly, who were to give a practical demonstration. As I sat in the car I watched two of her ten-week-old pups creeping around, in a half crouch position, rounding up a batch of chickens in the yard. The chickens clucked and dithered, running this way and that, as chickens will. Each way they faced there was a pup quietly staring them out and gradually pushing them into the corner. Eventually, one old bird flew over their heads and escaped. No doubt this little performance was re-enacted several times each day. Isn't life wonderful!

George Kinrade, the eldest son, had called me in a great panic. He had gone out before morning milking and found the old carthorse lying dead in the field, after being disembowelled by their boar.

Jeremy, the Large White boar, was about six hundred pounds of amiable muscle. Exceedingly handsome and covered with wiry bristles, he possessed a most delightful personality with human beings, but only a love-lorn gilt could home in on his smell!

In a fit of porcine 'joie-de-vivre', brought on by an amorous sow next door, he had leaned against the door of his pen, which shattered under his weight. Sensing freedom, he found himself outside the sow pen but was unable to force his way in. Somewhat irate and frustrated he rooted around in the pasture where the family horse had been grazing.

135

One never knows what sparks off boars but he ran under the mare and slit open her abdomen with his razor sharp tushes. Poor old Dolly, the mare probably didn't feel much, but was instantly disembowelled and died very soon after from shock. George had very strong Methodist leanings, but that morning his references to Jeremy's ancestors were extremely defamatory. He was too good a boar to put down, so I was assigned the task of removing his lower tushes, which protruded from his lips like a pair of scimitars.

We drove Jeremy into the feed passage in the cow shed. From behind, I slipped a wire noose over his snout, and into his mouth, so that it lay behind his top tushes. This slipping noose was attached to a rope, which George threaded over a beam. As George pulled on the rope Jeremy was appalled at this affront to his dignity and screamed out in anger. He could'nt turn around as he and I were jammed in the feed passage. The more George pulled, the more Jeremy dug in his toes and pulled the other way. The noise was ear shattering. For volume and pitch the squeal of a boar, at ear level, is deafening. The whole scenario is more of loss of dignity than pain.

My job was to remove those evil looking tushes without injury to myself. Fortunately, there is no central nerve canal in pigs' teeth so he felt nothing. I had chosen to use a hacksaw, which makes a clean cut, as opposed to shears, which can shatter teeth. It was quite a hazardous procedure, working beside the frothing jaws of a very cross boar, but his mind was too set on pulling backwards.

It took five minutes to remove both teeth and my head was reverberating with the squealing. Once the operation was over, Jeremy wandered off on his own, completely unconcerned, his mind intent on the delectable young sow down the passage. The whole process of removing tushes was to become much easier in the future, with the introduction of the plaited wire saw, which speeded up the work.

As we let him go, George said, almost regretfully, "We're all so fond of Jeremy. I never thought that he would do a thing like that. Many times our children have ridden on his back!"

" Makes no difference, "I replied, "Animals run on a different set of guidelines to ourselves. They can revert to their roots very rapidly!"

"Before you go," continued George, "Father wants you to call in for a word."

I had to stoop to enter the house. The low arched doorway had been made many years before and led into a flag stoned hallway and kitchen. I could hear a clattering of pans as Annie Kinrade scoured the pots in the little scullery.

Willie was sitting in his chair by the fireside, stirring up a few logs with the poker. He was a tall, rangy man, with a gaunt face and sunken eyes, who wasn't looking his best with twenty-four hours of grey stubble on his face.

"'Morning, Ned. It's good to have a sight of yer. I hope that you've taken the teeth out of that randy old devil. He's gettin' above himself. I don't suppose that George swore at him much. A good boy that, but a mite too holy, like his mother. When I were his age I was in town most weekends. Father said that I would come to no good!"

There was a pause, whilst he pulled out his wad of baccy, examined it, and then put it back again. This was followed by a 'kaak' and a 'psst' as he scored a bull's eye on the centre log in the fire.

"I wish I could have seen yer takin' the teeth out. Unfortunately, my arthuritis is bad at the moment and the blood flows cold as yer get older. Still I had my fun with the wenches in Douglas, when I was a young man. Daughter, Alice, took me for a run in the car along the promenade last week. All those young things in their summer dresses. Wigglin' along with their bottoms sticking out-like a couple of ripe pears, wrapped up in a silk handkerchief. That made my blood flow quicker!"

A silence gripped the room as Annie Kinrade entered from the scullery. All four foot ten of her was held upright in righteous indignation. Garbed in a flowered dress and with her iron grey hair pulled back severely into a bun, she glared at the luckless Willie through gold rimmed spectacles.

"William", she admonished. "You should not be putting wicked ideas into this young man's head. You are too easily led!"

Willie didn't even acknowledge Aggie's prescence. He became deeply involved in poking the fire with a long stick, apparently oblivious of her tirade as a consequence of selective deafness.

"Just look at him", continued Aggie. "He's just like that old tom cat curled up in the chair, with his turnip head and tattered ears. Every time I scold him for stealin' the herrin's from the pantry he goes all deaf and starts washin' hisself, as if I aren't here. The dear soul - he's so gentle - that is except when he's courtin'. My William is just the same - they're a right pair!"

It was fortunate for me that he had to have another chew and a spit as my imagination was running riot at the thought of Willie, let loose on Douglas promenade on a hot day. As I got up to leave, I picked up the two boar's tushes and handed them to him.

"There you are Mr Kinrade. Look how sharp the edge is on those teeth-you could almost shave with them." Watching him as I left him I knew that this had given him lots of ammunition for his next audience.

# Chapter 46

I was about to go an see Roy and Val Callin, at Lhergydhoo, when a message was phoned through to call out with John Corlett, at Quarry Bends, to examine a ewe. It couldn't have been farther away from Ballakissack. Right on the other side of the island!

I took my favourite route via Baldrine and then followed a steady climb up into the hills until I joined the T.T. race course at Creg-Ny-Baa. Past Kate's Cottage and Windy Corner where I'd spent many happy hours marshalling the T.T. races. Here the air was clear and I was driving along the top of the island, beneath the blue dome of the sky. These wild hills were part of me, as I'd spent many days shooting and fishing in their shadows. This was freedom!

Turning left at Brandywell Corner, towards Kirk Michael, the road opened on to the most captivating views across to Ireland, and I then headed for Ballaugh and the Quarry Bends.

I had been to the Corlett small holding twice, to treat red water cases. It was a small yard on the roadside and backed onto the "Curraghs", a wild area of marsh and willows, where wildlife flourished in peace.

As I drove into the yard, John was awaiting my arrival. "Sorry to call you out, Mr. Carson. It's a ewe lamb that got caught by the ram a bit early, and now she's having a problem."

"Can I have a bucket of warm water, soap and a towel?" I replied, "Then we can have a good look at her."

As he appeared with the pail, I was lead off to a small lean-to shed, beside the house. A young Suffolk ewe stood in the corner, straining spasmodically. I scrubbed up, and cleaned the ewe's hindquarters. It was quite difficult to insert my hand through the ewe's pelvis, where I found the lamb's head and feet, vainly queuing up to come out. The pelvis was too small and immature to deliver the lamb!

I looked up at John. " The lamb is much too large but I think he's alive. We're faced with two alternatives. Carry out a caesarean or slaughter the ewe on humane grounds.

After a brief hesitation, John said, "I think it should be a caesarean. She comes from good stock and she still has a long breeding life ahead of her."

Having made the decision, I suddenly realised that I'd left all my surgery kit back in Douglas for sterilisation. A return trip to collect it, a distance of thirty miles could easily result in the lamb dying. I had a mild panic, while I searched through the equipment in the back of my car for a means of operating. In total, I found that I had a bottle of anaesthetic; syringes and needles, antibiotics, scissors, methylated spirit and a packet of scalpel blades.

What else did I require? Suture needles and suture material and yes-then I remembered a roll of fishing monofilament on the back seat!

I had a word with Mrs Corlett, who had a selection of sewing needles, a spool of linen thread and also a sacking needle, which I might need for the skin. We were ready for action!

Needles and suture materials were boiled up in a saucepan in the kitchen, while John and I clipped out the fleece behind the ribs, on the ewe's left flank. We then injected a local anaesthetic nerve block, and sterilised the area with iodine and methylated spirit.

The patient was tied firmly onto an enamel topped kitchen table for ease of handling. Incising through the flank and uterus, I very quickly had a lively ram lamb sputtering and kicking beside me. We laid him out, beside his mother's nose, which kept her well occupied, licking him clean. This enabled us to proceed with the suturing without interruption. It seemed a bit strange using such basic tools to close up the wound, but they worked very efficiently and I learned that sophisticated tools and techniques are not always necessary. I had averted a possible disaster with one scalpel blade, linen thread and a couple of sewing needles!

On my journey home I called in to see Roy and Val Callin. They used to deliver our milk in the mornings and we'd become good friends since we arrived in Peel.

Roy had asked me to put a ring in his bull's nose, when I was passing the farm. Dealing with Roy, I had to be extra careful about carrying out this very simple operation. If I made a mess of it, or lost the screw, it could cost me quite a few pints as hush money when we next met in the Whitehouse Hotel.

We had christened his fifteen month old bull, "Tricky Dickie", because his temperament was already becoming a bit unreliable. We drove him into the milking shed and managed to chain him up before he knew what had happened. Roy slipped a halter over his head and fastened it so that his nose was facing up in the air, which semi-immobilised him.

The average bullring is about three inches in diameter and made of copper. They're made of two similar semicircles, hinged at the back and interlocking smoothly at the front, where a transfixing screw locks it into position.

The ring is inserted through a hole in the central division of the nose, not too far forward where it would tear, nor too far back in the cartilage where it would be ineffective. It has a point at one end, which makes it 'self piercing'. Once it is pushed through the nose, the halves are pushed together and the screw inserted.

The problem has always been the screw, which is very small and easily dropped. It gave the farmers a great deal of amusement to see the "vetinry" on his knees scrabbling through the straw after this elusive screw. That was, until someone came up with the almost fool proof idea of holding a cap underneath to catch it! We achieved a further technological breakthrough by tying a thread around the screw, which was supposed to make it completely idiot proof.

I grabbed "Dickie" by the nose, and despite his resentment, pushed the ring through the nose, and reached into my overall pocket for the screw. To my embarrassment, all I found was a hole, which I had forgotten about. Feeling slightly furtive, I excused myself on the pretext of collecting some healing ointment from the car.

I picked up the ointment, quickly opened another bullring box and borrowed the screw. Then I returned to "Dickie", and with a great flourish, tied thread around the second screw, twisted it in, and rubbed in the ointment. Packing up my gear I commented, "That was fairly simple." Roy looked at me rather dubiously and said, "Come on in. Val has a pot of tea on the brew." So we spent a pleasant twenty minutes chatting before I headed for home.

Now, the strange outcome of this story is that the hero went home to Moira, chuckling with mirth at outwitting his friend. It was Friday evening and we would call in at the Whitehouse Hotel later, for a social drink. Sure enough when we arrived, Roy and Val were sitting at a table. I asked Roy if he was going to buy the drinks and to my surprise he looked at me with the suspicion of a smile on his face and said, "I'm sorry about that but the answer is no. I forgot to tell you, back on the farm, that as you left to go out to the car I glanced down and there was a little copper screw sitting in the cow dung on the toe of my boot." He firmly placed a shiny copper screw on the table. "It's mighty nice of you to offer to buy the drinks, yessir!"

It was only a few weeks before our new arrival was due and Moira was finding life was more of an effort, so Brian's return from holiday was even more welcome.

# Chapter 47

Before heading for the surgery I had a couple of visits to make. I called in at Keillsluaig to check up on Ruby, the cow on which we had operated to remove the hydrops calf. I didn't expect her to make a rapid recovery after her ordeal.

As I walked into the cowshed I noticed her ears flicking and she was quietly chewing some hay from the rack. The wound was looking fairly clean, without any discharge, and her eyes looked bright but the mucous membranes were still very pale. I could see that she had a long way to go but she was certainly on the mend.

I was still very concerned about Alan Kermode's heifer and diverted down south to check it so that I could give Brian a full report, later in the day. As usual Alan was out in the yard building. The walls and gateways were all complete and his brand new calf house had its first occupants with their noses immersed in a pail of milk.

He greeted me with a smile on his face, which is always a good sign. "Well, Ned. You'll be pleased with the heifer. I sat up with her for a couple of nights and now she's on the mend, eating and drinking well."

She was so much better that Alan had to hold her to prevent me being kicked as I handled the sensitive udder. The abscess had burst and was draining well.

As I looked at her I said, "You've saved her life Alan. She's lost the quarter but you'll find that she'll yield nearly as much on the other three quarters. I could only do so much and the rest was up to your nursing."

"No, Ned," It was a team effort and I'd be delighted if you would take this box of eggs for your wife, as a thank you"

It's little gestures such as this that make practice so pleasurable.

Fortunately, I phoned the surgery after leaving Alan and found that Daphne Rylance wanted me see her horse urgently. A phone call from Daphne Rylance was generally couched in the terms of a command. Major Peter and Daphne Rylance were members of the pseudo - aristocracy, who regarded themselves as the leading socialites in the island - rather big fish in a very little pond! Their daughters had been exported "across the water" for a select education, and possibly to meet the right type of young man.

As I drove up towards the house a figure leapt out of the driveway, directing me through the field gate. I could see a crowd of people surrounding one of the daughter's show ponies. I was climbing out of the car when a pair of bolt cutters were thrust into my hand with the staccato command "You're right on time. Cut it out of there. 'There', being several coils of barbed wire that had been carelessly dumped in the hedge!

Little daughter Priscilla was crying. Ariadne, the young owner, talked to the pony, "Clarabelle", whilst mother shouted orders indiscriminately at all and sundry. On the fringe of all this chaos lollopped a mini-pack of variegated dogs, enjoying the situation to the full.

I moved in quietly, with the cutters snipping left and right, with what I hoped was the casual air of a veterinarian, accustomed to working his way through barbed wire entanglements. At last, Clarabelle stood in the field exhibiting her barbed wire ankle socks, and I looked around for an assistant to help unwrap this cat's cradle. The Major was too busy, shouting orders in the background, and deploying his troops. Anyway he was an infantryman, not cavalry. Daphne, on the verge of hysteria, was countermanding his instructions and creating bedlam.

I applied a twitch to Clarabelle's nose, to control her, as the next few minutes would be quite painful. I pushed the twitch handle into Daphne's hand and commandeered Ariadne and Priscilla to unwrap the wire surrounding the pony's fetlocks, while I held the feet steady. It took us several minutes, by which time the hubhub had quietened down.

The twitch had done the trick, and saved the day once more in an era when sedatives and anaesthetics were still in their infancy. Twitches have been used to control animals for generations and have saved thousands of human and animal lives.

The normal twitch consists of a loop of light rope attached to a short wooden pole. The loop is placed over the sensitive tip of a horse's nose and the pole rotated, causing the loop to contract down onto the nose, like a tourniquet. The pain must be excruciating and diverts the animal's attention, particularly if they are aggressive, to the extent that minor operations may be carried out in complete safety. I always took care to massage the nose afterwards to restore the circulation.

Clarabelle's fetlocks and legs were covered with a series of gashes caused by the barbed wire. A few of the wounds warranted stitching but as many of them were on mobile joints I suggested that we should use skin dressings as many of the sutures, on joints, would pull out. The dizzy and arrogant Daphne would have none of this. How could darling (and very embarrassed) Ariadne show a pony with scars on its legs? I was getting used to some of the amateur horse owners who felt that they were instant experts, so I agreed to try and suture the cuts.

We cast Clarabelle, using sidelines. This is a technique whereby, a loop of the correct size to rest around base of the horse's neck, is made in the middle of a long rope leaving two long ends. These long ends are passed around the inner side of the hind legs, so as to rest upon the fetlocks, and then taken forward again through the original loop. As one person pulls on each rope end and a third person holds the head, so the fetlocks are pulled forward to the shoulder and the horse gently falls over.

To give her credit, Clarabelle lay quietly with Ariadne kneeling at her head, talking to her constantly. I injected anaesthetic and sutured all the wounds, the Major holding my instruments and instructing the garrulous Daphne to shut up and go indoors.

It must have taken an hour to suture up all the cuts and as I straightened my back, with a sigh of relief, we let the pony stand up. The job looked perfect until, as forecast, every stitch on the joints split open and we had to cover the legs with skin dressings!

Arriving back at the surgery, I glanced at the daybook, which appeared to be filling up rapidly. Brian had no sooner returned from his morning round and snatched a quick lunch than he had to rush off to see a farrowing sow at Ballaragh, high above the sea at Laxey. Juan Qualtrough had just arrived in from The Braaid with a ewe in the boot of his car that had been savaged by dogs. As I opened the boot I saw her lying there, gasping her last, and immediately put her down on humane grounds. The dogs had torn her throat open and a large piece of her hind leg was missing.

Very rarely does one dog go off by itself and worry sheep. Generally, two or more animals are involved, forming the basis of a pack, with pack mentality. They initially chase the sheep in fun, and it ends up in wanton destruction as the animals revert to their hunting instincts. This can result in quite a few sheep being attacked, costing the farmer hundreds of pounds. Often they can be the most affectionate and home loving dogs, who go wild in a group. Unfortunately, they are punished by being put down, whilst it is in reality the owners' fault for not keeping their animals under control.

Various methods have been used to discipline dogs to prevent sheep worrying, from walking them, on a lead, through the flock, to shutting them in a pen with a ewe and newborn lamb. This latter method ends up with a very chastened and bruised dog, although I have seen them sustain broken ribs from an over protective mother.

As I finished with the ewe, a car drew up at the gate. It was Jack Comish from Ballavaish. " Bring the dog in, Jack," I said. "I've just returned and seen your message." Jack carried in his Springer spaniel, wrapped up in a large blanket. He was pale faced, with shock, and had tear stains on his weatherbeaten cheeks. So much for the tough, aggressive farmer that I had first encountered.

He gently placed his burden on the table and, in a choked voice, said," I hope that I haven't killed her. It was all my stupid fault. We were out shooting partridge at Mullinaragher and a wounded bird went down into a clump of gorse. Nell is as keen as mustard and was in there with her stern wagging. As I reached in past her to get the bird, I nudged her with the gun barrel and it went off. Call me a bloody fool. I forgot the first lesson in gun handling, to keep the safety catch on except when you are shooting!"

Nell lay quietly as I unfolded the blanket and removed a piece of bloodstained sheeting, covering her ribcage. It was a clean, saucer shaped wound, which appeared to have been sculpted in her side. By good chance, the gun had been lying at a tangent to her ribs as it discharged its lethal contents. Almost miraculously, it had cut a swath through the skin, without damaging the ribs.

"This is a lucky day for both of you," I said. " This should stitch up and heal fairly well. I may have a problem bringing the edges of the wound together. You go and get on with your milking and I'll get Alan in to help me to operate.

Jack went away much happier, and Alan and I set to work. There was a minor problem drawing the wound together, but I finished, quite content with the outcome.

When Jack came to collect her next day, they were overjoyed to see one another. As Jack said, " Nell is the sweetest natured dog I have ever possessed. It upset me so much, because as soon as the gun went off, she did'nt appear to feel the pain and came and sat at my feet, nuzzling my hand as if apologising for getting in the way!"

# Chapter 48

I was feeling the pressure of running the practice single-handed and was glad that Brian had just returned from holiday. As an assistant I had'nt appreciated the extra work and responsibility involved in running a practice. He had spent some time in England and been invited to the ball given by the Quorn and Belvoir Hunt!

My first patient in the surgery was the small fat Jack Russell terrier, Mouse, being carried in by big Jack Quayle. " How is she now, Mr. Quayle?" I commenced, determined to avoid any confrontations.

"Well," started Jack, "Oh! She's better than she was, thank you, but she's still havin' trouble passing her water. The missus and I have had a long talk about her and even though we can't afford a great deal, her health comes first, and we must leave it to you to make a decision on whether to operate. We lost our little girl with polio some years ago and after that I bought Mouse for my Rosie as we were both so upset. Now she's all we've got."

" Thanks, Mr. Quayle, if you would like to leave her with me, I'll consult Mr. Scanlon. Then, with your permission, we'll operate if necessary during the day. Can you 'phone me at tea time?"

As he turned to go, Jack said, "I hope that little old lady who was in the surgery last week doesn't bother you too much. She means well, but she's been worrying my Rosie somethin' awful this week, callin' in to see Mouse several times a day."

Shortly afterwards, Brian arrived in from his rounds and we discussed Mouse's problems. " I'm fairly sure that she's got urinary calculi," he said, "Under the circumstances, I feel that we must operate for her own sake and the Quayles' peace of mind. What a pity that we don't have X-ray facilities!"

I was glad of his guidance as we prepared for surgery. It was a double first for me. My first operation to remove stones (or calculi) from the bladder and the first time to carry out an operation on the surgeon's nightmare, a very fat patient. Meanwhile, Alan had been busy sterilising the instruments and gathering equipment together.

Looking back on the surgery carried out in that era, when we did'nt use sterile gloves, gowns, or masks, gives me great respect for the standards of hygiene that were drummed into us at college, resulting in minimal post operative infections.

We anaesthetised Mouse by injection and maintained the anaesthesia by bubbling air through chloroform into a leather mask, over her nose. Alan acted as the anaesthetist, which left us to concentrate on the operation.

The patient's abdomen was scrubbed, shaved and sterilised. I then made a mid-line incision, just in front of the pelvis. As the scalpel entered the abdominal cavity, a mass of fat welled up through the opening. Fortunately, Brian was there to push it aside as it threatened to obscure our view, and he talked me through the operation.

The urinary bladder was large and solid, and as I handled it I could feel the stones grating against one another. When I lifted it into view, there was a large gap left below into which all the offending fat vanished. A short incision on the top surface and we had calculi falling all over the table like pebbles on the beach. This was the time to remove all the stones and prevent contamination of the wound. Suturing up the thickened bladder wall was more difficult as I had to leave it completely waterproof when it filled up with urine again. There was a great sigh of relief as I inserted the final stitch. Only then did I realise the tension under which I'd been working.

We carried the sleeping Mouse into the kitchen and left her in the dog basket, to recover quietly beside the Aga stove.

Soon afterwards Jack Quayle was on the phone to hear the good news that she'd come through the operation. He made me promise to put all the stones in a jar, which he kept on the mantelpiece for several years as entertainment for his friends.

I had hardly put down the phone when it rang once more. " Good afternoon Mr. Carson, this is Mrs. Frensham speaking. How is dear little Mouse? I hope she didn't suffer too much."

" She's fine, Mrs Frensham, and just recovering from her anaesthetic beside a nice warm fire. She may even go home tomorrow."

"Oh! You have been so kind to her Mr. Carson. I have spoken to her mistress, Rosie, several times. They are so worried about her and about being unable to pay the bill. Anyway, I have spoken to Fred about it, and as we have nobody to leave our money to, we have decided to pay for Mouse's operation."

I was delighted for Jack and Rosie's sake and the strange quirk of fate that had brought this about.

After a very busy day, Brian and I decided that a convivial drink at the Woodburn Hotel would refresh us, whilst we compared notes.

"I've had my fill of amateur cow keepers today," Brian started off. " At seven a.m. this morning, Squadron Leader Jeffs, fresh out of the R.A.F. with a big bonus, was on the phone. He's bought a smallholding in Santon, which included the family cow. Apparently the cow calved yesterday and produced so much milk that she keeps leaking milk all over the place. He had brooded on the problem all-night and demanded a visit at seven a.m.. By eight a.m. he had phoned four times, in a terrible panic and when I arrived half an hour later he gave me a severe reprimand for not giving a good service. After reminding him that I could outrank him, he cooled down. I then explained that it was quite natural for some heavy milkers to leak milk and that there was only one cure."

"And what was that?" I enquired, intrigued by this magic remedy.

Brian chuckled, "I merely told him that he must hand milk the cow dry, every hour for the next twenty four hours. By now he must be getting tired wrists. Still, only another fourteen hours to go! Let's drink his health."

Whilst we were chatting, a figure at the other end of the bar sent us over a couple of pints of draught beer. We turned and recognised the figure of old George Kaighin, wreathed in a blue cloud of his favourite shag tobacco. He waved and came shambling across to speak to us.

"Well, Mr. Carson, do you remember when our little Danny died last year. I thought that it would never be the same again. No more walks to the pub in the evenings with my little friend. I kept seein' this little white shadow following me all over. I even got to the stage of taking down his lead from behind the door, to see if he was there. It was mighty awful for my Daisy too. It really got her down, with me sittin' inside every evening doin' naithin' but moping about the house.

Then one day she says that her niece, Molly Quirk, from out Kirk Michael way wanted to go on holiday and couldn't afford to put the dog in kennels. Anyways, she agreed to have the lil' mite for a couple of weeks. Well, when it arrived it looked a bit like Danny but not as smart lookin'. I had to take "Gyp" here, out for a walk every day. By the end of the fortnight she had developed this old habit of sitting looking up at her lead after tea and we were going off to the pub each night. I tell yer,' By then I was gettin' to the stage of grievin' at the thought of parting with her.

One day, in walks young Molly, smart as you like, gives me a kiss an' says 'Happy Birthday, Uncle George! Mind you I'd clean forgotten about the day it was. 'What would you like as a birthday present?' "Naw," I says, "You've given me present enough. I've had Gyp for a couple of weeks and we're good friends."

Well, she and Daisy burst out laughing. The whole thing had been a spoof. Gyp belonged to an old lady that died and they'd been havin' me on, hoping I would take to her. So now I'd like you to meet this little mischief.

At his feet Gyp looked up, gave us a knowing look and wagged her stern end.

After George and Gyp had gone off home, Brian continued, "I had Roger Nelson, the cattle dealer, on the phone this morning. He'd sold a freshly calved cow to an old couple up on the Lhergy Crippetty. They complained she wouldn't give any milk so I was asked to check her.

When I arrived at the cottage I had a good look at the cow. The udder was enormous and should have had lots of milk.

I checked her over thoroughly and popped a thermometer into her rectum in case she was carrying a temperature. Everything appeared to be normal so I tried to milk her. The teat openings were narrow and she was nervous so did not let her milk down easily. I told the owners that it was only a problem of being a hard milker!"

"Oh no it isn't," exclaimed the old lady, vehemently, "I was watching you!"
Rather taken aback, Brian said, "What do you mean?"

"I saw you mister. You lifted up her tail, stuck something up her bottom and pushed the milk down!"
There are some battles that you can't win!

"If you had come back a couple of days earlier you could have had the privilege of losing a client instead of me." I commented, looking at my empty glass in sorrow, as it was Brian's round.

"How did you manage to do that?" he said, secretly delighted that it had happened to me.

"It was about ten o'clock on a Sunday evening when the phone rang. A voice at the other end asked if I could come and see their dog, that was having fits. Of course I drove the ten miles into Douglas and arrived at the house on a rather run down estate. It was one of those evenings when winter was announcing its arrival. The rain was sheeting down and the last of the leaves were being torn off the trees by the strong sou'westerly gale. Huddled into the porch, I rang the doorbell.

The door was opened by the owner, Mr. Karran, unshaven, wearing a collarless shirt and a somewhat furtive expression on his face.

As I entered the sitting room, I could see a cocker spaniel, sound asleep in front of the fire. "Is this the patient?" I said, looking at the motionless animal.

"Oh yes!" was the immediate response.

" I thought that he was going in and out of fits?"

"Well," said Mr. Karran. "He was scratching his ear a lot as he lay in front of the fire and the smell was something awful. I could see that it was worrying my wife so we thought that we must call you. We didn't think that you'd come out for a little thing like that so we said that he was having fits. The cost of the visit doesn't matter."

"I see," I replied, trying to maintain a cool approach. "I'm glad of that because a ten mile journey at half past ten on a Sunday night can be expensive." I was wary of E.D.M., or "Expense Doesn't Matter" clients as many of them don't intend to pay anyway.

"Couldn't you have brought her into the surgery?"

"Not really," said Mr. Karran, "We haven't got a car and it seemed a bit unfair to ask the neighbour to bring him in on such a stormy night!"

I had a look at Posy, the Spaniel's ears. I had smelt them as soon as I entered the door. They were inflamed, painful and black with wax. Evidently they had been neglected for months.

"Right," I said, "She is in a lot of pain and should have treatment tonight, and then I shall see her in surgery during the week. Some of the lotions and tablets are in the surgery so you should collect them tonight. If you pay me now I'll give you a lift into the surgery and back."

After a great deal of mumbling and grumbling as I'd called his bluff, he went into the kitchen and then into the bedroom. After fossicking around for a few minutes he returned with the cash and handed it over with very little grace. By this time I was getting some pleasure from his discomfort. He climbed into the car beside me and I drove three miles into the surgery.

After dispensing his drugs I phoned through to Moira, who told me that there was an urgent call to a cow in Laxey, flat out with milk fever. Almost with tears in my eyes, I had to tell Mr. Karran that his taxi ride was cancelled as I had an emergency call. He would have to walk the three miles home in the rain. Life can be very tough sometimes!

# Chapter 49

Early next morning I had an urgent call from the Quirk brothers up on Lambfell. They were a hard working couple of men and never seemed to have much sense of urgency as not a lot seemed to happen on their farmstead. Probably the most exciting event of the day was to wave to the postman as he rode past on his bicycle. They didn't farm intensively and consequently avoided a lot of problems. They seemed to have taken Moira to their hearts because in the springtime they regularly appeared at the door with a bunch of daffodils.

When John Quirk's voice carried a sense of urgency in his voice it implied an impending disaster, so I leapt out of bed and headed for the hills very rapidly. As I drove into the yard, at the top of Creg Willys, I could see a crowd of men huddled around a large Friesian cow. The message had been that she was flat out on the ground and had put her body out. Whenever I receive such a message it is rapidly interpreted that she has prolapsed her complete uterus after calving and most probably has milk fever as well. The two main causes of uterine prolapse are an over large calf, which partly jams in the pelvis and pulls the uterus out with it, or more commonly when calving is associated with an attack of milk fever. In this instance the uterine muscle loses all its tone and may flop out whilst the cow is straining or be pulled out by the afterbirth.

I grabbed hold of my milk fever injection as I jumped out of the car. Indeed, the bottle of calcium had been clasped between my thighs, to warm it up, as soon as I had left home. If I'd been involved in a car accident, all sorts of problems could have resulted if the bottle had shattered!

There were a lot of grim faces on Lambfell that morning as "Blossom" was their first heavy milking Friesian cow to upgrade the herd, and had cost a lot of money. She was just breathing and had nostrils caked with stomach contents, which indicated that she may also have breathed some into her lungs. Straight into her jugular vein went the needle and slowly I let the life giving fluid flow into her vein. Looking at her rear end I could see the uterus lying on the ground covered in straw. Keeping an eye on her respirations I called for two pails of hot water, a clean sheet and two pounds of sugar.

She had an enormous udder, which was leaking milk on all four teats, and losing further calcium. Her eye blinked and the tip of the tongue twitched, which was a positive sign and slowly her faculties returned. The stomach started to move, she burped as the swallowing reflex returned and then she defecated all over her uterus. Not a pretty sight! I injected a second bottle of calcium under her skin and then concentrated on the prolapse.

The prolapse must have been out for several hours in the cold and pouring rain during the early morning. Fortunately, the placenta was still attached and provided a protection against further damage. I washed the uterus off as best I could and lifted it onto the clean sheet. An injection of pituitrin restored the muscle tone to the organ, and as I detached the placenta I could visibly watch the uterus contracting. We managed to sit her up in order to administer a nerve block into the spine and remove any straining during the next process.

Having prolapsed for several hours the uterus was extremely congested with fluid, so with due ceremony I poured all the sugar over the surface. I could see that the attending helpers thought that I had, at last, flipped mentally. In fact, I was using the sugar for its hygroscopic properties, which make it suck up fluid from the surrounding tissues and reduce the swelling. Once I had removed the placenta, and cleaned up the uterus I was faced with the problem of sending it back home into the abdomen. It's not easy trying to push a floppy balloon, weighing some eighty pounds through a small pelvic opening. It keeps popping out in other places. I called for volunteers to lift the sheet at both ends so that the uterus lay level or slightly above the entrance into the pelvis. This eased the situation greatly so that, after about half an hour of hard work, it disappeared into the pelvis with a satisfactory gloop! Once inside, the uterus has to be returned to its normal position. To do this we always carried a wine bottle to act as an extension for the arm. I often wondered how the most teetotal farmers could produce a wine bottle on such an occasion! Having carried this out in the traditional manner we inserted a couple of stitches in the vulva, and I promised to check her later in the morning.

I arrived back at the surgery, after leaving Lambfell, to be told that John Cretney was coming in with his Border collie that had been kicked by a cow.

Within a few minutes, John and his daughter, Ann arrived in with "Scot", the collie. Carrying him, between them on an old rug, they laid him gently on the examination table.

"Mr Bernstein brought this dog back from Scotland last month," commenced John. "He's well bred, from a working strain and has been settling in well. His only fault is that he's a bit headstrong with the cattle and will nip at their tails. One old lady got a bit touchy today, lashed out and knocked him over."

We stood "Scot" up on the table, and I could see that he was holding his right hind leg in the air. The top of the thigh was very swollen and painful. Gently manipulating the limb, I could feel "crepitus" as the two ends of the broken bone grated together, just below the hip.

As luck would have it, Brian arrived back at that moment and I was grateful for a second opinion.

"Nasty break!" he said, What are you going to do with it?"

"Not a lot," I replied, "It's out of the question to use a plaster cast or conventional splint. What about a Thomas extension splint?" Thereby, putting the final decision back into his lap.

" I don't know whether it would work with a live wire like Scot," Brian said, "He would probably spend much of his time chewing it. He'll have to be tied up anyway so why not use the traditional table leg technique, if Ann can keep an eye on him?"

"Anything to get him right," interjected Ann. "What would you like me to do?"

"Take him home and tie him to the leg of the table or in the barn for the next four weeks," Brian said. "There is so much bruising and swelling in that leg at present that it will act as a splint if we keep his movements restricted. As it starts to heal together in a few days the muscles will keep the bone ends in place. In about four weeks the fracture should have healed sufficiently for him to run around. Ned can call in once a week to check him."

I nodded appreciatively at the thought of such a pleasant weekly chore. There were no sophisticated techniques, such as bone pinning, or plating, available in many rural practices in the nineteen fifties. With good management most of the limb fractures could be treated satisfactorily.

When the time approached for the arrival of the baby we went to live with my parents in Douglas. Our reasons were twofold because it was near to the maternity home and as the birth might occur during T.T. race week the roads could be closed and we might be unable to reach the maternity home.

On a lovely day in June Moira produced a bouncing boy, which filled us both with delight. In some ways we felt sad that he might not grow up in our green and pleasant Isle, but we had to look to the future. We had not quite realised just how the focus of our lives would change, when Donal arrived as the centre of our household. We gave up the carefree life but gained much more in exchange.

"Ned," called Brian as I was leaving the surgery. "We've been working all hours these last few months. Do you feel we should take it a bit easier for a while?"

"You're the optimist," I replied. "We're the victims of our own success. We can't really let up now without someone to help us. Moira is beginning to wonder what kind of a job she married into! I think that we're both suffering from this condition called 'practice fatigue'"

"That's just what I wanted to hear," continued Brian. "Do you remember a student by the name of Mary Sutherland, who we had to see practice a few years ago? You probably will, as you were panting around after her like a young puppy chasing a bowl of milk! She's between jobs and wondered whether we could employ her for a few months. She wants to move out of purely equine work and become more involved in general practice?

I remembered her well. We'd spent a lot of time together when she saw practice as a final year student and I had just entered veterinary college. She was a quiet, likeable girl with a passion for horses, who had initially graduated in agriculture and then changed direction into a veterinary career. Mary was three years my senior and a very good tutor. I was somewhat in awe of her, as she appeared to have so much new knowledge and the latest techniques at her command. Several years later, she confessed that the situation had reversed when I, in my turn, introduced new skills into practice.

" It sounds like a good idea Brian. We've been so busy chasing the urgent cases that there is a build up of routine work that we should tackle." I commented, relishing the thought of long walks with Moira along the cliffs to White Strand.

"Well. I've suggested that she might like to come over for a chat next week, as she will be visiting her parents in Cheshire. If Moira and yourself are free we might all go out to the Carrick Bay Hotel for a meal."

"That's great I'm sure that we can arrange the evening. One little point does concern me. I wonder how she will cope with Mrs Corkish, the government Doberman?"

# Chapter 50

At two p.m. on Thursday afternoon, Brian and I were due at the Cooill Smithy to trim a bull's feet in preparation for the show season. Arthur Caley, at Ballabooie was a meticulous man and everything had to be exact in the show ring. This included his Aberdeen Angus bull, with which he intended to walk away with the best in show rosette.

He was a large, gentle bull who was more at home sniffing daisies than being belligerent. He took his time about doing everything, including fathering the herd. Why bother rushing about the place like those artificial inseminator chaps who were trying to undercut his services. He knew his entire harem by name and kept them contented. He had very aptly been christened "Traa-dy-Liooar!" which translated from the Manx for the "come overs" means "Time Enough!" Because he regarded exercise as an over rated pastime, his feet and toes had all overgrown until they curled up like a ram's horns.

The cattle truck arrived on time and Arthur led him out happily enough into the paddock behind the smithy. In retrospect we could probably have tied him up to a ring in the smithy and lifted his feet up one at a time. This wasn't good enough for Arthur who wanted the deluxe treatment for his pride and joy.

Once in the paddock we cast him, using Reuff's method. This consisted of a thirty-foot rope, with a loop around his neck continued to a second loop about his chest and a third turn around his belly. I was delegated the privilege of holding the bullring whilst three men pulled on the rope at the rear.

Looking rather bewildered at the whole procedure "Traa-dy-liooar" subsided gracefully to the ground, as the loop tightened about his abdomen. We rolled his one-ton weight onto his side and tied his legs up with sidelines. I sat on his head and chatted to him whilst the blacksmith settled down to trim all his feet. It was an education to watch him working with hoof cutters, knives and rasp. His skill enabled him to have the feet looking shipshape in no time.

All this time the bull lay happily on the ground with me scratching his ear. I was so engrossed that I failed to notice signs of restlessness. Eventually, even his tolerance must have worn thin so he flexed his rather cramped muscles. The casting ropes snapped like sewing thread, I somersaulted up in the air as the bull stood up and all was chaos. Stories of bulls kneeling on their victim's chest, so that they were crushed like a hen's egg, flashed across my mind. A very rapid word with my maker and I opened my eyes to look straight into those of "Traa-dy-Liooar" who looked almost apologetic for disturbing me. Everyone else was too busy laughing to come to my rescue as I stood up and dusted myself off, as the bull meekly followed his master into the cattle truck.

The decreasing numbers of farm workers during the post war years had forced farmers to adapt their husbandry techniques. All stock were reared more intensively and batches of cattle were fed from the same trough.

Horn damage became a problem, as in the excitement of feeding time they could readily damage another animal's eyes. Cows were crowded together to wait milking and inevitably disputes would arise. Attempting to suture a wounded udder from which milk was pouring is a thankless occupation.

Dehorning cows and removing the horn buds from calves was becoming of economic importance, and it was certainly altering the problem of bullying in herds where the cow with the most effective horns became the herd boss and could keep the others away from the feeding trough.

I called at Michael Kennaugh's farm up above Ballawilleykilley to check up on several lame ewes. I didn't really expect to find him in the yard as he was probably out doing fieldwork. Every spare minute of his day was occupied profitably as he was constantly chasing his dream of more acres to pass on to his two sons, who were still at school in Douglas. Normally, he left the sheep in a pen for me to deal with on my own.

My car roared into the yard in a cloud of smoke as I had left my exhaust perched on a rock in the middle of his lane. I saw Mike sitting on a straw bail outside the calf pen looking somewhat shaken and exhausted.

"What's the problem, Mike?" I said as I wound down the car window. He was normally fairly active and robust.

"Well, Ned," he said despairingly. "Everyone is talking about disbudding calves at the moment, so I thought that I would have a go. I was lent an electric debudding iron and some local anaesthetic by my brother-in-law who told me how to do it. I have now upset the calf and exhausted myself trying to do the job. No more disbudding for me."

"You mean old devil," I said, slightly irritated at his lack of thought for the animal and determined to make him see the error of his ways. "You've been trying to save a few pennies by cutting corners and not really knowing where to inject the anaesthetic. As a result you've caused the calf a lot of pain and you look pretty knackered as well! It's easy if you use the anaesthetic properly. Let me give you a demonstration!"

"Now, if you disbud the calves fairly young you have very little trouble. You and brother-in-law can help each other out."

I showed him how to hold the calf whilst I injected the anaesthetic around the nerves supplying the horn area. " Now leave it for a few minutes whilst we have a look at the sheep and sort out their problems and by that time the whole area will be numb."

Shortly afterwards we returned to the pen. "Now the disbudding iron is hot I can burn away all the horn growing tissue around the base of the horn, leaving a small hole in the skin, that heals very rapidly. Because the anaesthetic was injected in the correct spot she has felt nothing and stood perfectly still, making life easier for both of you. Let's get hold of another one and you can have a go whilst I show you where to inject the anaesthetic."

After we had finished disbudding half a dozen calves he was becoming very competent at the operation. As a result of this helping hand we were soon inundated with other requests to demonstrate the technique.

152

Whilst we worked with the calves our conversation turned to the sheep and Michael mentioned that he had received a good tip from Rodie Tait, the hill shepherd at Kate's Cottage. Whenever he had a ewe that would not allow a lamb to suckle, he would bring a strange dog into the pen. Immediately, the maternal instincts would take over as she defended the lamb, and afterwards she would accept it readily.

I collected Mary from the airport the following Friday evening. She was staying the night with Brian as they intended to exercise the horses early next morning. She was much more attractive and mature than I remembered. Very confident in herself she had overcome her original air of shyness. Perfect teeth and auburn hair enhanced her attractive smile. We started where we left off four years ago, enjoying each other's company and by the time we arrived at the surgery much of the Island gossip had been considered and I knew that we could work together as colleagues. The gossip network in the island was already buzzing at the sight of the vetinry driving around with a pretty young girl in his car!

The next evening we spent a very enjoyable few hours together having a splendid meal at the Carrick Bay. We had been given the centre table by the window, which overlooked the bay. The tide was full and the wavelets sparkled in the evening sun, as couples strolled slowly along the promenade, determined to take in all the pleasures of their holiday. As we sat drinking our coffee, watching the lights coming on across the bay, Brian arranged that Mary would join us in a month's time.

Little did we realise the repercussions that would arise from this pleasant evening and the manner in which it would shape our future but that was a story yet to unfold.